CRUEL SHADOW

'So what's it to be, Elune?'

'Trussed and stuffed,' Elune answered.

'Nude, or torn and dishevelled?' Juliana asked.

'Oh, torn and dishevelled,' Elune said immediately.

'I still say he won't believe it,' Thomasina stated. 'You've been caught, tied up, your clothes ripped off, but you haven't been had? I don't think he'll even do it.'

'He will,' Elune said confidently. 'He's a man.'

'A modern man,' Aileve pointed out. 'I say he'll untie you and try to take you down to the police station. I'll put a kilogram jar of Mrs Stewer's set honey against anything you care to mention that I'm right, Juliana.'

'You're on,' Juliana answered. 'I'll buy the honey, and if he fucks her first you get to eat it out of me. Fair?'

CRUEL
SHADOW

Aishling Morgan

This book is a work of fiction.
In real life, make sure you practise safe, sane and consensual sex.

First published in 2004 by
Nexus
Thames Wharf Studios
Rainville Road
London W6 9HA

www.nexus-books.co.uk

Typeset by TW Typesetting, Plymouth, Devon

Printed and bound by Clays Ltd, St Ives PLC

ISBN 0 352 33886 5

You'll notice that we have introduced a set of symbols onto our book jackets, so that you can tell at a glance what fetishes each of our brand new novels contains. Here's the key – enjoy!

cp (traditional)

cp (modern)

spanking

restraint/bondage

rope bondage/hojojutsu

latex/rubber/leather/enclosure

fem dom

willing captivity

medical

period setting

uniforms

sex rituals

One

The girl quite simply had the most delightful bottom Peter had ever set eyes on. Perfectly rounded cheeks of lightly tanned flesh thrust out from above the waistband of a pair of lowered white panties, just open enough to hint at the ruder details between without revealing. Twin dimples showed above the neat V of her crease, either side of the last lock of her long, jet-black hair. A lacy dress had been lifted to display the joys of her bottom, and it hid her chest, but it was tight enough, and her half-turned pose hinted at a firm, apple-sized breast. Her face added the final exquisite touch, a delicate oval, with full lips, large, dark eyes and an expression of shy vulnerability that went perfectly with the way her naked bottom was exposed.

He shook his head in regret as he returned the book to the shelf. She was beautiful, achingly beautiful, yet she was merely a model, just a pretty girl hired to pose for the cover of an erotic novel. Even if she did possess the qualities hinted at in her pose and expression, which seemed unlikely, he was highly unlikely to meet her and, if he did, she was still less likely to be interested in him, a brush salesman pushing forty. Most likely she would regard the modelling job as something dirty she had to put up with for the sake of the money, and the exposure of her bottom would have filled her with nothing more than embarrassment and self-disgust.

There was a bitter smile on his lips as he turned away from the bookstand. It had been a long day, out of the house at seven, breakfast at Scotch Corner at nine, appointments in Darlington and Middlesbrough, south again on the M19. It had been going well, a thousand units from Mike Barnes at Homeland, 750 from Steve Kendrick at The Kitchen Man. Then had come the broken appointment, leaving him two hours to fill at lunchtime instead of the one he'd scheduled. The services at J49 had seemed as good a place to kill time as any, and the girl on the book cover had drawn his attention as he'd been buying a paper.

He tried to shrug off an irritating sense of regret as he ordered coffee, egg and chips. The girl serving was pretty, and friendly, but even that failed to shake his mood. Taking a seat where he could keep an eye on his metallic blue Mondeo, he settled down to lunch. Outside, beyond the crowded car park, the countryside was a wet spring green, with the North York Moors a darker line across the horizon. For a while he watched the clouds drift east, his mind going with them, to thoughts of the band and the evening's jamming session. In moments he was lost in thoughts of chords and riffs, only to be brought sharply back to attention by a soft voice at his ear.

'May I sit with you?'

Peter's instinctive stab of irritation vanished as the silky, feminine tone of the voice sank in, to be replaced by surprise as he took in the young woman who had spoken, then astonishment as he realised it was the girl on the book cover. There was no question about it. It hadn't been clear from the picture just

2

how small she was, maybe not even five foot, but she was unmistakable, and every bit as lovely as her picture. She didn't wait for an answer, but slid herself smoothly into the seat beside his, the tight denim encasing her hip nudging his arm just briefly as she did so.

'Yeah, er . . . sure,' he managed, glancing beyond her to where a good third of the tables in the café were empty.

She smiled, revealing twin rows of small, perfectly shaped teeth. It was her, no doubt at all, the big, lustrous eyes, the full mouth, unmistakable. Yet in the flesh she was more lovely still, petite to the point of being elfin, with a vivacity no photograph could ever hope to convey, and a glitter of mischief, malice even, in the deep-green pools of her eyes. She had a coffee, and as she put it to her lips he found his eyes drawn down to where her apple-sized breasts showed round and inviting beneath a tight red skinny top, quite obviously unrestrained by any bra, her nipples large and perky. She giggled and he pulled his gaze quickly away, embarrassed.

'Look all you like.' She laughed. 'I'll show you, if you like?'

Instantly the slight flush of embarrassment at being caught admiring her body became a full-blooded blush. His mouth came open, but no sound emerged, and his brain struggled to find a hint of sarcasm or anything else negative in her voice as she went on.

'They are rather cute, aren't they? A nice handful, but not too big.'

As she spoke she put her coffee cup down, and briefly cupped her breasts, one in each hand, glancing down with a look of satisfaction. At last Peter found his voice.

'Er . . . very nice . . . yes. I . . . um . . . I'm surprised to see you here . . . I mean . . .'

3

'Oh I saw you looking at the cover of *Tease*,' she broke in. 'You seemed to appreciate the way I looked, so I thought I'd say hi.'

'Great ... er ... thanks ...' Peter managed. 'Hi. I'm Peter, Peter Williams.'

'Linnet,' she answered.

'That's an, er ... unusual name. Pretty though ... very pretty.'

'It's a sort of bird.'

'Yes.'

She took another sip of coffee, completely casual, while he was shaking inside and still trying not to stare too obviously at her breasts, despite her offer. He was already cursing himself for not immediately taking her up on her offer, although it was hard to imagine she was genuine. Certainly she was not going to lift her top in the middle of a crowded service café, but maybe, just maybe ...

'So you're a model, then?' Peter asked, keen to make conversation.

'Oh, no,' she answered, 'not professionally, but you know how it is with these photographers. Any excuse to get a girl stripped down, and all the better if she'll do it for peanuts.'

'Yes ... er ... right. I can imagine.'

'He was a dirty sod, that one,' she went on. 'Normally they just have a good stare and maybe a quick grope. Not Luke Richter. He wasn't content with making me show the lot and flogging the pics, or even touching me up. He wanted a blow job afterwards.'

'What a bastard!' Peter responded, struggling to sound sympathetic with the image of her exquisite face wrapped around a man's cock filling his head. 'I hope you told him where to go?'

'No.'

4

'You . . . you . . . don't mean?'

'I sucked him? Yes. I didn't get much choice.'

Peter swallowed hard. His cock was getting uncomfortable in his trousers, and not just from the casual way she was describing being pushed into giving a blow job, or her lovely body, but everything about her. She seemed to radiate warmth and affection, the promise of casual, playful sex. Even her scent was alluring, something he couldn't place, but which held a tang of sea-salt. She had taken another sip of her coffee, and reached out casually to take the very largest of his chips from the plate as she went on.

'He just told me I had to do it, and out came his cock. What could I do?'

'Refuse?'

'He hadn't paid me.'

She popped the chip in her mouth, chewing meditatively as Peter struggled to feel properly outraged instead of aroused. Yet his guilt was growing with his cock, and it was all he could do to hope she had really been willing.

'And . . . and you didn't mind?' he managed. 'I mean . . . you don't seem to?'

'A bit,' she admitted, 'but not too much. I quite like assertive men, and he had smacked my cheeks a bit to get them pink . . . my face, not my bum. That always makes me horny. He'd got in a right state too, what with groping me and everything, and maybe I had flashed a bit more pussy than I really had to, so I suppose it was only fair.'

'Only fair?' Peter asked, wishing he'd just once in his entire life met a woman who thought it was 'only fair' to satisfy a man she'd accidentally turned on. Now he had, and the temptation to do something about it was growing by the moment. She took another chip, blowing on it before she went on.

5

'Yeah, I suppose so. I mean, I wouldn't have minded so much, only he was such a bully. He was big, and he really hurt my jaw. When he did it, he held me by the hair, so I had to try and swallow the lot. I couldn't, and it all came out my nose. Gross.'

She prodded the chip into the middle of one of his fried eggs, to scoop up a blob of glistening yellow yolk. As she lifted it, a long strand of runny white came up as well, breaking halfway to her mouth. Her little pointed tongue flicked out, catching it, but not perfectly, so that her lower lip and chin were soiled.

'Go ahead,' Peter offered. 'I'm not all that hungry.'

She didn't answer him, ate her chip and took another, once again dipping it in the egg. He watched her, picturing her in his mind, in the lace dress and little white panties she'd been in on the cover photo, only kneeling between the photographer's knees, his hand twisted hard into her hair, his erection in her mouth. No doubt he'd have made her pull her top up, to get her breasts bare, and it seemed unlikely he'd have let her pull her panties up. She'd have been nude from neck to knees, nude and sucking cock.

It was an alluring image, impossible to dispel. She was so petite and so pretty that it was hard to see how any man could resist her. Her face, her breasts, her svelte waist, her little round bum, everything about her just cried out for sex. She seemed so vulnerable too, for all her teasing ways, yet for all that he wanted to protect her he also wanted to see her stripped down for sex, on her knees with his cock in her mouth, gagging on his come.

'Men always love to make a mess of a girl's face, don't they?' she continued around a mouthful of egg and chip. 'Mine anyway. Do you do that?' She giggled, and went on, cutting him off before he could find an answer. 'I bet you do.'

6

He didn't try to deny it, but sipped at his coffee, watching her over the rim of the cup. Everything about her was casual, save for the glint in her eye. Was it mischief, malice, caprice? Was she teasing him, or daring him in the hope that he would treat her with the same forceful machismo the photographer had done? Was she simply after a free meal, and maybe a lift? Possibly she was down on her luck and needed help? It seemed likely, and fresh guilt hit him as the thought of taking advantage of her rose up unbidden. Yet it could do no harm to offer her help.

'I'll buy you some lunch if you like?' he asked.

'No, thanks.'

She took another chip.

'Where are you headed? I'm going south, Doncaster, then down the A1 for Peterborough and Milton Keynes. I'd be happy to give you a lift, if you're heading that way . . . at all?'

'I've got a car, thanks. The green one.'

She jerked her thumb casually over her shoulder, in the general direction of the car park. Peter followed the gesture. There was only one green car in view, an MG TF 160 Roadster with the latest plates. Sure he must have insulted her, he hastened to make amends.

'Not that I thought you wouldn't have a car . . . I was just . . . er . . . wondering.'

'Whether I'd suck your cock for a lift?'

Peter just managed to catch his coffee cup, spilling some down his tie and the front of his shirt. Linnet burst into giggles.

'Whoops!'

He hastily dabbed at his front. Peter could feel himself going red in the face and was praying nobody had heard her above the din of conversation, cutlery and canned music. Linnet was smiling, her eyes brighter than ever as she went on.

'Yeah, OK, if you fancy it. Not here, but there's this place near Huntingdon, Mapley's. It's just a garage with a row of loos out the back, on the old road.'

'Just north of Buckden. I know it. Been the same for ever.'

'That's the one . . . I think. Anyway, six o'clock, if you see my car, you'll know I'm waiting.'

She winked and leaned forwards, her hand finding his thigh beneath the table as she whispered into his ear.

'I'll be in the loos, the end cubicle. Choose the next one and you'll find a glory hole. Stick your cock through, and I'll suck you, all the way . . .'

Her hand had been moving up his leg as she spoke, and as she finished she gave his cock a gentle squeeze. He was rock hard, and as she felt him her eyes went wide for a moment.

'Now that I am going to enjoy,' she said as she stood up. 'See you later.'

She waved and stepped away, swaying her hips with deliberate insolence, to make the little rounded cheeks of her bottom rise and fall with the motion. At the door she turned and smiled, then she was gone, only to reappear moments later in the car park. He waved, trying to seem cool although his heart was beating crazily. She smiled back as she reached the MG, took hold of her top and quite casually flipped it up, exposing two round little breasts, each topped by a large and erect nipple, so perky they seemed to point at the sky. It was only an instant, then she had covered herself, but it left him with his eyes popping and his mouth wide, while several other people had seen.

He got up, sauntered over to the till, paid and left, all the while feigning indifference to the looks of envy and disapproval that followed him. She had flashed her tits for him. She had offered to suck his cock. A nagging voice at the back of his head was telling him she was teasing, that it was all just a wind-up, designed to keep him on edge all afternoon only to discover that she wasn't there. Yet she had been so open, so easy-going, and, if there had been the light of mischief in her eyes, then that mischief seemed to include him.

As he left the services he seemed to be walking on air. One moment he had been ruefully considering the seeming impossibility that any girl that beautiful would be interested in him, and the next that very same girl had propositioned him. It still seemed far too good to be true, and he was shaking his head as he put his foot down on the slip road, pushing the Mondeo up to over ninety as he joined the A1. A moment of concentration as he passed a string of lorries, and he was cruising, and running over what had happened in his mind.

Traffic was light, and within a mile the speedo needle of the Mondeo had crept up over the hundred mark. The exhilaration of fast driving began to get to him, putting a grin on his face as he thought of what she had offered, and done. Ten, maybe fifteen, men had seen her flash her tits, and everyone would now be boiling with jealousy. She was class, more attractive by far than any other women who had been there, more than most women a man could expect to meet in a lifetime, and she had flashed at him – Peter Williams. It felt good, and the prospect of her beautiful face wrapped around his cock better still.

He was past Pontefract before he managed to turn his attention to what he was supposed to be doing – selling Truwood bath brushes to Simon Mawby of Status Interiors. By then he had decided there was no question of what he would do. He had to go to Mapley's. Perhaps she would not be there, and that would be that. Yet, if he didn't go, he would never know, and that would be intolerable.

Simon Mawby was a hard man to bargain with at first, but now loyal. Peter knew he had the measure of Simon, but still pulled over to check his file before he reached the trading estate on which Status Interiors was based. With the tip of his pen in his mouth he quickly went over the facts he already knew. Simon was a family man, married since 94, to Marcie. There were two children, Andrew, seven, and David, five. Marcie had wanted a girl but they didn't feel they could afford a third just yet. Simon was interested in moving up the property ladder, had a moderate interest in sport, supporting his local team with the same dogged loyalty Peter had worked so hard to win for himself. His only hobby was angling.

Peter moved on, the way he would play it fully formed in his mind. As he entered Simon's office he was chanting softly, 'two–nil', 'two–nil', the score Simon's team had lost by the previous Saturday. Sure enough, it was received in good humour. A couple of carefully placed remarks about how he envied Simon his stable marriage and family life, an entirely fictitious description of how he had landed a fifteen-pound carp, and he was leaving with an order for five hundred units.

Peterborough was easier still. Derek Pitt was one of his oldest clients, a tough, hard-drinking Londoner who now ran a chain of bathroom shops across the Midlands and East Anglia. Peter knew enough about the old East End to wing the conversation, while always deferring to Derek, and had his knowledge of West Ham United and canaries well up to date. The result was an order for a thousand units, leaving him well pleased with himself as he once more turned the Mondeo south.

Only as he pulled back on to the A1 did another, and unpleasant, possibility occur to him. Could it be that Linnet was setting him up? It certainly fitted the circumstances, a pretty young girl luring an older man to a lonely spot where her accomplices would be waiting, and where he would be robbed, maybe beaten up for daring to think he was going to get his hands on her. His grip tightened on the steering wheel at the thought. If it was true, then they might find they'd bitten off rather more than they could chew. Certainly it wasn't going to stop him going to Mapley's Garage, but it was sensible to look around first.

He drove hard for Huntingdon and Mapley's Garage, pulling off the motorway and on to the old road well before six. There was an immediate sense of nostalgia, the broad, now empty road one of those he had driven so often in his days as a junior. Back then, Mapley's had been a busy place, frequented by an endless stream of truckers, tourists, businessmen and more. Now it stood almost deserted. He slowed as he approached, bringing the Mondeo to a halt on the verge a good two hundred yards before the slip road left the main carriageway.

Getting out, he spent a moment listening, but nothing was evident over the drone of the traffic on the new road. He approached, cautiously, crossing the road to peer out from among a stand of pines. Everything looked normal, the double row of pumps, the red-brick kiosk, the cracked and dirty awning, as he remembered it, except that grass had begun to push up between the slabs of concrete. Only one person was visible, a bored-looking woman with dyed blonde hair in the kiosk.

He crossed back, entered the kiosk, bought a bar of chocolate and asked casually if his young friends from the rugby club had been in. The answer was no. Still cautious, he walked round to the back, to look out over the great lorry park, a huge expanse of windblown concrete occupied by a single cableless rig, and a Le Mans green MG roadster. His mouth curved up into a knowing smile.

Across the park were the loos, five boxes on a concrete platform, with a set of steps at one end. The door of the last in the row was shut. Briefly he inspected the MG, but nothing hinted that anyone other than Linnet had been in it. There was evidence of her, a make-up set open on the passenger seat, a brilliant scarlet lipstick still out, as if freshly used.

Now confident, he strode towards the loos, his heart hammering in his chest and a tight knot in his stomach. She was going to suck him, and with any luck it would go further. He could offer her dinner, take her home, get her out of her clothes, enjoy the pert breasts she had flashed so cheekily and her beautiful bottom. It was just a matter of playing cool.

He opened his chocolate bar as he approached the loos, and bit off a chunk. His cock was already beginning to swell, with his mind fixed firmly on Linnet's beautiful face. There was something about having a really pretty girl suck cock that added the final touch and, if he wouldn't be able to see her, then her image was very clear in his imagination. Besides, that was for now. For the time being he would play her games, but in due time she would learn that, when it came to games, nobody beat Peter Williams.

It was dim inside the loo, the bulb long gone, and a grimy panel of frosted glass in the roof the only source of light. The walls were covered in scrawl, rude pictures, dirty poems, invitations to sex, either the numbers of girls who were presumably prostitutes, or man to man. To either side of the loo were large glory holes, one with 'suck me' written above it, the other, on Linnet's side, decorated to resemble an anus. He gave a sniff of distaste, but sat down.

'Linnet?' he asked.

Her voice came back, as smooth and sexy as ever.

'Are you eating chocolate?'

'Yes.'

'Gimmee, gimmee, gimmee!'

Amused, he broke off half the bar and pushed it through the glory hole. It was taken immediately, Linnet sighing with pleasure as she ate. Peter waited a moment, picking out the straight graffiti from the walls. There was an invitation from a man to fuck his wife while he watched, a claim that somebody called Kev had taken his girlfriend's virginity with her bent over the very loo he was sitting on, another that a Laura Simmons liked to be fucked up her bottom. He chuckled as he read them, wondering which were real and which mere boasts, and if he should add his own experience.

'Are you ready then?' Linnet's voice came from beyond the partition.

'Sure,' he answered, 'how about a little show first?'

'No,' she answered, 'I want to suck you. Stick it through, your balls too.'

As she spoke he peered close, to find himself looking right into her mouth, the red lips parted to reveal the perfect teeth and pointed tongue, sticky with chocolate. The mouth closed and she blew a kiss, her scarlet lips puckered up to the hole. He chuckled, amused by her enthusiasm, and swallowed the last of his chocolate. Standing, he undid his trousers, and pushed them down along with his pants. His cock was already half stiff, and he fed it through, pushing

13

his balls afterwards. Immediately he was taken in, Linnet's mouth warm and wet around his shaft.

He closed his eyes, in instant ecstasy as his cock began to swell in her mouth. She took his balls in hand, stroking and teasing with her fingernails, until he had begun to shake. It was going to happen, at any moment, his head full of images of the girl sucking him, the way she had posed her bottom for the book cover, her breasts tempting beneath a taut top, then bare as she flashed them for him, round and pink and lovely, the hard nipples pointing up, so pert, so sexy . . .

She was good, the best, her little pointed tongue everywhere, her lips always moving. Again and again she brought him to the edge, teasing his helmet and the meat of his foreskin, only to stop at the last possible moment, as if she knew exactly when he was starting to come. Soon he was moaning aloud, lost in ecstasy, and then gasping as she suddenly took him deep, his helmet pushing into the tight passage of her throat, sudden and unexpected.

It was too much. Peter groaned as he came in Linnet's mouth. She swallowed dutifully, sucking and squeezing on his balls until every last drop of spunk had been milked into her mouth. When at last she let go and he pulled back, he sat down, gasping and weak-kneed from the experience. A ring of scarlet lipstick and brown chocolate marked the very base of his cock, showing just how deep she had taken him, right into her throat.

'That was great,' he managed eventually. 'You are quite something, Linnet. Now how about I take you out to dinner?'

She didn't answer.

'Linnet?' Peter queried.

Again there was no answer. He put his eye to the glory hole, but could only see the curve of her hip in dark blue denim. She was standing, apparently pressed to the wall beside the glory hole.

'Linnet?' he repeated. 'Are you OK?'

There was a faint giggle.

'See you outside, yeah?' he tried. 'I'd really like to get to know you better.'

Still there was no answer. Puzzled, and somewhat annoyed, Peter adjusted himself and opened the door. Hers was still shut, the car as before. Tentatively he pushed her door, to find it locked. Irritated by what seemed to be childish behaviour, he stepped away. Evidently she still wanted to play games but, if she could, then so could he. He walked away, deliberately nonchalant, his hands in his pockets, cool and casual.

Not once did he look back, sure that she would be watching him from the door, until he had reached the trees where the slip road came in. Sure enough, the door of the loo she'd been in was open a crack. She was watching. He walked on, sure that if he pretended to ignore her it would pique her interest. Reaching the Mondeo, he got in and drove back, stopping once more at the edge of the lorry park. Her car was still there, the loo door closed once more.

He got out, to lean against the bonnet of the Mondeo. She had to come out eventually, and when she did she could either come to him or drive off. If she drove off he would follow, and the woman who could outdrive Peter Williams had yet to be born. Either way he would get to talk to her and she would end up accepting a date. After all, deep down, she had to want it, or she wouldn't have sucked him off.

Five minutes passed, and ten. At last the loo door opened. A slim figure stepped out, in dark blue jeans, but baggy; with dark hair, but short; with a red top, but long; with scarlet lipstick, but on lips that were anything but kissable – a man.

15

Interlogue

Elune spooned a dollop of crabmeat into her mouth, immediately regretting her choice. It was cooked, and tasted very dead. She made a face at Thomasina, who took no notice but continued to eat her scallops with every evidence of relish. Shrugging, she turned to the man in the seafood stall.

'Do you have any strawberry sauce to go with this?'

'Strawberry sauce, on dressed crab?' he queried.

'Or chocolate.'

'You taking the piss, love?'

'No,' Elune answered. 'How about maple syrup?'

'Look, love, I sell seafood. What you see is what you get. Try an ice-cream stand.'

'Good thought,' Elune agreed, and turned away to glance down the line of stalls.

There were over a dozen, set out in a long line beside the fair that occupied the entire area of the market-place. The next one sold hotdogs and burgers, the one beyond a huge assortment of sweets, the third ice-cream. She started towards it.

'I'll have that if you don't want it,' Thomasina offered, and smacked her lips to take in the last of the juice from her scallops.

'I need feeding,' Elune replied. 'It takes it out of me, that stuff.'

'Me too,' Thomasina agreed, 'but I don't really see why you bothered.'

'It was fun!'

'You really are a disgrace,' Thomasina remarked. 'Perhaps I ought to spank you?'

'You wouldn't dare!' Elune taunted. 'Not here.'

'Maybe I wouldn't,' Thomasina answered, 'or maybe I would.'

'Don't,' Elune answered, 'I need to eat.'

'Very well, but you do deserve it.'

'You're such a Victorian. Grow out of it.'

'Well, you do! I'd do it too, and I'd have thought people would be happy to see a brat like you get her bare bottom smacked, or just not care.'

'Oh they'd care,' Elune assured her, 'or at least those two would. I expect most of them would like to watch.'

She nodded to two policemen who were walking slowly towards them between the twin lines of rides and booths. Thomasina chuckled and turned to the man in the ice-cream booth.

'A triple please, mint-chip, honeycomb and English toffee.'

'I'll have the same,' Elune added, 'only that pink one with the bits in instead of mint-chip. Can I have some strawberry topping for my crab?'

The man gave her an odd look but complied, Elune holding the half-shell up until the meat was thickly topped with sauce. As soon as he'd lifted the bottle away she began to spoon the mixture into her mouth, now eager, and relishing the sweet salt flavour. The man busied himself with their ice-creams. Thomasina paid and they walked away from the stall, down the middle of the fair, eating as they went.

'This'll be enough for now,' Elune said after a while. 'Shall we go down to the water?'

'Why not.'

17

They turned aside, walking the long familiar path between King's Lynn's ancient houses, down a narrow street, and an alley, which brought them out on the bank, with the Ouse stretching away arrow-straight to north and south. A man passed, middle-aged, huddled into a dirty brown Mackintosh despite the warm May weather. His eyes flicked first to Thomasina's ample chest, then to Elune's legs. She bent, pretending to adjust the laces of her trainers, far enough down to make sure her little skirt rose and he got a flash of taut white panties. He tripped and nearly fell, leaving Elune giggling and Thomasina struggling not to join in.

'Really,' Thomasina said when the man was safely out of earshot, 'do you always have to taunt them?'

'Not always,' Elune replied, 'just most of the time.'

They walked on, along the bank to where the houses finished and in among a tangle of willows and young birch. Neither spoke, taking their time over their ice-creams. Only when they had finished and reached a place well screened by trees where the hulk of an old barge lay rotting on the bank did they stop. Thomasina seated herself cautiously on the gunwale and patted her lap.

'And now,' she announced, 'I am going to pull those little panties of yours down and give you the spanking you so well deserve.'

Elune giggled and laid herself across her friend's legs.

Two

Peter Williams sat on his sofa, beer in hand, feeling slightly sick. It had been the same ever since the incident with the girl Linnet and the gay bloke three days before. Not only had he let himself be sucked off by a man, but it had been the best blow job of his life. Just to think about it made his stomach turn queasy.

The moment he had realised what had happened he had left, unable to bring himself to accost the man, or to look for Linnet, or anything else. He had driven back to Milton Keynes at speeds high even by his standards, found himself unable to face eating and gone straight to his jamming session at The Pig and Whistle. Even jamming with the band had failed to shake the horrible memory.

On the surface it looked obvious what had happened. The lonely toilet block at the back of Mapley's was a perfect place for gay men to meet for sex, as was obvious from over half the graffiti scrawled on the walls. One man had been waiting to meet another, a man into sucking other men's cocks. He'd come along, assumed the effete little bastard was Linnet and got his blow job. Simple, and utterly disgusting.

Unfortunately, it didn't add up. For a start he had spoken to Linnet, and she had used the same smooth-as-silk sexy voice as when they had first met.

No man spoke that way, gay or otherwise. Then there was the car, her car, the unmistakable Le Mans green MG TF 160. He hadn't actually focused on the plates, beyond noticing that they were new, but the chances of it being a different car had to be minuscule.

So Linnet had been there, and she had spoken to him, but the only explanation that made sense was that the effete young man had been in the loo with her. That made it possible that it had actually been her who sucked him off, but he knew with dull certainty it wasn't.

She had tricked him, the whole thing an elaborate joke to humiliate him, or more likely her gay friend got some sort of weird kick out of sucking off straight men. Maybe it was a bit of both, but the more he thought about it the more the second option seemed likely. If he'd simply driven away he would never have known. For the rest of his life he would have been imagining that he'd had a wonderful experience with a girl who was quite simply the sexiest he'd ever met, while all the time it had been a man. Somehow that made it worse.

Another thing that didn't seem to fit was the effort she had gone to. It was a long way down the A1 from the J49 services to Mapley's, and it was pushing coincidence to assume it had just been chance. After all, he'd been looking at the book cover, and suddenly she'd turned up. Then the gay guy had been ready to do his part, just six hours later and one hundred and fifty miles away. Much more likely it had all been worked out in advance, but he had never met her, or the man. That meant he had been set up.

The more he thought about it, the more likely it seemed. In the end he was sure, but one important question remained, who by? If it was a joke, it was a pretty gross one. More than one of his friends had a sick enough sense of humour, but it was hard to see any of them going to so much trouble. It couldn't have been any of the boys in the band, for certain. No way could they have kept their faces straight during the jamming session.

It seemed a pretty childish prank for a rival, even though the country was dotted with men, and women, who resented his success, salesmen in both competing companies and his own. Otherwise, it was hard to think of anyone who might have a grudge against him. When it came to work he might take no prisoners, but in general he was a pretty easy-going guy. Whoever it was, they had done him up like a kipper, and he, Peter Williams, was going to get even, no mistake.

As he'd been set up, that made the man who'd sucked him a rent-boy. He'd certainly looked as Peter would have imagined a rent-boy to look – small, thin, effeminate. He'd also been very, very well practised at giving blow jobs. However sickening the memory, there was no denying the pleasure. For three whole days it was as much as Peter could do to hold his own cock in the loo, much less masturbate, because he was sure that the moment he tried his mind would go back to Linnet and the rent-boy. What he needed was a woman.

It was a decision he reached on the Friday afternoon as he pulled out of Solent Accessories in Southampton. Dave Niven, the buyer, was usually good for five hundred units, but had got away with an order for a miserable two hundred. Normally Dave was easy, a pushover in fact. All it needed was for Peter to put in his Man Utd tie-pin and check up on the latest team news. This time he'd been distracted, and had got the scorers for the team's three goals in the wrong order. From there on it had all been downhill, and that was not good.

As he turned down the M27 for Portsmouth he knew exactly what he was going to do. There was no point in hanging around in bars, it was just too chancy, and, besides, not just any woman would do. He needed a girl the complete opposite of Linnet – big, blonde, busty, bouncy. She had to be sweet too, somebody who would put him first. It was best to pay.

That he could do. With his commission on top of his salary he had pulled in over a hundred thousand the previous year, and it had been looking better than ever up until that week. He could afford the best. No, he could afford two . . . no, three girls, the finest the city had to offer, with more tit and arse between them than a barrowload of watermelons. He was grinning as he pulled on to the 275. There was one more call and his time was his own and, boy, was he going to use it.

Half an hour later he had a signed order for one thousand five hundred units from Jeff Mitchell at The Home Maker, double the usual and most of it from the deluxe range. He was back on form, and he hadn't even dipped his wick yet. The next step was a hotel, somewhere they didn't ask questions but still provided a decent service. He chose The Ship, a big pub on a corner in Eastney, with spacious old rooms and a back staircase he could let himself up any time he pleased with little chance of being seen and just about nobody objecting.

A leisurely dinner of steak and chips washed down with real ale, a bath, a smart yet casual look and he felt ready for the girls. Street walkers were out. He needed class, and that was going to take a little inside knowledge, something he possessed in spades. One quick phone call to a certain Madam, a brief discussion as he explained what he needed, and he was set. All that remained was to pick them up, pay, treat them to a few drinks, and he'd be up to his balls in pussy.

It was beginning to get dark outside, with revellers already on the streets. There were many small groups of teenagers of both sexes, as urgent for each others' company as they were unsure how to go about getting it. There were also sailors and other servicemen, older men in twos and threes, some on their own. A few, Peter knew, might get lucky. A few more would end up with an unsatisfying grope or a snog in some grimy alley. Some might pay. Most would end up frustrated. Not one would be going to bed with three partners. He would be.

Not that there was any shortage of girls, young and not-so-young, short and tall, slim and plump, in a half-dozen shades of skin and two dozen shades of hair. Nearly all looked as if they were out to enjoy the fine May evening, and more than one glanced his way, letting him know he still had the old magic, that he could have had any of them, for free, and that paying was a choice. One in particular he noticed, because for one shocking moment he thought it was Linnet. She had the same long black hair and a petite figure beneath a heavy black overcoat, but as she turned in at the door of a pub he saw that her face was quite different, plain, with an unfortunately large nose and thin lips.

He shrugged inwardly, instinctively sorry for her, but he was still smiling as he pushed in at the door of the Green Dragon behind her. Smoke, noise, heat, the smells of beer and perfume hit him immediately, a long-familiar atmosphere. It was crowded, but he knew where he was going – to the back bar. There, sure enough, was Annie, and his three girls.

He paused a moment to take them in. As he had ordered, all were blonde and buxom. One, beside Annie, he recognised as her senior girl, Cherry, who he'd had before. She was certainly everything he wanted, perhaps a little plump, but tall, with breasts like a pair of footballs and a big, firm bottom. Beside Cherry was a girl who might have been her younger sister, a little shorter, a little slimmer, not quite so luxuriously endowed, but with the same pleasant face and gentle brown eyes. The third girl was smaller still, and plumper still, a regular butterball, with big, baby-blue eyes and a tumble of blonde curls spilling down over huge breasts barely restrained within her halter top. All four were giggling together, and well down bottles of alcopop or glasses of gin and orange. They were certainly as different from Linnet as a woman could be, and also as female as a human being could be. Peter found himself smacking his lips in anticipation as he moved towards them.

Annie recognised him immediately, greeting him with a big, cerise smile. The girls straightened up immediately, tits out, backs in, their expressions of casual good humour changing to sultry promise on the instant. Peter responded with a casual nod and took his place on the padded bench as Annie patted it, squeezing between her and Cherry. Just the feel of their thighs against his, soft and full, was enough to make his cock twinge, and the first of his worries was immediately dismissed. The experience had not turned him gay.

'Well, it has been a while,' Annie said cheerfully, 'and you must be doing well for yourself. Three at a time!'

The little plump blonde dissolved in giggles. Annie went on.

'Three girls, all blonde and busty, just as you

24

asked. You know Cherry, and this is Zoe, and the one who won't stop her giggling is Katie.'

Peter gave each of the girls a friendly nod, not bothering to hide his interest as he took in their ample chests. Katie looked to be in danger of spilling out of her top, and she clearly had no bra, her tits quivering like two big, water-filled balloons within her top, her huge nipples making bumps at least as big as the ends of his thumbs in the thin cotton. Cherry and Zoe, too, were both braless under thin dresses, but firm enough not to need much in the way of support, for all their size.

'Now,' Annie went on, leaning close and speaking in a confidential whisper, 'normally I'd want extra but, seeing as how you and I go back so far, we'll say three hundred all in, shall we?'

'Sure,' Peter answered, and reached into his pocket.

After taking out a bundle of notes, he peeled off six fifties, held well under the table but not so far that both Annie and Cherry couldn't see. Zoe leaned forwards to look, and gave a little coo of surprise as she saw the size of his bankroll. He slipped the six notes to Annie and casually returned the rest to his pocket. Both Zoe and Cherry were looking at him wide-eyed, and quickly moved closer. Katie caught the implication and put her hand to her mouth, her magnificent chest quivering to a fresh giggle.

'Champagne, girls?' Peter asked casually, putting his arm around Cherry's shoulders.

She felt soft and warm, her hair silky, adding to the stiffness of his cock. He passed Zoe another fifty and as she scampered away to the bar he followed the rotation of her bottom beneath her dress, twin bulges that promised as much delight as her chest. Again he smiled, relaxing into Katie's embrace as Annie stood up.

'Well,' she said, 'I'll be leaving the four of you to yourselves. Now, you send them back the same way I left them, young Peter.'

'Oh, you know me,' Peter assured me, 'nothing worse than a little tired and a little sore.'

She favoured him with a smirk as Cherry slapped his leg playfully. Katie moved in beside him, her flesh soft and ample against his side. His cock was a hard bar in his trousers, and he gave a contented sigh at the prospect of the evening ahead. Already he was the envy of every other man in the bar, including two with their wives from whom he had caught wistful looks. There was a group of sailors too, naval men, whose gaze he carefully avoided in case they should decide he was getting too much of the action. Another group of four sat in one corner, three more in the other, none with partners. There was only one single woman other than his girls, the ugly one who had walked in before him, propping up the bar with a look of sad dejection on her face as she sipped an alcopop, her overcoat still on.

He gave her a smile but she merely looked away. Zoe came back to them, with four glasses and a tall green bottle, the surface misted from the chiller. He took it, adroitly pulling the foil back, twisting the wire closure and popping the cork, the sight of the froth spurting from the bottle neck sending Katie into fresh giggles.

'This is the way it works,' Peter stated as he poured. 'You do right by me, and I'll do right by you. I want you to have fun, but I want you to do as I say too, got it?'

'Yes, sir,' Katie answered in mock trepidation. 'I promise to do as you say, sir.'

She batted her eyelids at him, pouting at the same time, and Peter promised himself that he would fuck her first. Both the other girls nodded their under-standing. He passed the glasses out and took his own, nestling back into the comfortable pillows of the girls' arms as he sipped the cool champagne. Under the table, Zoe's hand had found his thigh, moving quickly up to his crotch. She gave a delighted purr at the discovery that he was erect.

'You are eager!' she cooed.

'Ever ready, that's me,' Peter answered. 'So, here's to us!'

He drained his champagne, the girls immediately following suit. Again he poured, and drank, and again, their conversation growing quickly more cas-ual and yet more intimate. By the time the bottle was finished he felt he could wait no longer. They left, Peter walking with his arms around Cherry and Zoe, then Zoe and Katie after they had stopped to buy three more bottles of champagne and some plastic cups. Again and again envious male glances were cast in his direction, and his frequent explorations of the girls' meaty bottoms met only with giggles and coy requests to be patient. By the time they reached The Ship he felt like the king of the world.

In his room he laid himself down on the bed, his head propped up on the pillows. Cherry began to play mother, opening the champagne while Katie quickly climbed on to the bed beside him, her hand going straight to his chest, stroking with delicate, podgy fingers. Zoe made to join them, but Peter shook his head.

'Go over to the window, darling, and strip for me, nice and slow.'

Zoe giggled and skipped over to the open area of the floor, quickly shut the curtains before striking a pose, her hands on her head, her chest pushed out, then turned slowly. As Katie's hand began to sneak

27

lower, Peter took in Zoe, a pretty face framed in bobbed blonde hair, bare, pale shoulders, ample breasts straining out of her cheap red dress, tight waist, full hips, long womanly legs. As she turned she pushed her bottom out, stretching the thin cotton over twin globes of heavy flesh, full and inviting.

Cherry handed him his champagne and bounced down on the bed, beside him, her arm behind his head, her breasts just inches from his face, her scent strong in his head. Zoe began to dance, wiggling her bottom and smoothing her hands over her curves, slowly, teasing, and yet with the promise of going all the way, and more. He pulled Katie closer, squashing her fat breasts to his side as his hand found her well-rounded bottom, squeezing a cheek. She responded by putting her hand to his crotch and easing down his zip. He smiled as her hand burrowed into his boxers, and sighed as his cock was pulled free and she gave a little squeak of delight.

'Slowly does it,' he instructed as she began to wank him, 'no rush.'

Her hand moved down to tickle his balls as the three of them gave their attention to Zoe's strip. Even with no music she was dancing well, swaying to an imaginary rhythm, while her opulent body just spoke sex. She could tease too, turning as she slid down her zip to reveal the soft white flesh of her back, but only as far as the twin dimples above her bottom. Again she turned, giving him a coquettish glance as she cupped her breasts, the dress now held on only by her shape. She jiggled them, making Peter's cock twitch, and then, suddenly, they were bare, two plump balls of ripe girlflesh spilled free and into her hands, her big nipples erect. Her eyes never leaving his, she began to touch herself, stroking and tweaking her nipples and bouncing the fat globes in her hands until

28

he had to close his eyes to stop himself coming in Katie's hand. Katie giggled and let go of his cock, to tug up her hopelessly inadequate halter top and spill out her own breasts, right into his face.

'You too, Cherry,' Peter ordered. 'Boobs out, darling.'

Cherry obeyed, moving quickly to pull her pale blue mini-dress up over her head, then snuggling up to him again, so that his head was pillowed between four big breasts. He took a nipple in his mouth, sucking as he continued to watch Zoe. She had turned her back, and was wriggling her dress down over her bottom, to make her meaty cheeks quiver, first encased in tight red cotton, then bare and lovely. The dress came down, and off, leaving her in nothing but white thong panties. She turned, smiling right at him as her thumbs went into the waistband, and pushed.

Katie's hand found Peter's cock again as Zoe's knickers came down. He watched in delight as the full globe was revealed, the tiny thong slid down over meaty cheeks well stuck out, to show off her slit, the tight pink dimple of her anus, the pouting lips of her pussy, shaved and pink and wet. He swallowed hard, once more shutting his eyes to stop himself coming. There was no holding it though, Katie's little hand doing wonderful things to him, too good to resist.

'Take me between your tits, Katie,' he ordered, his voice hoarse. 'Make me come.'

Immediately she scrambled around, not as he had expected her to, but by climbing over his chest, to leave him faced with her ample bottom, just inches away, her beefy cheeks straining out from her little jeans shorts. He took hold, stroking her bottom as she folded his cock in the warmth of her cleavage. She began to jiggle her breasts, and as her mouth found the head of his cock, Zoe reached back to spread her bottom, exposing every detail of ready pussy and tight bumhole, flaunted for him.

It was too much. He came, Katie squeaking in shock as he gave her a faceful of spunk, but dutifully sucking it down, his cock jerking again and again in her mouth even as Cherry leaned forwards to nestle her chest into his face. It seemed to last for ever, Peter lost in a welter of plump female flesh, all three of them attentive to his needs, all three willing and bare and lovely.

As he came down from his orgasm, his ecstasy was replaced by an overall feeling of well-being. It felt good to be alive, in control and, above all, male. Any suspicion he might have had was an absurdity, the incident with Linnet and the rent-boy more amusing than anything.

Katie hurried off, cheeks bulging with his sperm, to be sick in the loo. Zoe went to help, and Cherry passed him his cup of champagne. He took a meditative sip, wondering what he should do with them next. First of all it seemed a nice idea to be served, with all three of them in the nude. A bath might be pleasant, then perhaps a leisurely massage, by which time he was sure to be ready again. He would take his time, and fuck all three, perhaps lining them up on the bed, perhaps making them watch, perhaps making two be rude with each other while he fucked the third.

'Strip off while you're in there, Katie, love,' he called, 'and run me a bath. You're going to give me the works. You too, Cherry.'

Cherry obeyed without hesitation, standing to peel off her panties and stockings before walking into the bathroom, her full rump rotating sweetly behind her. He could just see Katie, and watched as she too stripped off, pushing down her shorts and the knickers beneath, then tugging her halter top off over her head. All three were nude, and after swallowing his champagne he climbed off the bed to watch them work, filling his bath and getting soap and shampoo ready. He began to undress, and Zoe quickly came to pick up his clothes, gathering up each garment as he dropped it. When he was naked he sent her into the main room with a firm swat of her meaty rump, making her squeak.

'Fold them on the bedside chair,' he ordered, 'then come back here. How's the water, Cherry?'

'Just right, I'd say,' she answered.

He reached forwards, dipping his finger into the water.

'Hmm, a trifle hot perhaps, but never mind. Katie, fetch my champagne.'

As she scampered away he climbed into the bath, immersing himself neck-deep in the steaming water. It felt glorious, immediately easing away all the aches and pains of the long day. He settled back, taking the cup of champagne as Katie offered it to him, leaving all three girls in the room.

'Shall I soap you?' Cherry asked.

'In a minute,' he answered. 'First, I want a good look at you. Line up.'

They moved into a line, Katie giggling as usual. Peter took a sip of his champagne, his eyes moving slowly over the three naked girls, considering the virtues of each. Katie was perhaps the prettiest, with her upturned piggy nose and apple-cheeks framed by golden curls. Her boobs were the biggest too, real melons, making her waist seem tiny for all her chubby tummy and little fat love-handles. Even her pussy was fat, the twin lips peeping out from between her thighs, shaved – as were all three. Her looks went with her nature too, soft and bubbly, eager to play and eager to please.

Cherry was more sophisicated, with a sensible, matter-of-fact air about her, motherly really for all that she couldn't be over twenty-five. As the tallest, she had perhaps the best legs, and her long blonde hair exaggerated her height and set off her chest and hips nicely. As he knew from when he'd had her before, she was at her best when he was tired, ministering to his needs without complaint and never demanding. She also sucked cock well, almost as well as –

He pulled his thoughts back from the edge, to Zoe. She was the slimmest of the three, but still curvy, all boobs and bum, a figure straight out of a porno mag, something she had more than likely appeared in. She had danced well, a natural for striptease, and for posing, the most elegant of the three, the one he would most like to be seen with, for all that Katie turned him on more.

'Turn around,' he ordered, 'hands on your knees, stick your bottoms out.'

Cherry and Zoe obeyed instantly, Katie with just a touch of reluctance, throwing him an uneasy glance across her shoulder as she got into position.

'What's the matter, Katie?' he queried. 'You don't mind showing your bottom, do you?'

'No ... I ... you're not going to spank us, are you?' she questioned.

Peter laughed and put down the bathbrush, which he'd picked up only because it was one of the new models from his main rival.

'No, of course not,' he assured her, amused at her discomfort, 'at least, not if you're good girls. Now stick those bottoms out properly, show it all.'

They obeyed, their cheeks parting as three full bottoms were pushed out, quivering with their giggles, the cheeks well parted to show off pouting pussies and puckered bottomholes. Each was as delectably feminine as the next, plump and round and soft, their holes moist and ready for his cock. He rubbed his hands, wondering whether to fuck Zoe or Cherry once he'd had Katie.

He took another sip of champagne, admiring the line of naked bottoms and the way the lewd pose made the girls' heavy chests swing forward. Already his cock was beginning to respond, and the temptation to make two pose while the third tossed him off was considerable. He resisted, telling himself to be patient as he put his cup down.

'OK, girls,' he announced. 'Cherry, you're to do my hair. Katie, get the soap. Zoe, put some more towels out to warm and then help Katie.'

He closed his eyes in bliss as the girls busied themselves with their tasks. Utterly relaxed, he let himself melt under the gentle touch of their fingers, all the while with his cock slowly growing, to Katie's giggling delight. He was half stiff even before her soapy hands found his balls, and fully erect just moments after she had taken his shaft in her hand.

'You are a big boy, aren't you?' she purred. 'And ever so randy.'

'That's me,' Peter answered, 'and you're going to get it first, my darling.'

Katie burst into giggles, then stopped at an abrupt rap on the door.

'Whoever that is, get rid of them,' Peter instructed. 'Zoe, you do it.'

Zoe had been soaping his chest, and stopped. He heard the wet pad of her feet as she left the bathroom, then her voice.

'Who is it? I'm busy.'

The answer was too faint to catch.

'From Annie?' Zoe responded, puzzled. 'Here, Cherry, there's a girl here says she's from Annie, sent over special for the gentleman.'

'Who is it?' Cherry called out.

'Let her in, let her in,' Peter instructed.

'OK,' Zoe answered, and he heard the door open, then shut. 'Who're you then? Ain't seen you around.'

'Linda,' a voice answered, soft and sweet. 'I was on this bloke's yacht. Bastard dumped me here when his wife turned up. Annie says I can work a couple of nights to get the cash home, so long as I do this job.'

'Oh ... yeah, right ... Come on in. Peter, this is Linda, she's got a treat for you.'

Peter raised one lazy hand in greeting.

'Hi, Peter,' Linda answered, her voice full of rude promise, then stopped. 'Oh, can't you see?'

'Sorry,' Peter answered, 'I can't open my eyes, I'll get soap in them. Pass a towel, Cherry darling.'

'No, no, wait,' Linda said quickly. 'Stay just as you are.'

He caught Katie's giggle, then felt the bath move ever so slightly. She had climbed up on it, her legs braced to either side. Her voice came again, smooth and sexy.

'If your eyes were open, Peter, you could see right up my skirt. It's very short, and red tartan, like a little tiny school skirt. I've a white blouse on too, and a little tie, and no bra, and no panties. Want a peep?'

'Yeah, sure I do,' Peter answered as Cherry pressed a warm towel to his face, wiping the shampoo bubble away.

He opened his eyes, to find Linda as he had been imagining her, square-heeled calf-length boots planted firmly apart across the bath. Long, coltish legs rose from them to a skirt so short any schoolgirl wearing it would have been sent home immediately, and a bare, furry pussy, held wide to show the pink sex lips. With her pussy spread right in his face it took him a moment to register her face, black hair, deep green eyes, a full mouth curved up into a smile of impish malice that could only possibly belong to one girl – Linnet.

The realisation came an instant before she let go of her bladder. Her urine caught him full in the face. He shut his eyes only just in time, and then he was gasping and batting futilely at the thick yellow stream to the sound of Linnet's crazy laughter and the blonde girls' screams and squeals.

'Go on!' Linnet cackled. 'Take it in your mouth, take it in your mouth! You know you want it! Come on, bitch-boy, drink my piss!'

Peter didn't answer, still struggling to keep the powerful stream of urine out of his face and too shocked to do anything sensible. All three of the blonde girls were squealing ineffectually, Katie giggling too.

'Go on, drink!' Linnet crowed. 'You know you want it! You do, you do! Come on, girls, help me! You with the fat tits, you look fun, piss on his balls while he licks my cunt. Come on!'

Not one of the girls answered, and urine still pattered down on Peter's head and chest as he struggled for a grip on the edge of the bath. Finally he got it and lurched up, pulling himself from the bath and clutching for Linnet at the same time. Unable to see, he missed, catching only her derisive laughter as she sprang away. There was a patter of pee on the floor and Zoe gave a squeal of disgust. Peter snatched out, missed again. His face was dripping urine, and as he struggled to stand he put a foot in a suspiciously warm pool, slipping and going down hard on the floor.

'Get the little bitch!' he ordered.

Katie was giggling crazily, Zoe squealing in disgust and alarm. Neither responded. Cherry ducked down to help him but it was too late. Linnet's laughter sounded from the next room, then the stairs, and at last outside, a demented cackling of raw, vicious joy.

Interlogue

'I can't take any more,' Elune gasped. 'I can't!'

'Oh nonsense,' Juliana answered. 'You wanted to be fed, and I'm going to feed you. Now open wide, and do stop struggling.'

'Wait, please!' Elune begged. 'I mean it ... I'm going to burst!'

'Open wide,' Juliana ordered, her voice suddenly hard.

Elune hung her head, panting softly as she struggled to contain the pain in her belly. She was naked, her body bare to the cool sea air, and the gentle waves washing around her waist. Her arms were spread wide, as if on a crucifix, each was lashed tightly to the rusty iron struts of the old pier. She was kneeling, her legs a little apart, her bottom pressed to a barnacle-encrusted pillar, her pussy gaping to the smooth, rounded stone Juliana had pushed up it before the feeding began.

'Open wide,' Juliana repeated, her voice harder still.

'No, please ...' Elune stammered, 'wait just a little ... please ... I'm not as big as you, I can't take it in this fast. Anyway ... why does it have to be seaweed?'

'Seaweed is good for you,' Juliana answered, 'and, besides, there's lots of it, and it's free. I suppose I could get something else though.'

'Please. Honey sandwiches, and ice-cream, and lots of choccy –'

37

'Do you think I'm made of money?'

'You've got lots of money!'

'Maybe, but not for fattening up little sluts. Besides, that sort of thing is no fun, you like it.'

'Oh please, Juliana!'

'Butter?'

'No.'

'Lard?'

'No!'

'Dog food?'

'Juliana!'

'Well, that's my final offer, so if you're not going to be reasonable it'll just have to be seaweed. Eat up.'

She stretched out her hand, offering a heavy wad of bladderwrack to Elune's mouth. Elune turned her face away, her lips tight shut, sure that if she swallowed one more mouthful either she would be violently sick or her stomach would burst. After a moment Juliana gave a sigh of resignation.

'Oh you are boring, Elune. OK, have it your way.'

Juliana's hand disappeared under the water, to come up again a moment later holding a large green crab, its pincers spread in defiance. She smiled at the crab, then at Elune, her gaze directed to her eyes, then to her breasts. Immediately Elune began to babble.

'No, not my nipples, Juliana, please! Please! Please!'

Elune shrank back against the pillar, her skin crawling, as Juliana shuffled close. Her nipples were stiff from the cold water, twin buds of firm flesh sticking out from her breasts, each completely vulnerable. As the crab was moved slowly closer to her skin she began to struggle, writhing in her bonds to make her tits quiver.

'Stay still, Elune,' Juliana instructed, 'or I'll just have to do your pussy instead. I don't imagine you'd like that at all, would you?'

'No,' Elune sobbed, 'OK, OK, I'll eat . . . I'll eat!'

'Sorry,' Juliana answered, 'I'm enjoying this now. This is going to hurt, darling . . .'

Elune pressed back hard against the rough iron of the pillar, whimpering, her whole body shivering violently. She felt the prick of the crab's claw on her breasts and she screamed, then louder still as the sharp little pincer closed on her nipple, the scream blending with Juliana's liquid laughter. Then the crab was withdrawn and she was gasping for air, her bloated stomach churning with fear and reaction. When she finally managed to open her eyes it was to find Juliana smiling sweetly at her, once more with a big handful of seaweed held out. It was put to Elune's mouth, and she forced herself to take it in, to chew on the salty, slimy, rubbery mass, and to swallow.

'You see,' Juliana remarked after a while, 'life would be ever so much easier if you did as I said in the first place.'

Three

If there had been any lingering doubts in Peter's mind that he was being set up, they were gone. There was simply no way Linnet could have known where he was without some inside information, let alone pretended to have come from Annie. Like before, it was the only sensible explanation, and this time it was the only possible one. He was also sure he could work it out.

She had wrecked his night of triumphant sex. Even after Cherry had cleaned him up and nursed the bruises he'd got when he fell on the floor, it had been impossible to recapture the mood. He had managed to fuck Katie, half-heartedly, making her kneel on the bed while Cherry and Zoe had danced for him, and later dip briefly into the others. None of them had really been into it, not the way they had been at first, least of all Peter. His mind had been on Linnet, and whichever misbegotten son of a bitch had sent her.

Back at his comfortable semi in Milton Keynes the next evening he sat down to work it out. Only a handful of people had even known he was going to be in Portsmouth. It had to be one of them and, if several could be dismissed out of hand, he was determined to be sure, and, after a solitary meal of curry and beer, he began to write down all the possibilities. First were the boys from the band, Baz, Jack and Zen. Then there was Jeff Mitchell from The Home Maker, John from The Ship and Annie. That made six.

He thought for a while, then added the names of several of his mates who drank in The Pig and Whistle, any of whom might have talked to Baz or Jack or Zen. There was John Walsh, the landlord, just possibly Jackie, his wife, John Evans, the barman, Pete and Dave, and both Greg Waite and Greg Disley, Barry Langley, John the butcher, Den, Steve from the music shop, Stan, Ed the biker, a dozen others. Then there was his boss, Phil; there was Roger, and Dex, and anyone else in the sales team, anyone in the company who could have checked his itinerary. His mouth twitched up into a wry grin. The list was not so short after all, but some at least he could cross off.

For one thing it couldn't be Annie. She might give the impression of being soft, but she was a shrewd businesswoman at heart and valued his custom. Besides, he had spoken to her the next day. Her amazement and sympathy had been genuine, and he had been a salesman too long to be taken in by a lie. Even when a buyer claimed he had more stock than he really did it showed in his face.

She had never even heard of Linnet, Linda, or any other girl dumped off a yacht that evening, yet Linnet had used her name and knew he was at The Ship, which was another clue. It meant somebody had either followed him, or overheard him talking with Annie and the girls in the back bar of the Green Dragon. The sailors didn't seem very likely, or the couples, leaving the single men and the ugly girl in the overcoat. She alone didn't seem to have had any reason for being there, and was the most likely candidate. Not that it helped much, but at least he could remember her face.

Jeff Mitchell could be counted out. He was a quiet, straightforward man, into angling and blues music. Nor did he have any reason to bear Peter a grudge. Most importantly, he knew nothing at all about Peter's private life.

Peter struck a line through Jeff's name, then hesitated. Jeff had known he would be in Portsmouth well in advance, and also had a fair idea who else Peter sold to. Possibly he might have known when Peter was doing the North-East. He could have had Linnet waiting at Homeland or The Kitchen Man, the rent-boy paid and ready at Mapley's. He could have had the ugly girl follow him from The Home Maker. Just possibly he had worked up some weird resentment of Peter over the years. Very carefully, he wrote Jeff's name down again.

The same went for Phil. Phil had been his boss for years and they had always got on well. While Phil was a bit of a joker, and might well think what Linnet had done was funny, he wasn't the sort to go to so much effort just for a laugh. If he had done it, he would have been sure to get photos. On the other hand, he always knew where Peter was, he knew about Annie's services from his own days as a sales rep, and that Peter frequented the services at J49. For years now Peter's combination of salary and commission had brought in more than Phil earned. Possibly there was resentment. Possibly there was a lot of resentment. Phil's name could not be struck off.

Then there was the band. He told them everything. They knew about Annie, his schedule, the places he liked. Any one of them could have done it, with just a little effort and expense. Zen wasn't likely, too laid back, too unworldly. There wasn't a bad thought in

42

his head, and nothing really interested him except his keyboard and keeping up his supply of weed. Baz wasn't much more likely, his best mate since school, co-founder of the band, and a guy he had total faith in. Jack was the only real possibility, a major joker who liked to play hard, but they got on great. Then again, maybe they were pissed off at him for taking on the role of frontman. He'd had to; they'd urged him to, but maybe they'd decided he was getting too big for his boots. Maybe the three of them were in it together? Maybe they were all in it together?

He went to bed feeling thoroughly paranoid and none the wiser as to who was responsible. Only in the morning did inspiration strike him. They'd done it twice, and they were likely to do it again, especially if he didn't react. So he would say nothing about it, not at work, not down at The Pig and Whistle, not anywhere. Whoever it was would be well pissed off that they'd failed to get a decent rise out of him, even if they had had Linnet's report of what had happened. They'd do it again, and this time he'd be ready.

First he had to lay the bait. Peter and Pizazz were playing the Dog in Luton at Sunday lunchtime, and on the way down he made sure to describe in glowing detail the new singles bar in Swindon he planned to try on the Wednesday night. It was a real bar, and after the gig he added a bit more detail, the name, Fat Sam's, the location and the motel he intended staying in afterwards, Midlander's. Nobody showed unusual interest, if anything the opposite, but that was just what he would have expected.

On Monday he repeated the same process at work, extolling the glories of Fat Sam's for pickups and Midlander's for shagging to both Phil and two of the others on the sales team, Roger, who did London, and their European man, Dex. Again, none of them showed any special interest, but he left feeling well pleased with himself. Unless the culprit was really Jeff Mitchell, they knew, and he was sure they would go for it.

Monday was East Anglia, an easy day picking up orders from clients in Norwich, Lowestoft and Ipswich. The only awkward moment came when he found Dave Pickering of Interiors, Interiors with a rival firm's product mag on his desk. A bit of banter, and bit of serious talk and it was sorted, Peter leaving with two hundred units over what he had expected in his order book.

Tuesday was Birmingham, always a hard one, slow traffic and two small local operators he'd yet to really see off. It was hard work, and twice he had to ring in to Phil to get discounts confirmed, but again he came away with better sales than he had estimated for in the morning.

Both evenings he'd been in The Pig and Whistle, but nobody's behaviour there or at the office had seemed unusual. It was the same Wednesday morning, Phil warning him that there was a quality control issue he'd have to settle with Roma in Newbury, but otherwise completely unremarkable. The day went easily enough, the complaint at Roma trivial, the new female buyer at Luxury in Bath an easy target for his charm. He pulled into Swindon just before five, scored two hundred units on a cold call and arrived at Midlander's well contented.

From the moment he was in his room he was cautious, checking the car park for Linnet's green MG, taking a seat in the restaurant from which he could watch the whole space, even checking the cupboards, shower and under the bed in his room. There was nothing.

He bathed, shaved, dressed, all the while expecting a knock on the door, even keeping an eye on the window. A casual yet sophisicated look was right for Fat Sam's, not too flashy, not too rough. It advertised itself as a piano bar, and customers could play if they chose. He could hardly fail to impress, with his skill on the ivories second only to his guitar-playing. Between that and his cool, easy-going look, he was sure he'd stand out from the crowd. Somewhere in that crowd would be Linnet.

It was just two blocks to the bar, and he walked, enjoying the warm spring evening. Now that he felt he was getting the upper hand there was a strong sense of adventure and, while he wasn't quite sure what he would do with Linnet once he'd got hold of her, he was determined that he would.

Fat Sam's was already busy, the bar lined with men and women, some chatting, others drinking as they took in their surroundings and the night's talent. Many of the tables were occupied too, and the discreet alcoves further from the bar, either by established couples, those who'd just met and wanted to get to know each other a little better, or a few pure and simple music lovers. A lanky man in a blue suit was picking out an Elton John tune at the piano. Peter ordered whisky and propped himself on the bar, no different to a half-dozen other men.

There was no sign of Linnet, but he was content to wait. After his first whisky he took a turn on the piano, going through a Jerry Lee Lewis number and a piece of his own impro fast enough and well enough to earn a round of applause. As he sat back at the bar a short-haired blonde slid on to the stool next to him, her face half turned to catch his eye. She was not Linnet, obviously not Linnet, too tall by maybe six inches, ten years older and with an air of easy charm in place of maniacal vivacity. He still grew instantly alert. She might not be Linnet, but that didn't mean she wasn't in on it.

'Can I buy you a drink?' he offered.

'Vodka and tonic, thank you,' she answered. 'You play well. Are you professional?'

'Amateur,' he answered, 'Peter and Pizazz, I don't suppose you've heard of us?'

'Oh, yes, I saw you at Crazy in Pimlico, I'm sure.'

'We've played Crazy, yeah,' Peter answered. 'Hang on, let me get you that drink.'

He was fighting to keep his laughter down as he turned to catch the attention of the barman. The whole thing was completely transparent. It wouldn't have fooled a newborn baby. Here he was at Fat Sam's, and a woman had come up to him and asked if he was a professional musician, claiming to have seen him play at Crazy. Only when they'd played Crazy the band hadn't been Peter and Pizazz, just plain Pizazz. She was in on it, and the boys from the band were the ones setting him up, maybe one, more likely all three.

Knowing who it was made it hard to be angry. OK, so maybe he had been a bit tough in the last few months, but he'd had to be, or the band would have fallen apart. Jack just didn't take life seriously enough. Zen was smoking way too much dope. Baz ... well, Baz was just Baz, a great guy, the best, but ...

It would be Jack who was the instigator, Jack who had hired Linnet and the rent-boy. That was just Jack's sense of humour, both having him sucked off by a man when he thought it was a girl, and having Linnet piss on him. Not that Jack would have told her to do it in the face, Peter was sure; that was her choice, the mad bitch. In fact, it seemed likely that after that the boys had decided to hire somebody else, the cool blonde now sitting next to him.

'Here's to you, and the boys,' he said, passing her drink.

Her answer was a little cool smile, nothing more, but to Peter it was the final confirmation. They certainly chose well. Linnet was truly gorgeous, mad bitch or not, and the blonde wasn't far behind. She was older, perhaps a little above thirty, with a compact figure and a mature, easy charm. Her suit of fine pale grey wool was designer, beautifully cut to enhance her neat figure yet retain an air of professionalism. The white blouse beneath was unbuttoned just far enough to hint at her cleavage without being blatant, the skirt knee-length, revealing silk stockings on nicely turned calves. Everything about her radiated the urbane, the refined, a style as far from Linnet or Annie's blondes as he could imagine.

'I'm Peter, but you'll have guessed that,' he remarked.

'Linda,' she answered.

Again he had to fight not to leave. They'd even chosen the same fake name Linnet had used to get into his room at The Ship, and they expected him not to notice! He allowed himself a chuckle.

'That's a very pretty name. I knew a girl from Portsmouth named Linda, a friend of Baz and Jack and Zen.'

She was good. Not a flicker of disappointment or surprise, just a slightly puzzled look. He pressed the point.

'The boys from the band.'

'Oh, I see. Sorry, I was a little lost there.'

She gave a light, silvery laugh and flashed a smile, a definitely encouraging smile. Peter smiled back and took another sip of whisky. Linda had that rare knack of being able to make a man feel completely at ease with just a look or a word. He was going to have to be careful, because he could be very sure they wouldn't have simply set him up for a night of fine sex. Somewhere along the line there would be a horrid surprise. Perhaps she'd just tease him and then turn him down, but it didn't seem likely, not after Linnet's behaviour.

Whatever it was, he knew how to deal with it, and turn the tables. He'd charm the knickers off Linda, enjoy her all night long, and then admit he'd guessed in the morning. That was if she didn't admit it first out of a sense of guilt and new-found loyalty to her lover. It was just a question of applying the old Peter magic.

He went into overdrive. He talked about her. He talked about himself, less. He talked rock and roll and blues and jazz. He played the piano, fast, improvised jazz that had the whole bar in applause, two blues numbers, three rock and roll classics, and 'Bridge over Troubled Water' as a finale. By then Linda had sunk five large vodkas and was wearing a lazy, come-to-bed smile. He took her hand, smiling.

'No pressure, but I'm in Midlander's, just a couple of blocks away. If you'd like to –?'

Her answer was to lean forwards and kiss him gently on the cheek, then whisper in his ear. 'I'd love to. One minute.'

She slipped down from her barstool and walked away towards the ladies' powder room, all elegance and poise, even drunk. Peter watched her go, admiring the trim swell of her bottom beneath her skirt. There was a knot in his stomach; lust and whisky were beginning to tell, and he had to force himself to remember that things could still go wrong. She seemed genuine, more so even than Linnet, but maybe Linda was just a smoother operator.

As he waited he was trying to imagine what the catch would be. Maybe he had charmed her past playing whatever trick the boys had paid her to, maybe not. He had to be careful. They'd know where he was staying, and it was sure to happen there, or on the way. Maybe they'd somehow got access to his room. Maybe they'd be waiting with cameras. Maybe Linnet was about, ready to leap in on him and Linda in bed, pretend to be his wife, piss all over them . . .

Linda emerged from the Ladies, as cool as ever. Peter took her arm as she reached him. She gave no resistance, only a knowing smile, allowing him to steer her out into the street. It was cool, and strangely quiet after Fat Sam's, the streets near empty. He found himself glancing around, for the boys, for Linnet, for the green MG. There was nothing, but he knew that even if he had charmed Linda it would be impossible to relax at Midlander's. Revenge could wait. He wanted sex.

'The hell with Midlander's,' he offered, 'for you, the best. Let's get a suite at the Royal.'

'But you've already got a room,' she answered. 'I don't mind, really.'

'No, no,' he insisted. 'The Royal it is.'

She hesitated, then seemed to make a decision, relaxed once more as they started down the street. He was smiling, sure she'd just made a decision to give in, and enjoy a night with him rather than whatever scheme she had been put up to. She felt warm beside him, and a little unsteady, leaning on his arm. He could smell her perfume, something expensive, alluring. Already his cock was beginning to stiffen.

Three blocks and they were at the Royal, a huge Victorian pile of red brick with rooms big enough to fit two of the box-shaped efforts at Midlander's. He booked the George suite, and signed them in as Mr and Mrs Smith. The manager didn't so much as raise an eyebrow. The suite was everything he could have hoped for, a large main room complete with well-stocked bar, a bedroom with a magnificent four poster and a bathroom with a tub big enough to float in.

Cautious to the last, he checked the shower and the wardrobe, then went to the bar for the complimentary bottle of champagne he'd been told to expect. It was there, a Veuve Cliquot nestled in an ice bucket, the glasses beside it. He pulled it out, listening to Linda singing one of the songs he'd played that evening in a gentle contralto as he worked on the foil. It took a moment, the wire unexpectedly stiff, and as he twisted the cork free he caught the hiss of the shower from the bathroom.

He chuckled, leaving the bottle a moment as he quickly undressed, piling his clothes on a chair. Naked, he filled two glasses and made for the bathroom. Linda was already in the shower, the svelte contours of her body visible through the frosted glass, the curtain pulled close. He stepped close, the knot in his stomach tightening, and pulled the curtain open. Linda simply smiled.

Her hands went to her hips, posing unashamedly for his admiration, her own chin lifted, her eyes fixed on his. He let his gaze travel down her body, taking in her smooth, pale neck, her firm, compact breasts, her well-sculpted midriff, the gentle bulge of her hips, her beautiful legs. One thing she did have in common with Annie's girls, she was shaved, her pussy a neat pink slit in the V of her thighs, her outer sex lips a touch parted to show the inner.

She reached out and took the glass, and he stepped in. They linked arms, drank, then kissed, Peter tasting the wine and her lipstick as their mouths opened together. She put an arm around him, her fingers splayed out on the muscle of his back and he returned the embrace, stroking the nape of her neck as they kissed, until she had began to shiver and her breathing grown deep. He could feel his cock growing, pressed to the smooth wet flesh of her thigh, and with it the urge to fuck her.

He held back, knowing she deserved the respect of his patience, contenting himself with kissing and stroking her neck and back, but slowly moving lower. She grew more urgent in turn, pausing only to take a swallow of her drink and once more let their mouths open together in a champagne-flavoured kiss. At that he let his hands drift lower still, to cup the neat globes of her bottom, holding her to him by them as he squeezed and stroked her flesh, his need rapidly getting the better of her reserve. Daring more, he let the tip of a finger touch her bottomhole, tickling the little star. Her response was to cling tighter as a shiver went through her body, then to break away.

Her mouth stayed open, her eyes bright with lust, her nipples erect, shower water running down to cascade from the tips. Briefly her tongue flicked out, and then she kneeled down to take his cock in her hand as she swallowed from her glass, then into her mouth. Peter gasped as cold champagne engulfed his cock and spilled down over his balls, then she was sucking, the warmth of her mouth building quickly. He took hold of her head, smoothing his fingers over her wet hair as he settled back against the shower wall, his eyes closed, in ecstasy as she brought him up to erection. She was bold, sucking him deep as she tickled him under his balls with her long, painted fingernails. He could picture her, so refined, so beautiful, now with his cock growing rapidly in her mouth, and shortly to be inserted in her pussy.

That was where it was going, no question, his resolve to take his time with her breaking to his need. He reached down, took her gently under the arms and lifted her. His cock, now fully erect, came free of her mouth, and she gave no resistance, anything but, as he lifted her, put her back to the wall and slid her down on to his cock. Her arms went around his neck, riding him, her face set in bliss. He took her by the bottom, slipping one finger into the mouth of her anus as they fucked, to tease the little hole as his cock slid in and out of her pussy.

Linda was quickly moaning, and wriggling herself against him, with her breasts quivering and water splashing from her body. She had lost all her poise, all her sophistication, now fucking like a horny girl, with raw animal passion, naked and shameless, bouncing on his cock. He was no better, thrusting hard into her, raw, dirty passion burning in his head. He pushed his finger further up her bottom and she merely sighed in pleasure. He pulled her close, kissing and biting at her mouth and shoulders and she grew more passionate still. He forced her hard against the wall, ramming his cock in and out, his finger jammed to the base in her anus, her body jerking helplessly, spitted on his erection.

He came, deep up her, clinging on tight in ecstasy, and in a savage joy at his success. They'd paid her to lead him on, to make a mockery of him, to frustrate and humiliate him. All that and more, but there he was, her naked and penetrated in both holes, his sperm pumping into her as she gasped and wriggled on his cock. Even when he had finished she didn't stop, clinging on tight as she writhed against him, rubbing her little bald cunt on to his pubic hair, and he realised that she too was coming, taken to ecstasy by what he had done, the final triumphant detail to his evening.

Interlogue

Elune cupped her heavy breasts. They felt strange, but nice, more as if she was playing with another girl than touching herself. Her nipples were exceptionally sensitive too, popping out to the slightest touch, and swollen, each the width of a wine cork and half as long. Even when not erect they showed through her top, straining out from the tips of her bulging breasts, with the cotton of her light T-shirt stretched so tight it looked as if it would burst. As she walked up from the estuary to the university just about every male pair of eyes had turned to her, and not a few female, looks of lust, astonishment, even disgust. Aileve had taken a moment to recognise her for all the years they had known each other.

'So what do you think?' she asked.

'I think you should stop playing with yourself,' Aileve replied. 'Somebody might come in, and I can't very well lock the door.'

'I just love these new titties,' Elune responded, but folded her hands in her lap. 'Seriously, though, what do you think?'

'Obscenely fat,' Aileve replied, 'are you sure you haven't overdone it?'

'No,' Elune replied, 'they're about right. OK, maybe my nipples are a bit bigger, but I doubt he'll notice.'

'He'll notice your hair.'

'Yes, I was going to ask you if you knew a good salon.'

'I use Mirabelle, just off the Honiton Road, but you should really go up to London. There's a place I know behind Euston Station, Simon Simone it's called. They specialise in transvestites. Apparently they can do amazing things with hair, and they do wigs and extensions and so forth too.'

'Sounds good. How does the extra-respectable Dr Alice Chaswell know about a place like that?'

'I was seeing a lecturer from Social Studies. He was into cross-dressing.'

'Any fun?'

'Not much, he took himself far too seriously. It was strange, at first, seeing a man in tights again after all these years. Do you remember the way they used to cut their jackets, so their bottoms showed under the hem?'

'Sure. So you dumped him?'

'Yes, after about a month. It was fun at first, but he was always analysing himself and it got boring. He couldn't get an erection unless he was in women's clothes, and even than I had to beat him first.'

'Juliana would have loved him.'

'He'd have run a mile from Juliana.'

'Don't they all. So I'm getting the tits, and my bum's just about fat enough. What else? Do you think I should be a virgin?'

'A virgin?'

'Sure, you know how men love to pop a cunt. It makes them feel big.'

'Maybe, if not so much nowadays, but it hardly goes with the image, does it?'

'Why not? Fat girls can be virgins too.'

'Yes, but you're not just a fat girl, are you? And for heaven's sake, buy some new clothes!'

'I did. I'm already bursting out of them. The button on my jeans broke earlier.'

'Get some with an elasticated waist, and some baggy tops. Odd, isn't it, about virginity? When I was young people were obsessed by it, but now it's regarded almost as a burden.'

'Times change. We used to go in for ritual defloration, some of the time. Do you think he'd fancy that?'

'Is he into paganism?'

'I don't think so.'

'Then presumably not. Frankly, he's likely to think it's extremely odd if you turn out to be a virgin at all. They've probably fucked already.'

'True,' Elune admitted, 'but I'm tempted anyway. Perhaps as I fatten?'

Four

Peter stretched as he came awake, the events of the night before filtering slowly into his mind. His mouth curved up into a smile as he remembered Linda, and the truly glorious night of sex they had enjoyed together. He could hear the shower, and was not surprised when he opened his eyes to find her side of the big four poster empty, the sheets dishevelled. Again he stretched, letting the blood flow into the muscles of his shoulders and arms, and into his cock.

Every moment of the night before was clear in his head, for all that he had lost count of the number of times he'd come. Just the thought was giving him a morning erection, and he took hold, playing with himself as he went over the details in his head. There had been the first time, in the shower with Linda up against the wall and the water cascading over their bodies. Afterwards they'd dried and sat down on the settee in the main room in their robes, to sip champagne and watch a late-night film. They'd soon been kissing again, and before long he'd been between her thighs, pumping into her as she gasped and shivered to his thrusts.

The third had been in bed. They'd been fooling around, fighting with the pillows and tickling each other. When they'd got into a grapple he'd found his cock against the warm slit of her pussy and fucked her, then and there, Linda with the pillow she'd been trying to hit him with still clutched to her chest as she moaned beneath him. Afterwards she'd gone to wash, but he'd been on a roll and caught her in the bathroom, bending her across the sink to fuck her from behind with her pretty bottom spread to let him watch his cock go in and out. After that they'd meant to go to sleep, but with her bare bottom in his lap it hadn't been long before he was erect again, and once more he'd fucked her from behind.

That made five fucks, five orgasms, and, if his cock was a little sore, it was also rock hard, ready for another. He grinned, wondering how many teenage boys could manage to come five times in as many hours and still be ready for a sixth in the morning. The shower was still going, and he decided to sneak in and surprise her, perhaps from behind, popping his erection into her at the same moment she realised he was there. His grin was broader still as he climbed from the bed and padded into the bathroom, to find the shower running, but empty, Linda nowhere to be seen.

Puzzled, and disturbed too, he hastened into the main room. She wasn't there either, and the empty bottle and their glasses stood as they'd been left. Something was missing though, and it took him an instant to realise what it was – his clothes. They were gone, all of them, even his boxer shorts. He was cursing himself, Linda, Linnet, Jack and the boys as he began a frantic search of the suite. Again and again he threw open a drawer or peered beneath something, hoping they'd merely been hidden, but they hadn't. Nor had something even more important – his wallet.

It had gone beyond a joke. He was stark bollock naked, without a penny on him, in a hotel suite he was supposed to pay nearly four hundred pounds for, and a good mile from where the rest of his clothes were. They were probably about, perhaps even in the hotel, having a good laugh at his expense. Yes, that would be it, they'd be downstairs in the breakfast room, Linda and the three boys, maybe even Linnet, all waiting to poke fun at him when he came downstairs in a sheet.

He forced himself to stay calm. The only possible thing to do was accept it, to take it as the joke it was supposed to be, to laugh along with them and apologise if he'd been driving them a bit too hard. Only he was not going to do it in a sheet. He'd be smart, out-think them, keep at least some of his dignity and show them he could keep his sense of humour too. He could even laugh off the rent-boy if he really tried.

Meanwhile, they could wait. Picking up the phone beside the bed, he asked for a full English breakfast to be sent up. By the time it arrived he was wrapped in the coverlet from his bed, and looking only a touch sheepish as the maid wheeled in a trolley. She gave him a slightly wary look, evidently cautious of male customers who ordered breakfast and accepted it with nothing on but a bed cover.

'It's not what it looks like,' he assured her, sitting down, 'just a stupid joke some mates of mine have played on me. They're nothing but big kids, really.'

'Yes, sir,' she answered, still doubtful. 'Shall I pour coffee, sir?'

'Yeah, sure, black, two sugars . . . no, make that three. Look, I'm in a bit of a spot here. They've taken my clothes, everything, my wallet too. Do you think you could do me a favour?'

'What would that be, sir?'

She did not sound happy about it, but he perse-vered.

'I'll make it worth your while, believe me,' he said. 'All I need are some clothes.'

'Clothes, sir?'

'Yes. You must have something in a place this size. Even some overalls would do, or perhaps some of the guys you work with change when they arrive? My mates'll be down in the breakfast room, I expect, and there's a hundred in it for you.'

'I'll see what I can do, sir,' she answered, straightening up from the coffee she had made him. 'I'll put everything here, shall I, sir?'

'Yes, do,' he answered, rising to cross to where she had begun to lay his breakfast out on a table. 'And try and get something roughly my size, yes? A suit would be nice.'

'I'll see, sir,' she answered, and stepped back, hiding a giggle as she left the room.

Peter made a wry face as he began to butter a piece of toast. He smeared it with egg and ate it, then a second. He started on his sausages, ate his bacon, his brownies, the other sausage, the last of the egg on a third piece of toast. All the while he slowly calmed down, and all the while he was plotting revenge. It had to be done. It was one thing to take the joke, and to admit that he'd deserved it, in a way, but they really had gone too far. He'd get them back, the same way they'd got him, with something sexually humiliating and each to his own style. Peter Williams did not go down that easily.

He was still drinking his second cup of coffee when the maid returned. She looked flustered, and had no clothes with her, or anything else. Before he could ask what was wrong a second person had stepped into the room behind her, a man, and wearing an uncomfortably recognisable blue uniform. A third person entered, another woman, but a policewoman, a sergeant.

59

'Mr Peter Williams?' she asked.

'Yes, that's me, Peter Williams,' he managed.

'If you could, sir,' she went on, 'we'd like you to accompany us to the station. We have reason to believe you have been the victim of a confidence trickster who goes by the name of Linda Armitage.'

Peter closed his eyes as he sank into the comfort of his armchair. It had not been a good day. In fact, it had been the worst day he could remember in a very, very long time, and that included the disasters in Portsmouth and at Mapley's. What with losing his clothes, several hundred pounds and all his cards, wandering around the Swindon Royal in a bed sheet, the hours spent answering questions at the police station, and coming home dressed in some gear that looked and smelled as if it had been taken from a dead tramp, it just about took the biscuit.

He had really fallen for it, letting her charm and his own self-assurance lull him into a false sense of security, and when he'd been on the lookout for trouble! Admittedly he'd been on the lookout for mates playing stupid games and not a skilled and experienced confidence trickster, but that was not much consolation. Having fucked her was no consolation either, given that she'd clearly enjoyed it as much as he had, and known what was really going on. It just left him feeling used. What little consolation there was resided in his having left his car keys and case at Midlander's, saving him at least something.

Apparently, so the police had told him, it was Linda Armitage's standard MO. She would find a man in a singles bar, get him thoroughly drunk and thoroughly horny, let him think he had seduced her, go back to his hotel room, have sex while she got him drunker still, and decamp at dawn with his money and if possible his clothes. Taking the clothes was apparently as much to humiliate him in some sort of weird revenge for giving into sex as to slow him down in the morning, or so the police psychologist had said.

It made perfect sense. Looking back, he could see that she had been way too easy. She had also been a great deal less drunk than she pretended. Most of her champagne had gone down the plughole in the shower, via his cock and balls, and even at Fat Sam's it was easy to see how she could have disposed of her vodkas while he was at the piano.

As a final irony, when he'd thought he was laying a trap for the boys in the band, he himself had been trapped, and with consummate ease. His own trap, meanwhile, had failed miserably, presumably because they'd spotted it. All in all, he seemed to have made every mistake there was to make, and then some.

He downed a slow whisky, then a second. As the alcohol worked its way into his system he began to calm down a little. He knew he needed to. They were playing in The Pig and Whistle that evening, home turf, and he needed to be on form. Amateur he might be, but he was good, and there was a chance it would be the night somebody from a record company chose to drop by and listen. They'd issued enough invitations, and it did look as if they might finally be given their chance to impress. A rumour had come back from a mate in London, an ex-drummer turned bike messenger, that Retro Records had scouts out to check out the covers bands. Quite possibly it would be Peter and Pizazz that night and, the way his luck had been, everything would go wrong.

It wasn't going to happen, not if he could help it. Zen would not be too stoned to do anything but weird improvs; Jack would not get so pissed he fell into his own drumkit; Baz would not be too shaky to string one bassline together. He, Peter, would make sure of it, and they would play a blinder.

One thing he was not going to do was mention what had happened. If he did, he knew he would never hear the end of it, either down the pub or at work. It was bad enough having to face the prospect of what had happened with Linnet coming out, without adding Linda to it. He would stay firmly quiet and pray it didn't get back to anyone he knew.

After a third small whisky he felt ready. There were still a couple of hours to go, but he'd always found it paid to be ready. For one thing John could not be guaranteed to have cleared the stage, and the amps were more than likely hidden behind stacks of beer crates. He couldn't expect much help from the others either. Baz might be a good bass player, but he'd been known to forget to switch his amp on. Zen seemed to think his sound would sort itself out by some magical means, and Jack was more than likely to be chatting up the new girl behind the bar.

He dressed carefully, a loose black waistcoat over a red shirt, worn denims, shades, boots. It didn't pay to be too flashy, or to seem to be trying too hard. Cool and easy was always best. Ready, he took his Stratocaster from its case, lovingly running a finger over its smooth red paintwork. It was impossible to hold it and not feel good, a true gem of an instrument, and with a history. Pete Townshend had played it, back in the heyday of The Who, and it still bore a dent where it had been smashed into a big Marshall. So went the story, anyway, and, as with any good story, it was better not to question it too much.

The Strat back in its case, he set off, working out the set in his mind as he went. It was best to start with numbers everybody knew, covers, and nothing too difficult. Once the drink had started to flow and the vibe had begun to infect the crowd they could go for some of their own stuff.

As he came in at the door of The Pig and Whistle he pushed all his bad feelings down, greeting John and Jackie with a friendly wave and a peck on her cheek. As he had suspected, the stage was bare, although they had at least moved the tables that occupied it on normal nights. He put the Strat carefully to one side and went into the back, finding the gear half hidden behind stacks of beer, tonic and soda, again just as he had anticipated.

He continued to work on the details for the set as he began to haul things around. When he came out again after ten minutes of hard work he found Jack had arrived, and was at the bar, pint in hand, cocky smile large on his face, the new barmaid giggling at some joke he'd told. A few others had come in too, regulars, except for one. Immediately he felt his pulse quicken, wondering if she could be the scout. He'd never seen her before, and she appeared to be on her own, and if she'd didn't look like a stereotypical record company type, then that might well mean she was one.

As he moved the amps and monitors into place he kept a cautious eye on her. She was pleasantly plump, her face soft and easy, making it hard to tell her age. Her manner spoke confidence though, very relaxed, and her dress, a dark blue trouser suit, well cut and expensive, a crisp white blouse beneath, her hair up in a slightly severe bun, ostentatious gold jewellery. She was drinking what looked like Crème de Menthe, also unusual in The Pig and Whistle.

He nodded to himself as he went backstage again. She did look the part, and she was sitting in a place that would give her a prime view of the stage.

Abruptly nervous, he ran through his choices for the set again. Were they right? Should he fool around less, jazz it up a bit, put in something with a good guitar solo?

As he hauled the bass amp out on to the stage he was already going through the chords for 'Hotel California' in his head. It had to be done, just to show her what he could handle, and, if she turned out not to be the scout, it was a great piece to play anyway. Only when Peter had called twice did Jack manage to wrench himself away from the barmaid's side to set up his drumkit, then Baz arrived, followed by Zen, looking no more than usually dazed.

Halfway through the soundcheck, the pub was already beginning to fill up. Most of the regulars were there, and a good number of others, many of whom he recognised from other previous home gigs and even from other venues. Every time they played it got a little more crowded. They were on the up, no question, and if he could only hold it all together they might just go all the way.

The others were ready, the juke box off. John threw Peter a quizzical glance. Peter raised a hand in response, his five fingers splayed out to indicate that he needed a little time. Quickly he beckoned the others to him, putting his arms around their shoulders as they gathered together.

'See the woman in the corner, with the blue suit on?'

'Sounds like a song that,' Jack answered, glancing over, '. . . *short fat woman with the blue suit on . . . dah dah, da da . . .*'

'Shut up, Jack, I'm being serious,' Peter interrupted. 'I think she's the scout for Retro Records.'

'You're fucking joking!' Baz answered, all nerves on the instant.

'No, I'm not,' Peter answered. 'So no fuck-ups, and no clowning around. Yes, I'm looking at you, Jack. Play it straight, strictly on my lead, got it?'

Baz and Jack nodded, serious for once. Zen gave him a lazy peace sign.

'OK, he went on. We kick off with "Hound Dog" . . .'

'Elvis?'

'Sod Elvis, the original, Big Mama Thornton style. That way she'll know we're for real. Let's go.'

They moved back to their places, Peter's nerves strung high as he took his place at the front, the Strat suddenly heavy in his hands. The plump woman was now standing, her glass in her hand, looking at him, her eyes reflected red in the spots to give her a weird, demonic appearance. He raised his hands and a hush fell over the audience. He caught the mic as John flipped it to him, spun it once and put it to his mouth.

'Ladies and gentlemen, here we need no introduction, but I'll give one just the same. I'm Peter and this is Pizazz, playing retro rock for you here at The Pig and Whistle. And that's about all I've got to say. Take it away, boys, one . . . two . . . three . . .'

He launched into the opening of 'Hound Dog', fast and smooth, and the instant he'd picked out the first chord he knew he was on a roll. Linnet was forgotten, and Linda, and the stress of work. All that mattered was the music, the tune flying from his fingers as he belted out the words he'd known by heart since childhood. He followed 'Hound Dog' with 'Johnny B. Goode'. He gave them James Brown, and Lou Reed, the Beatles and the Stones. He gave them Freddie and the Bellboys and Rufus Thomas. He gave them 'Hotel California' and took the solo without a single slip.

By then he was buzzing, high on the sheer joy of his music, barely aware that there might be a scout in the audience, let alone caring. They moved on to their own stuff, songs written by Baz and himself, some of them dating right back to his schooldays. The regulars knew them, and clapped and cheered each and every one with the same gusto they'd given the classics, until Peter was sure that if he played the theme from *Thomas the Tank Engine* he would get rapturous applause.

They moved into improv straight from the end of their most popular number, altogether, to end with Jack belting out a thunderous drum solo that ended only when a stick broke on a rimshot. Peter had caught the rhythm on the Strat before the clash of the cymbals had even died away, then the others moved smoothly in, and the drums joined them once more. A final crescendo, ending with him kneeling at the front of the stage, the Strat across his knees, and it was done, every single man and woman in the place clapping and cheering and stamping on the floor.

Shouts were going up for more, but John was already ringing the bell for last orders and Peter shook his head. The woman in the blue suit was still there and, while he knew too well to press his attention on to her, he was at least determined to give her a chance to speak up. Sure enough, no sooner had he got a welcome drink in his hand at the bar than he saw her coming towards him through the crowd, her pleasant face lit with a beaming smile. He quickly moved back a little, making space at the bar, and signalled John.

'Another, Peter?' John asked.

'For this lady,' Peter explained and turned to the woman. 'If I may?'

'Thank you,' she answered. 'Crème de Menthe please.'

'A double,' Peter instructed John.

Baz was nearby, and moved close, also Jack.

'D'you know the joke about the Pope and Crème de Menthe?' Jack asked.

'If it's the one that ends "Two pints of Crème de Menthe please, Jimmy", then yes,' she answered. 'Billy Connolly.'

'Hey, a real woman,' Jack answered.

John served the drink, a tumbler half full of the thick green liquid, along with a couple of ice-cubes, more likely four shots than two. She picked it up and took an appreciative sip. Peter took a swallow of his whisky, tongue-tied for once in his life and more sure than ever that she was the scout. There was an air of confidence about her, the manner of somebody who is ultimately in control, and her green eyes showed a twinkle of humour uncomfortably reminiscent of Linnet. In fact, he considered, so far as looks went, she might have been Linnet's mother.

'What do they call you then, love?' Jack asked, as unfazed as ever.

'Patricia,' she answered after an instant of hesitation. 'Patty more often.'

'Patty's nice,' Jack answered, 'a friendly name. So what d'you think, are we the business, or what?'

Peter winced, but she answered casually enough. 'You're great. You've got a lot of talent.'

She took another sip of her drink, evidently not wanting to be drawn. Peter made a frantic grimace at Jack over the top of her head. She gave a light chuckle for no obvious reason and took another swallow, downing about half the tumbler of liqueur. In the background John was ringing the time bell. She spoke.

'So, boys, what else do you for fun in Milton Keynes of an evening?'

Jack answered. 'Drink, shag, eat curry.'

67

Peter groaned inwardly. 'Don't mind Jack,' he apologised. 'He's pissed. We'd like to think we're about the best entertainment you can get, as it goes. After a Pizazz gig everything else is downhill.'

He'd kept the humour in his voice, trying to sound jokey more than arrogant. She smiled.

'You certainly play well. I wonder, do you play as well?'

Jack responded with a dazed look. Peter caught her meaning. It was not what he'd been expecting, but if that was the way she wanted to play, then who was he to protest?

'We play,' he answered. 'Anyone in particular in mind?'

She looked straight at him.

'All four of you.'

Peter swallowed hard, his immediate thought whether he would be able to get an erection in front of the others. Somehow he knew Jack wouldn't have a problem, even if what was on offer didn't quite seem to have sunk in.

'What about the amps and drums and that –' he had begun, and stopped abruptly. 'Shit, you mean?'

'I do,' she assured him.

'She does,' Peter added.

Jack gave one glance towards the barmaid, who was collecting glasses, and nodded.

'I'm on. Let's go.'

Baz shot Peter a worried look, but Jack had already taken his arm. They moved towards the door, Peter quickly collecting Zen from where he was deep in conversation with Steve and Ed. Zen came, protesting only when they were outside.

'What's up, man?'

'What's up, man,' Jack answered, 'is that we four are going to take this nicely rounded piece of totty back to my gaff and fuck her four on one, eh, babe?'

Peter hid his face in his hands, but to his amazement Patty didn't kick Jack in the balls or even slap his face. Instead she answered quite coolly.

'That's about the size of it, if you think you can handle me?'

'Yeah, cool, I'm on,' Zen answered, his eyes going straight to her chest. 'Nice.'

They moved off, walking down the gentle slope towards Jack's house, a new semi in a cul-de-sac, one of thousands like it. Jack had his arm around her, Peter by their side, Baz hanging back and Zen with him, trying to roll a joint as they walked through the uneven glow of the street lamps. Peter's throat felt tight, his fingers twitchy. It had been a long time since he had shared a woman with another man, and never four. She was no groupie either, whatever Jack seemed to think, but someone who mattered, someone who mattered a lot. As he glanced sideways to admire the way her big breasts bounced in her blouse he tried to psych himself up, to fuck her the way a rock-star would fuck her, without a thought for who was watching, or joining in.

Until they reached Jack's house he held the lingering hope that she would expect to go upstairs and take them one by one, but it was soon dispelled. The moment they were indoors she took charge, ordering up beer and settling down on the settee. Peter joined her, determined to keep the boys, and more especially her, in mind of just who was band leader. Jack dished out the beers and settled down on the far side of her, immediately leaning close to kiss her. She responded for a moment, then pulled away, smiling as she popped a beer can open, her lipstick already smudged.

'So, boys,' she demanded, 'let's see what you've got. Willies out for Mama.'

'Let's see what you've got and all,' Jack responded, unzipping without a moment's hesitation. 'Those fine-looking titties for a start.'

Patty merely gave him a knowing smile, and was shrugging her jacket off even as he flopped a large and ugly penis out from his fly. Remembering the rent-boy, Peter winced, but followed suit, taking out his own cock, embarrassed, yet with a touch of pride. He was bigger than Jack, and a good deal better formed. Patty gave a purr of appreciation, all eyes on her as she fiddled with the buttons of her blouse. She already had a fair bit of cleavage on display, more as the first button went, and about as much as any man could reasonably want with the second. Proud and unselfconscious, she pulled it wide and flipped her bra up, leaving two plump pink breasts sticking out from among the twin nests of her dishevelled clothing. Her nipples were big, red and erect, each bud stiff, ideal for sucking. Peter felt his cock twitch and he began to stroke it, suddenly sure he would be able to make it.

'Here, let me,' she offered, and reached out to take him in hand, her soft fingers sending a shock right through him the instant they closed on his cock.

She took Jack in her other hand and began to masturbate them both, glancing from one to the other with her face set in a happy smile, then opening her mouth and batting her eyelids at Zen. There was no mistaking the gesture. He too had taken his cock out at her command, a skinny white thing, thin but long like his body, the red tip already protruding from the end of his foreskin. He moved forward, immediately, cocking one leg up on the sofa to feed his cock into Patty's mouth. She immediately began to work on him, her plump cheeks sucking in, her eyes closed in bliss.

Baz had held back, and was watching in open-mouthed amazement, one hand clutching his beer, the other tentatively rubbing at his crotch. Peter gave him a grin, wanting to support his friend. Baz moved close, watching as Jack began to fondle one of Patty's heavy breasts. Peter took the other, feeling her cream-smooth skin and full flesh, firmer than he had expected, and warm to his touch. She was almost as big as Katie, whose huge globes had been the largest he could remember seeing on a young girl, and, if Patty seemed older, it was not by much.

Not that her age mattered, or much else aside from the fact that her hand was around his cock. His cock was growing rapidly stiff and the urge for sex was rising in his head. Leaning down, he took her nipple in his mouth. She gave a little sigh of pleasure around Zen's cock and began to tug harder on him. A glance showed that Jack was hard, his cock rigid in Patty's other hand. He realised that unless he took control he was unlikely to be the first in her.

'Come on my lap,' he breathed, sliding his hands around the softness of her hips.

She made a muffled swallowing sound as she responded, lifting, her mouth still on Zen's cock, to pose her bottom above Peter's crotch. She looked round and inviting beneath the tight blue material of her skirt, and he lost no time in tugging it up, exposing big lacy panties simply bulging with plump female bottom. He whipped them down, catching the scent of her arousal as she was stripped, and took his cock, pressing the head to the warm, wet slit of her pussy. She wriggled down, her full bottom settling into his lap, plump and soft and delicious. His mouth came wide in ecstasy as she began to squirm on his erection.

Zen was hard, and taking his time in her mouth, letting her do the work with his joint still hanging from the side of his lip as she sucked on him. Her hand was still busy with Jack, jerking clumsily on his erection. Baz had his cock out, still limp in his hand, his face full of nervous energy and lust as he watched Patty being fucked.

Peter put his arms around her, taking one plump breast in each hand, feeling the big nipples beneath his fingers. She had cocked her thighs open over his, and the feel of her boobs in his hands and her bottom in his lap was bringing him up towards orgasm. He closed his eyes, shutting out the distracting sight of his friends' cocks and concentrating on wallowing in the delights of female flesh. He heard Jack grunt, mixed ecstasy and disappointment as he spunked over Patty's hand, then Zen, and he knew her mouth was full too.

Both men moved back, leaving Peter a free field. Grinning broadly, and now revelling in his control, he took a firm grip on Patty's waist and lifted her bodily, still on his cock. She gave a squeak of delight and surprise as she lifted, and another as he put her to her knees on the carpet. Once more he began to fuck her, now doggie-style, her big bottom wobbling to his thrusts. He took hold, spreading her cheeks to show off the tight wrinkle of her bumhole.

Patty was gasping, her eyes closed, her mouth wide, spunk and drool hanging in a curtain from her chin. Baz was right in front of her, cock in hand, looking worried, then abruptly going down, kneeling on the floor to feed his cock into Patty's willing mouth. She was sucking immediately, lewd and eager, a cock in each end, her big boobs swinging under her chest, and as Peter picked up his rhythm inside her she put a hand back to masturbate.

Jack began to clap to the rhythm of Peter's fucking and the sway of Patty's body. Zen caught the beat, clicking his fingers in time, and even Baz was grinning as he fed his cock in and out of Patty's mouth. Peter fixed his eyes on the spread of Patty's bottom, her lifted skirt, her dropped knickers, her big creamy cheeks, the rude brown wrinkle of her bottomhole, the plump pussy lips with his erection pushed between.

Zen and Jack began to pick up the time, and so did Peter, faster and faster, jamming himself deep, making Patty's whole body quiver to the thrusts. Her breasts began to bounce and slap together to the same beat; her pussy began to contract on his cock and Peter was coming. Her body went tight, her sex in urgent contraction, milking him into her as he built to a final crescendo of hard thrusts, in perfect time as she too came, and Baz slipped free to coat her face in thick white come.

Peter sank back, his cock slipping from Patty's hole. She was still in orgasm, her fingers busy between her plump sex lips as she licked and sucked at Baz's cock and balls, taking down as much come as she could get. Her pussy was running spunk, her bottom smeared with it. As Baz stood back she moved into a lewd squat, her bottom pushed out and her knees well spread. She was still masturbating with furious energy, her big breasts bouncing crazily on her chest, and as her body went into a fresh set of spasms, she pushed a hand down between the cheeks of her bottom, inserting a finger well up inside her rectum. She cried out; her whole body went tense and she stopped, holding her orgasm with her face set in absolute rapture, then rubbed again, now slow and gentle as the tension drained from her muscles. All four watched her as she finished herself off, Jack planting a heavy smack across her bottom as she finally took her hands away.

'Dirty bitch!' he crowed. 'Hey, lads, we just had us our first groupie!'

Peter threw Jack a dirty look, but Patty merely rolled over, sitting down on the carpet. Her hair had come loose; her face was plastered in come, her make-up ruined, but her beautiful green eyes were full of sleepy pleasure. She smiled, oblivious to Jack's crude remark, right at Peter, once more reminding him of Linnet as she spoke, her voice pure silk.

'Just let me brush up a little, we'll have a beer, and you can all fuck my tits, OK?'

Interlogue

Elune slid herself into the pond. Cool mud squelched up between the cheeks of her bottom and over her pussy and she sighed in pleasure, closing her eyes. It was a favourite place, hemmed in by reeds with the flat fenland stretching away to every side, making it invisible save from a few feet away or the air. Nobody could reach it without either crossing one or other of the broad, muddy dykes to either side. Miles of bog, bramble and willow scrub between the dykes cut it off from road and sea. Not even the sand banks in the wash provided better basking.

Her face was set in a gentle smile, her thoughts drifting. The sun was warm on her tummy and face, her breasts too, which felt sensitive and a little sore. They'd felt good, the pleasure they gave just about balancing their clumsiness, although it did make her wonder how Thomasina, and even Juliana, managed all the time. Running was awkward, and anything that involved jiggling about, but yes, the sex was excellent.

Stretching her arms out, she scooped her hands into the thick muck, enjoying the feel of it between her fingers, cool and slimy, before slapping a heavy handful to each breast. Her back arched as she dirtied herself, smearing it over her chest until her nipples had come erect making twin humps in the wet black muck. The effect was instantaneous, soothing away the stresses of being so big and so well used.

Six or seven hours of basking, and she would drive on to King's Lynn for food, then to Thomasina's caravan. Possibly Thomasina would want to spank her, or there might even be men around, dirty ones. There was something about Thomasina that attracted older men with a penchant for spanking, strip and generally lewd behaviour, perhaps not so much her voluptuous curves as the way she behaved. It suggested that they might get what they wanted. Often they did.

Her smile grew broader at the memory of Thomasina down on an old man's cock, her big bottom stuck out behind, her skirts thrown up on to her back, her drawers wide apart to show cheeks red from spanking. Even during the punishment he'd been embarrassed to have Elune watching, for all his claims that Thomasina needed discipline, but it hadn't stopped him making her suck him off. Afterwards, once he'd filled Thomasina's mouth with spunk, he'd given them each a penny and then spent an hour in guilty prayer.

She chuckled at the memory. It was tempting to come one more time before she began to bask in earnest. The mud was making her pussy and anus tickle, tempting her to stick a finger into each hole. To think was to act, and her legs came up and open, spreading her muddy pussy to the air. Her hands went down, finding her pussy hole moist and easy under the mud, her anus tight but yielding. She purred as two fingers went into her pussy and one into the tiny ring beneath. It felt delightful, making her want more.

Her eyes came open, fixing to the fat green seed pods growing from the flags around her head. They were just formed, hard and waxy, each as thick as two fingers and just right for filling her cavities. She pulled her fingers free and reached up, tugging the thick stems

76

down one by one to pluck the seed pods and pile them on her belly. A dozen seemed enough, and with her legs cocked as wide as they would go, she began to feed them into the muddy hole of her sex. They went easily, quickly giving her a delightfully full sensation that grew with each one. Ten went in, leaving her pussy packed, the tips of three protruding from the stretched hole.

She began to tease herself, stretching out the moment before she invaded her anus. Her hands went to her breasts, squeezing them to break the crust of mud, already caked dry on her skin. It felt odd, and hurt a little when she broke bits from her nipples, leaving them poking up red and sensitive from the brown of her dirty boobs. Suddenly urgent, she pulled her legs up again, rolling herself high to pull her bottom from the mud with a sticky sound. Once again her hands went down, taking the seed pods with them. One she pressed to her anus, gasping as her slimy ring stretched open to take it, and wriggling her bottom against her hand as it went in.

A second seed pod followed the first up her bottom, and a third, each packed into her rectum. With the fourth she began to feel bloated, but she pushed a fifth in without hesitation, and a sixth, to leave her bulging in pussy and anus both, and slowly gyrating her bottom into the mud. She tried to poke the last pod in, not quite succeeding, to leave the mouth of her anus agape on the tip.

One hand went to her pussy, rubbing as the other explored between her thighs, touching the protruding tip of the seed pods and feeling the sensitive, penetrated flesh of her holes. She arched her back, revelling in the bloated, bursting sensation in both cunt and rectum, sighing as she picked up the pace of her masturbation before screaming as she came. Her body went into violent contraction, pods squeezing from her pussy and *her anus too, only to be jammed firmly back up as she writhed in the mud, her whole body jiggling to her frantic masturbation.*

Moments later she was fast asleep.

Five

Patty had been as good as her word. She'd washed and come down stark naked, drunk a leisurely beer with her head in Peter's lap so that Jack and he could fondle her boobs, then offered her cleavage for fucking. They had taken turns, Peter first, all four of them reaching their second orgasms over her breasts and in her face, with Patty casually mopping up with tissue between each titty-fuck. Nor had that been the end. They had taken her upstairs, to suck and fuck until dawn had begun to lighten the sky outside the windows. Peter had been the last to collapse, still immersed in her pussy when the others were sprawled in drunken sleep on the floor, and slept with her in Jack's king-sized bed. In the morning she'd been gone.

His first thought had been to check his pockets, but nothing had been missing. The boys had still been asleep, although unconscious was perhaps more accurate. In between bouts of sex they had drunk every beer in Jack's fridge and then started on the bourbon. The bottle, now empty but for a drop, was still clutched in Baz's hand. Peter felt a certain pride as he picked his way through the debris. He'd drunk as much as any of them, but he'd been the last to pass out, the last to fuck Patty, and he was the first up.

79

Jack also had taste in breakfast, starting every morning with a fry-up before going down to the garage he ran. Peter found sausages, eggs and black pudding in the fridge, but nothing to fry them in. After a moment of fruitless searching he put the grill and a pan of water on instead and made coffee. There was still no sign of the others, and for all the throbbing pain in his head there was a wry grin on his face as he ate and drank.

He was sure Patty would be impressed. They had given her what she wanted, and plenty, although he had a suspicion that she had still been up for more when he had finally collapsed. It was extraordinary how much she had soaked up, not just being repeatedly penetrated, but enduring Jack's crude language, jokes and generally laddish behaviour. At one point Zen had put the tip of his joint in her bottom to see if she could smoke it with her anus, and Jack had poured cold beer all over her head while she was sucking him, joking that it was to cool his balls down. She had taken it all.

Whether it would be the same in the morning he wasn't sure, and his grin faded as he considered the consequences. How much would their behaviour influence her report on the band? Had she just been testing them? Had she actually liked being called a groupie, and a fuck-dolly, and a fat tart, all expressions Jack had used during the evening. She had seemed to, and it occurred to him that she might actually get off on being insulted. It also occurred to him that women's behaviour in the heat of the moment did not necessarily reflect their long-term reaction, Linda being a case in point.

Unfortunately they had no choice but to wait and see. He had tried to ask her about Retro Records, during one of the lulls in the sex, but her response had been to push one of her huge nipples into his mouth, which had set it all off again. That had ended with her getting topped and tailed by him and Zen, then by Jack and Baz in turn. Jack had come in her face again, and the image of her with one beautiful green eye half closed by a blob of spunk came up in his mind, to set him on a new train of thought.

The only other girl he had ever met with such vividly green eyes was Linnet, and Patty had been similar in other ways. The evening before it had occurred to him that Patty was similar enough to Linnet to be her mother but, on sober reflection, the age difference was not big enough. It was hard to imagine Linnet as much above twenty, more likely eighteen. At first glance he had put Patty at mid-thirties, but once they'd got down to it her body had proved remarkably firm and her energy abundant. He was still considering the question when Jack appeared, red eyed and sleepy.

'Morning, Jack,' Peter greeted his friend, deliberately cheerful.

Jack responded with a grunt as he staggered to the fridge.

'How old do you reckon Patty is?' Peter asked as Jack upended a carton of orange juice over his mouth.

'Who gives a fuck?' Jack answered after a pause. 'She still around, is she?'

'No, she went before I woke up,' Peter answered. 'Don't worry, she didn't pinch anything. I've checked.'

'Why would she pinch anything?' Jack queried.

'Oh, nothing,' Peter answered. 'Pays to be careful, that's all.'

Jack responded with another grunt and began to assemble breakfast ingredients. Peter went back to his coffee, still considering Patty. After a while Jack spoke again.

'Where's the fucking lard? Nah, thing is with these fat bitches, you can't really tell how old they are. She could have been sixteen, could have been sixty.'

'Twenty-five?'

'Yeah, maybe. Dirty cow, eh?'

'Let's just hope you didn't put her off.'

'Nah, they love it. Rock bitch, ain't she? You've got to treat 'em rough; they get off on that stuff.'

'I hope so.'

'Take it from me, mate. If we hadn't been up for it, or if we hadn't given her a proper fucking, she'd have given us the kiss off. I know women, me.'

Peter shook his head. Patty's behaviour certainly suggested that what Jack said was true, in her case anyway. Then again, if Linnet really was Patty's little sister, there might be a lot more going on than they were admitting. Possibly the whole thing was a set-up, including the rumour about Retro Records. Certainly Patty and Linnet were suspiciously similar in appearance, and the rent-boy not so very different. Had Jack unearthed an entire family of sex maniacs? He felt a sudden flush of irritation and turned back from the table to speak, just as Zen and Baz appeared in the doorway.

'Cards on the table,' Peter announced. 'What's going on?'

Not one of them answered.

'A joke's a joke, boys,' Peter went on, 'but not when it fucks with the band. Who was Patty?'

'Patty?' Zen answered. 'The girl we fucked last night, yeah?'

'Yeah,' Baz agreed, 'we've made it now! Nobody's anybody 'til they've had their first groupie!'

'And got ourselves a deal and all!' Jack put in.

82

'Don't count on it,' Baz answered him. 'I reckon she was just some chick on the make, eh? Great fuck anyway!'

He thrust his hips out, at the same time pretending to hold on to a woman's hips as if entering her from behind and contorting his face into a look of mock ecstasy.

'Quit clowning around,' Peter insisted. 'You know what I mean. Was Patty really from Retro Records, or what? I know, I'm not stupid. Linnet's a model you hired, yeah? And Patty's her big sister. Am I right?'

'Linnet?' Jack queried vaguely as he peered dubiously at the mixture of lard and bits of burned substance in an unwashed frying pan.

'Linnet,' Peter insisted, 'green eyes, black hair, gorgeous arse, cute as a button. A model, a model you lot hired to ... to take the piss, yeah?'

He had stopped an instant before mentioning the rent-boy. Over the years he had learned to judge a great deal from the tone of voice of customers and prospective customers. Jack sounded genuinely puzzled.

'You're not making any sense, man,' Zen answered him.

Zen also sounded genuinely puzzled.

'And this doll's Patty's baby sister?' Jack queried. 'Bring her on, we'll fuck 'em side by side! Yeah, boys?'

'Yeah, cool,' Baz agreed.

'Great, eh?' Jack went on. 'I've always fancied having two sisters in bed together.'

'Twins, twins would be good,' Zen added.

'Yeah,' Baz put in, 'but how about a mother and daughter, eh? That would be something else.'

'Nah,' Jack argued, 'they'd just cramp each other's style. Sisters, that's what you want, a pair of right dirty bitches who'd go down on each other.'

'Nice, man,' Zen agreed, Baz nodding vigorously.

'You're a bunch of perverts, you know that?' Peter put in. 'Look, tell me straight out, no more messing. Do you know who Linnet is? Or a girl with that description, maybe she's used a different name?'

Baz shrugged.

'No, worse luck,' Jack stated.

'So,' Zen queried. 'I don't get it. You knew Patty before, if she's got this little sister, or what?'

'Don't worry about it,' he answered.

They were telling the truth. Hung-over, still high on the triumphs of the night before, both musical and sexual, they could not possibly be lying. His mind turned to work, yet by and large he kept his business life and his private life separate. If it was Phil or somebody who had set him up with Linnet, then the resemblance between Patty and Linnet became more puzzling still. Alternatively, if for some bizarre reason the people at Retro Records were responsible, it was hard to see how they could have known his movements so precisely.

Just thinking about it made his head hurt, and he abandoned the effort in favour of more coffee.

Peter spent the Sunday in his garden, not working, but reclining in the shade with a jug of chilled fruit juice at his elbow and the papers beside it. Monday was the North-West, Tuesday Scotland, two days of hard work with a stay in a hotel between, it not being worthwhile to return from Carlisle to Milton Keynes. After the indulgences of the Friday and Saturday nights he badly needed rest, and was promising himself to do nothing more strenuous than ring for a pizza all day.

His resolve lasted until the evening, by which time his head had cleared and thoughts of Patty, of Linnet and of Linda began to intrude again. Determined to get his rest, he phoned through his order for a stuffed-crust meat feast with extra mushrooms and washed it down with orange juice instead of beer. An hour later he retired to bed, stuck *Busty Beauties get Dirty VIII* on the video and within another hour was asleep.

He awoke refreshed but regretting the extra mushrooms, having dreamed of being held down by a dozen naked girls including Patty and Linnet while Linda went through his suit pockets and lectured him on respect for women and politically correct principles. Now knowing that he had been wrong to suspect the boys in the band, he was especially vigilant at the morning sales meeting but, if Phil or any of the others were hiding anything, it didn't show.

By ten he was on the road, by eleven thirty in Manchester, explaining the virtues of their range to a Geoff Sullivan of Price Slash, a chain of mini-markets who had begun to expand into household goods. He came away well pleased, with an order for two thousand units in his pocket, the commission on which just about made up for what Linda had stolen from him.

He celebrated with a glass of champagne over lunch, then moved on, with three established clients in the afternoon, in Oldham, Blackburn and finally Carlisle, which left him dead on his feet but with a sales total for the day a hundred short of the five thousand mark. Too exhausted to make much of the evening, he booked in at a Roadlodge and for the second night running wanked himself to sleep.

Tuesday dawned in brilliant sunlight, with the chill gone from the air by the time he let the clutch in. By nine he was in Glasgow, by five in Aberdeen, with another three thousand five hundred units in his order book. Though even more tired than before, he was beginning to see the humour of the incident with Linda, and even allowed himself to dwell on his memories of her compact curves as he took his cock in hand at the hotel that night.

He had deliberately avoided making any appointments for Wednesday, setting it aside to drive back and sort out the paperwork at the office. It proved convenient to lunch at the J49 services, and he sat at the very same table he'd occupied when he met Linnet. As he ate he was half hoping, half dreading that her green MG would pull into the car park or that she would suddenly appear at his elbow. Nothing happened, and he had to fight down a pang of disappointment as he left.

A hard drive south, seldom dipping below ninety, and he was back at the office in plenty of time to do what was needed and get home in good time. Even allowing for Wednesday, his total for the week was impressive, and Phil had reacted with good humour, if perhaps a touch of envy.

The rest of the week was not going to come up to the same standard, with a conference on the Thursday and the weekend given over to a team-building exercise, playing silly buggers on Dartmoor. Only the Thursday evening promised any fun, and that limited. Faithful Copy were performing at the Snappin' Squirrel in Hemel Hempstead, a band they'd shared many a gig with, but who had managed to attract an agent, then a European tour. Ever since then they'd been giving themselves airs, demanding top billing at every event with their name in letters at least twice as high as any other semi-pro act.

Peter was not impressed, convinced that Pizazz had the edge on them in every department except luck.

Yet it paid to keep an eye on the competition, and to be seen, while there was every chance that Patty and other scouts might be there. So after work he collected the others and drove south, and pulled into the pub car park as the support band, Sixty Vibe, were already playing inside. There were posters, huge pictures of the three members of Faithful Copy with their name splashed large across it, and 'Sixty Vibe' in plain black print at the bottom left.

'One day, mate, one day,' Jack remarked, pausing to draw thick-rimmed glasses on to the face of the Faithful Copy lead man.

'Now he looks like Buddy Holly,' Peter commented. 'You'll give him ideas.'

Jack grunted and quickly added a large drooping moustache.

'Could be the other way around next year,' Baz remarked.

'More like our name on top and both those suckers down where they belong,' Jack said, standing back to admire his work. 'Let's go in, I could murder a beer.'

They moved into the bar, loud with music, but no more crowded than The Pig and Whistle had been the previous week. Sixty Vibe were doing the Stones' 'Wild Horses', or trying to, their lead singer struggling even to approximate Jagger's voice. Peter bought a round, all the while scanning the crowd in the hope of seeing Patty while trying not to be too obvious.

She was nowhere to be seen, bringing him regret for his own sake and relief that she hadn't come to see Faithful Copy, or not yet. With the glasses in his hands he returned to the table the boys had managed to find in the far corner of the pub, put them down and took a deep swallow from his own.

'No sign of Patty.'

'Shame,' Jack answered, 'still, there's plenty of

other totty. What d'you reckon to her in the white mini-skirt?'

'I reckon you're old enough to be her Dad, you –' Peter began, and trailed off, thinking of Linnet.

'She's eighteen, she's fuckable,' Jack remarked flatly.

Peter sat down, still scanning the crowd. A man was coming towards them, white haired, smartly dressed in a mid-blue suit and a collarless shirt. As he approached he extended his hand to Peter. Peter took it and shook, slightly puzzled.

'George Marks, Retro Records,' the man introduced himself.

'Hi, take a seat,' Peter managed, struggling to get his brain into gear somewhere between being a salesman and a musician. 'I'm Peter Williams, this is Jack –'

'Sure,' Marks broke in, 'I know you all. Saw you play the other day.'

'Last Friday?'

'Nope, the week before. I called in at The Pig and Whistle while you were jamming. I reckon I can tell a whole lot more about a band from half an hour's jamming than any number of gigs. That's the way you see if they've got flair, that and listen when they don't know I'm about.'

'Well, you caught us there!' Peter laughed. 'Drink?'

'Sure,' Marks answered, 'a glass of red wine, if you'd be so kind.'

'Baz, get a bottle,' Peter instructed quickly. 'Down to see Faithful Copy, Mr Marks?'

'George, please. Yes, as you may have heard on the grapevine, we're going to be releasing a set of cover albums, fifties stuff mainly. Faithful Copy seem to be the men of the moment.'

'They're good,' Peter stated cautiously, 'Dan has one of the best voices on the amateur circuit, certainly among those cover bands focusing on The Beatles and Beatles derivative bands. Ken's not a bad drummer, either. Still, maybe I'm not the best judge . . .'

Marks laughed gently. Peter smiled, indicating that he knew his effort to put Faithful Copy down by damning with faint praise had been rumbled. It was a gamble, going for the friendly, slightly cheeky angle, but his at-a-glance assessment of George Marks suggested it was the best way.

'I like it,' Marks stated after a moment. 'You're a player, Peter, in more ways than one.'

Peter smiled and shrugged, reflecting that he hadn't sold nearly two million bath brushes for nothing. Marks went on.

'So I'll cut to the chase. We're after four bands, first off, and we've three, Pickin' up Steam, Gold Seal and Habanera Hellcats.'

Peter nodded, knowing far better than to pick fault with a choice already made.

'We need one more,' Marks stated, 'and it's down to Faithful Copy, or your good selves. Would you be able to come down to the studios and do a demo, maybe in three weeks' time?'

'No problem there,' Peter answered as Baz returned with an open bottle of Shiraz. 'Baz, George wants us to do a demo.'

'Great!' Baz answered. 'You are so right in making this choice, George . . . er . . . Mr Marks. Believe me, you won't regret your decision. I –'

He shut up abruptly at a glance from Peter. George Marks was smiling indulgently as he filled his glass. Jack spoke up.

'May as well just sign us up, George, save yourself the trouble of the demos. We're the best there is.'

Peter winced, but Marks simply took a sip of his wine, then chuckled as he answered.

'That remains to be seen. You can play, yes –'

'Everything from Jelly Roll Morton to The Clash,' Jack cut in.

'– but a recording studio is a very different environment to what you'll be used to, no disrespect intended.'

'None taken,' Peter said quickly.

He raised his glass as Sixty Vibe launched into a new and louder number, one of their own, drowning out his voice. Marks responded, half-turning to watch the band and Peter sat back. For all his outward calm, his mind was a whirl. Even when his teenage fantasies of becoming a rock star had foundered on the harsh reality of having to keep body and soul together he had never entirely abandoned his dream. What George Marks was offering would not make him rich, or famous, but it still meant a great deal, to see his name on a record, on sale in high street stores . . .

'So,' Jack began the moment the music began to fade, with a distinct snigger in his voice, 'you Patty's boss then, eh, George?'

Jack winked, lewdly. Peter felt his stomach go tight inside. Marks returned a look that at first seemed irritated, then merely puzzled.

'Patty?' he queried.

'Your colleague,' Peter replied quickly, 'who came to see us last week at The Pig and Whistle. A nice lady. She seemed to like our music.'

'A very friendly lady, eh?' Jack laughed.

'I'm sorry,' Marks replied, 'I'm at a bit of a loss here. I don't have a colleague called Patty, and nobody from Retro came out to you last week. I'd know.'

'I said she wasn't –' Baz began, only to be cut off by an abrupt gesture from Peter.

'Our mistake,' he said quickly, 'she must have been from another label.'

'Another label?' Marks queried.

'I assume so,' Peter went on, extemporising frantically and praying Jack kept his mouth shut. 'She was a scout, certainly, and we'd heard a rumour Retro were looking out for cover bands, so we thought . . .'

'Not one of ours,' Marks replied, now looking a touch worried. 'Seems you're in demand, Mr Williams.'

'Seems so.' Peter laughed.

Another song had started, Sixty Vibe's invariable finale, 'If You're Going to San Francisco'. Peter took a swallow from his pint, well pleased with himself. Jack's comment might so easily have led to disaster, and he had not merely turned it around, but also gained an advantage from it. If George Marks thought another label was interested it was sure to help.

The brief conversation also raised the question of who Patty had been, if not a scout from Retro. Possibly Baz was right, and she had simply been out for sex. Even the way she'd been dressed could be accounted for if she'd come straight from work. Or possibly she was a scout from another label, or something to do with whoever was setting him up with Linnet. He shook his head, unable to find any solution that accounted for all the facts. Something odd was going on, no doubt at all, but what, and why, were questions that only seemed to grow harder to answer with time.

Sixty Vibe's set came to an end and George Marks rose from his seat.

'It's been a pleasure, gentlemen, and we'll meet again shortly, but I'm sure you'll appreciate that it won't do for me to be sitting with the competition. Fair's fair.'

'Absolutely,' Peter agreed, extending his hand.

Marks took it and shook, beaming, then withdrew a card from his pocket and passed it across.

'Give me a call.'

He moved off towards the stage, leaving the band members grinning at each other like schoolboys.

'Champagne, boys?' Peter suggested.

'Yeah,' Jack answered, 'but not here. Sod Faithful Copy, let's go to a titty bar and celebrate.'

'Yeah, nice,' Zen agreed, Baz nodding and giving them a dirty grin.

'They're a rip-off, those places,' Peter objected. 'How about a singles bar? We could get to Benji's in maybe twenty minutes?'

'Too chancy. I say titties,' Baz answered him.

'Only for an ugly fucker like you, Baz.' Jack laughed. 'I'm easy, just so long as there's booze and there's cunt.'

'Zen?' Peter queried.

'Whatever.'

'Benji's it is then,' Peter announced.

They trooped out, just as Faithful Copy were being announced. Peter caught a dirty look from the singer, Dan, and returned a cheerful wave. It was cool outside and oddly quiet after the heat and noise of the pub, and he drew in a deep gulp of air as they made for Baz's Astra.

'Some people, bet it's a woman,' Jack joked from beside him.

Peter turned, to find a car parked almost sideways across three spaces of the car park, not only taking up extra space but partially blocking the way out. It was a Le Mans green MG Roadster with the latest plates.

'Hang on a minute . . . I . . . I just need the Gents,' he said quickly, and hastened back towards the pub.

Inside, Faithful Copy had begun to play and the area around the stage was thick with people, their faces uncertain in the multicoloured spotlights sweeping over them, features briefly outlined in red or blue or green, with sharp black shadows. He tried to peer in among them, cursing under his breath at the realisation that the tiny Linnet would be extremely difficult to see. Certainly she was not obvious.

He bit his lip in frustration, telling himself that he would be better off at Benji's but filled with the need to see Linnet again, to confront her, but also because just seeing her car again had given him a hollow ache of longing. Whatever she had done, there was something entrancing about her, which combined with an urge to tame her, even punish her.

She had to be there, but it was impossible to pick her out from among the crowd, try as he might. He also knew that she could not be there by chance yet, if she was looking for him, why had she not approached him? It was ridiculous to suggest that she could be shy, which either meant that she had just arrived and did not know he was there, or that she was deliberately taunting him. He had a nasty suspicion it was the latter. Still he searched the crowd, until he felt a tug at his arm and turned to see Zen.

'What you doing, man?' Zen shouted.

'I . . . nothing . . .' Peter yelled back. 'I thought I saw somebody I knew, that's all.'

'We're waiting, yeah?'

Peter moved back towards the doors, filled with regret and not a little anger. She had to be taunting him, and it did not feel good, while he was unable to understand why he felt he needed her so badly. They hadn't even had sex. For all his anger at Linda, it made no real difference to him if he never saw her again, or any of the other women he'd had one-night stands with. Linnet was different.

He swallowed his anger as they stepped back out into the night. Her car was as before, not so much badly parked, but parked with an insolent indifference to others. As he passed he shook his head, but took the trouble to memorise the number plate before climbing into Baz's Astra. They set off, down the A41 towards Watford and Benji's, Baz driving with his normal nervous caution.

Peter stared out at the night, trying to get his thoughts in order. The green MG shot past them, doing at least a hundred, the driver's profile visible for just an instant. Peter turned sharply, a demand to follow on his lips only to abandon the idea. Baz had stuck to a single pint, but it would be tempting fate to speed, and he was no driver anyway.

He forced a resigned laugh. Linnet did not matter. He was going to go to Benji's and have some fun, toast the band's good fortune in champagne, maybe pick up a girl, somebody sensible who didn't trick him into being sucked off by a man, or piss all over him, or steal from him, or even demand group sex. She would be sensible, fun but not crazy, the sort of woman who would make him feel like a man all night, then bring him breakfast in bed in the morning.

Benji's proved to be half empty, a typical Thursday night, with a scattering of hopeful men propping up the bar or trying to chat up the three women present. They chose a table and ordered champagne, eyeing the talent as they waited for the barman to bring it over.

'Nah, nothing special,' Jack remarked after a while. 'I'd give the blonde one, but –'

'You'd give anything that moved one,' Peter put in.

'That is not true,' Jack answered. 'I'll have you know that where women are concerned I am something of a connoisseur.'

'Sure, Jack.' Baz laughed as an ice bucket was placed on their table.

'I've a few up on you at any rate!' Jack answered.

'Yeah,' Baz retorted, 'because, like Peter says, you'll go with anything that moves.'

'I –' Jack began, and stopped. 'Fucking hell, will you look at the tits on that!'

Another woman had entered, young, with curly blonde hair and a voluptuous figure. She was dressed as a schoolgirl, her red tartan skirt indecently short, to show almost the full length of her creamy white thighs above the tops of white knee socks. Her white blouse was full to bursting point with two overripe breasts, held up within a big, lacy bra the pattern of which showed through the thin material. Three buttons were undone, displaying a generous slice of cleavage only partially obscured by her tie.

'Pro,' Zen suggested in a half-whisper.

'Nah,' Jack answered him, 'it's well in, that school stuff. They have nights down Hammersmith, thousands of the little darlings, all dolled up like they just stepped out the school gates, half of 'em in skirts so short you can see their panties. Enough to give a bloke a coronary just driving past, it is.'

Peter watched the girl as she moved to the bar. She was small, making her curves seem more exaggerated still, her breasts bigger even than Patty's, if not quite so huge as Katie's. Her nipples were just as prominent though, even through her bra, which spoke straight to his cock. Big-breasted girls had always been a turn-on for him, small ones especially, as they always seemed deliciously vulnerable.

Jack was already on his feet, going to her side as she tried to attract the barman's attention. They exchanged greetings, the girl smiled, then she was walking back with Jack. Peter was immediately cursing himself for not being quicker on the uptake, but she made a point of sitting on the stool beside him and he realised that all was not lost.

'This is Sally,' Jack announced. 'Sally, these are my mates, Peter, Zen, Baz. We, all together, are Pizazz, the best covers band this side of Memphis, and we have just agreed our first recording contract. Champagne?'

'Good for you,' she purred. 'Yes, thank you.'

Jack had already secured a fifth glass, and as he poured he slid his arm around Sally's waist. She didn't resist, and was all smiles as she lifted the glass to her painted lips.

'Here's to you then,' she said, drank, then winked at Peter, slow and deliberate, and judged so that Jack didn't see.

'Cheers,' he answered, and took a swallow of champagne.

'We're going to be big,' Jack went on, 'you wait, six months and our faces'll be on posters wherever you look. Pizazz, remember the name.'

His hand had slipped a little lower, to cup the cheek of her bottom where it stuck out over the edge of the stool. Still she gave no complaint. Peter smiled to himself. He seemed to be on a roll, Sally the fourth woman in a row who had picked him from among many others. Jack could flirt, and Jack could push, but, unless she was like Patty and wanted more than one man, it was going to be him, Peter, who ended up dipping his wick.

Pleased with himself, and with Linnet pushed once more to the back of his mind, he relaxed. It was amusing to watch, Jack growing ever more turned on but ever more aware that it was not going to be him who took Sally to bed. She made no effort to resist his groping, but her attention was firmly on Peter, and her admiration. He didn't even bother to flirt, chatting casually about this and that, music and the band, his job, and the training exercise on Dartmoor at the weekend.

By the time Benji's was due to close Sally was snuggled up next to Peter, the side of one full breast pressed against him, drunk and amorous and quite plainly willing. When they stood to go she took his arm, and the moment they were in the street he kissed her, marking her as his woman. Jack swore softly under his breath.

'So where to?' Peter said casually.

'Your place?' she suggested without the slightest hesitation.

'It's a fair way,' he answered, and went on, seeing no reason to be any less bold than she was. 'You're probably a lot nearer.'

'Exeter?'

'Exeter!?'

'Bit out of your way, aren't you, love?' Baz queried.

'It's a long story,' she said, 'but basically I was out with my boyfriend, we had a row, 'cause we were going to this school night and he said I was dressed too tarty. I asked him how else he thought a sexy schoolgirl was supposed to dress. After all, it's just a laugh, isn't it?'

'Yeah, dead right,' Baz agreed.

'What a prat!' Jack added. 'You're gorgeous, a fucking doll!'

Sally smiled. A single, straining button was holding her blouse closed over her breasts, now tauter even than when she had first come into the bar, or so it seemed. Peter swallowed, remembering the pleasure of titty-fucking Patty. Sally was younger, and bigger, and he told himself he'd be sure to do it before the morning.

'So I was passing the bar,' she went on, 'and . . . well, here I am.'

'Come back with us then, if you like,' Peter offered. 'We live in Milton Keynes.'

'Sure,' Baz added, 'my car's over there.'

'I think we ought to collect a taxi fee here,' Jack suggested.

'I don't mind putting something towards the petrol,' Sally answered him.

'I wasn't thinking of money,' Jack stated. 'How about blow jobs all round?'

'Hey, come on, Jack,' Peter answered him. 'Show the lady some respect.'

'No, that's fair,' Sally said with shrug. 'I mean, if it wasn't for you guys I'd be sleeping on the street tonight, so I suppose sucking your cocks isn't too much to ask.'

'He's just trying it on, love,' Peter told her, 'don't worry about it. Come back with us, no strings and you can stay at my place. If you don't want to come to bed with me, that's fine, if you do, I'd be honoured.'

'Hey, Peter, she just offered us blow jobs!' Jack objected.

'Yeah, man,' Zen added.

'Easy for you to play the white knight!' Baz put in.

'Look, boys,' Peter objected. 'We can't just push her into sex, that's not right.'

'Why not?' Jack demanded. 'She's all right with it. She said so.'

'Because it's really taking advantage of her!' Peter pointed out. 'I mean, come on, what if you were stuck miles from your place and some bastard demanded a blow job to give you a lift home? You'd kick his head in, that's what you'd do!'

'Yeah, but I'm not a poof. It'd be all right if I was a poof, wouldn't it? Now, if it was a chick and she wanted me to go down on her, that'd be different.'

'Sweet Jesus!' Peter began, only to be cut off by Sally.

'Hush, Peter. I said I'd do it, and I will.'

'You don't have to,' Peter insisted.

'Maybe she wants to,' Jack suggested. 'Thought of that, Peter?'

Peter threw his hands up.

'How old are you, Sally?' he demanded.

'Twenty-two,' she answered, immediately defensive.

'Really twenty-two?' he queried.

'Eighteen,' she admitted, 'but –'

'Eighteen!' Jack interrupted. 'I think my balls are going to burst, right now.'

'Oh thank you, Lord!' Baz added.

Sally giggled, making her huge breasts quiver. The button between them gave up the unequal struggle and popped, leaving a good six inches of fat pink cleavage on show and a fair bit of lace from her bra. Her hand went to her mouth.

'Whoops!'

'Looks like your clothes could do with loosening,' Jack joked, 'and I know just the place to do it. Let's go.'

Peter shook his head in despair as they moved towards the car. The others were eager, and hurried, hustling Sally with them. Jack and Zen had climbed into the back with her by the time he reached the car but he didn't protest, telling himself he'd be warm in bed with her when all three of them were alone. She was giggling as Baz set off, and when Peter turned he found that Jack already had her school blouse open, and her bra undone, her huge breasts sticking out, plump and pink and naked, her nipples erect. Jack was fondling one, cupping the big globe in one hand and licking her. Zen had the other, rubbing one elongated nipple as if he was rolling a joint.

Baz drove a great deal faster than he had on the way to Benji's, with Jack giving occasional instructions from the back. For a while they were on the

M1, turning off at J9 and Jack speaking almost immediately, telling Baz to pull over. By then Sally's school top was fully open, showing a puppy-fat tummy and the full glory of her chest, with her green school tie hanging down between her boobs. Jack's cock was already out, and erect in her hand.

'I'm first,' he demanded as the car pulled off the road into a lay-by well screened by trees. 'Come on, Sally, love, get your laughing gear around that.'

'No,' Sally answered him, sweet but firm, 'I'm not doing it in front of all of you.'

'Get out, you lot,' Jack instructed.

Peter climbed out, shaking his head but secretly glad Sally had shown at least a spark of old-fashioned modesty. Zen and Baz joined him, walking over towards one of a line of picnic tables illuminated by the distant security light from a lorry park further down the road. As he passed the car he had a brief glimpse of Sally as she went down on Jack. He was holding his cock up for her mouth, and she was scrambling up on to the seat, exposing the seat of her white schoolgirl panties, absolutely bulging with firm teenage bottom.

There was a touch of guilt for her age as he considered the prospect of sucking and fucking with her, but his cock was responding anyway, and he knew he would go for it. They sat down, Baz grinning shyly, Zen with his tobacco tin of roll-ups already out. Peter accepted one, not his usual habit, but his nerves were strung out. Even with the prospect of the delicious Sally he had found it hard not to be on the lookout for Linnet's car, and it seemed that whenever he thought he'd put her memory aside she somehow managed to work her way back in.

The clang of the Astra's door signalled that Jack had finished, and Peter rose to take his turn. Jack was grinning, and still tucking in his shirttails as he approached, speaking as he slapped hands with Peter.

'She gives great head, man, the best!'

Peter managed a smile. His cock was ready despite himself, half stiff in his pants just from the thought of Sally with her flesh spilling from her school uniform. He slid into the car to find her waiting, green eyes shining in the interior light, bright with desire, her lipstick now a little smudged. Her blouse was still open, her bra off, her fat pink breasts heaving gently to the rhythm of her breathing. Her panties had been pulled down too, and were stretched between her knees, with her skirt so high her bare pussy was peeping out from beneath the hem, just visible in the shadows. She licked her lips, gazing right at him as she took her boobs in her hands and bounced them, then squeezed, as if trying to milk herself. Peter closed the door and put his hands to his fly, trying to tell himself there was nothing wrong at all in being sucked off by an eighteen-year-old schoolgirl in the back of a car after they'd saved her from a night sleeping rough.

He pulled out his cock and put an arm around Sally's back as she went down, meaning it as a gesture of reassurance. She took his cock in, purring as she mouthed on it, and wiggling her bottom in open invitation. Peter gave in. His hand slid further down, lifting her skirt and she was bare, her plump rear end stuck high, panties well down, her pussy available. As she began to work on his cock he cupped her mound. Her lips were shaved, her slit moist. He began to stroke her, again trying to tell himself that it was OK, that he wasn't molesting her, but doing her a favour by masturbating her while she sucked him.

She responded well, squirming her bottom into his hand in encouragement, and he let his fingers slip between her sex lips, rubbing on her clit. Immediately she grew more urgent, sucking him deep and starting the same trick Linnet had used ... no, that the rent-boy had used, rubbing her tongue on the sensitive underside of Peter's foreskin. He forced his mind away from the rent-boy, concentrating on the glory of Sally's indisputably female bottom. She was all girl, plump to the edge of being fat, but firm and round and gorgeous, her waist slim between a wide chest and broad hips, her boobs magnificent, her bottom a delight.

With his cock now fully erect in her mouth, he slid a thumb into the mouth of her pussy, only to discover that it wouldn't go in. A taut membrane blocked the hole, and his mouth came open in shock and surprise as he realised he was being sucked off not only by an eighteen-year-old schoolgirl, but by a virgin.

It was too late anyway. She was doing amazing things with her tongue and at the same time had his helmet jammed deep into her throat. Her hand had found his balls and a finger was tickling beneath them, an inch from his anus, then on it. He came, his cock jerking in her mouth, his spunk pumping into her throat, his hand rubbing hard at her bare pussy. She began to make gulping noises, struggling to swallow his load, and then she was coming herself, her bottom and thighs tightening, her pussy going into spasm. He put his thumb to her bottomhole, knowing he had to penetrate her but unwilling to break her virginity, and in, her ring sloppy with her own juice and hot and wet inside.

She was still coming as she milked him into her mouth, and after, sucking on his cock with real urgency, her body shuddering in orgasm. He kept rubbing, his thumb still in her bottomhole, masturbating her on and on, until she finally came off his cock with a deep sigh. He stopped, pulled his thumb out and relaxed into the seat, his breathing still hard.

'Nice?' she asked.

'Beautiful,' he breathed, 'and so are you. Thank you.'

'Any time.' She giggled.

Peter opened his mouth, wanting to say something about her being a virgin, at least to tell her to keep it special, and not to lose it in a gang bang with a bunch of rowdy musicians twice her age. Nothing came out, but he kissed her before climbing from the car, feeling more drained than satisfied and guiltier than ever.

Zen stood up from the table, slapping Peter's hand as they passed, just as Peter had with Jack. Both Baz and Jack were smoking joints, and Peter took a drag as he sat down. Sally was willing, no question, yet he still felt that they were taking unfair advantage, four men who should have been old enough to know better, taking turns with a teenage girl as if she was some kind of trophy. He was still brooding and still smoking when Zen came back, well pleased with himself. Baz hurried to take his turn, stumbling in his eagerness to get at Sally.

'Nice,' Zen stated as he sat down, 'and, man, does she know how to suck cock! She may be just eighteen, but that is not her first time!'

'She's a virgin,' Peter said.

'She is?' Jack demanded. 'Shit, to think I pulled down her panties but didn't bother to fuck her!'

'Yeah, I felt that tight little pussy myself,' Zen confirmed, 'all yours, Peter, later tonight.'

'Lucky bastard!' Jack added. 'Still, who cares? That was one ace blow job! She took it right in her throat, and did this trick with her tongue – fucking unbelievable!'

He chuckled and turned to the car, in which the back of Baz's head was visible by the interior light.

Sally was invisible, down on his cock, presumably with her bottom stuck up, just the way she had sucked Peter, virgin pussy bare and vulnerable. A strong shiver went through him at the thought of fucking her. It was wrong, he was sure, something that should be done by a loving boyfriend. Then again, he had the experience, the patience. He could get her properly horny, perhaps lick her to the edge of orgasm first, certainly set her completely at ease, so that she was ready to surrender herself, to offer her sweet little cunt to a man's cock for the first time . . . Yes, he was going to fuck her.

The car door banged. Baz got out, walking towards them, a big sloppy grin on his face, his fly still undone.

'She just wants to tidy up,' he announced, jerking his thumb over his shoulder, 'and she says she's got a surprise for you, Peter.'

'You bet she's got a surprise!' Jack laughed. 'Her cunt, first time, eh, boys?'

'Show some fucking consideration,' Peter answered him, 'or at least keep your voice down. I mean, it's a big deal for girls, first time. She's probably scared, and the last thing she needs is –'

He stopped at a sudden sound, the engine of the Astra. They turned as one, to see Sally's arm extend from the window, something held between two fingers, her bra. She dropped it, the tyres screeched, kicking up gravel, and she was gone. For a moment Peter could only stare, and then he found his voice.

'Why . . . why me? Why do I always seem to get the demented bitches!'

Interlogue

'I used to know someone who lived here,' Elune remarked, idly kicking one of the stones that protruded from the turf in a rough circle. 'He had twelve goats and used to make the most beautiful jewellery.'

'There aren't as many goats around as there used to be, are there?' Juliana said. 'I wonder why?'

'Simple economics,' Aileve answered her. 'Within a generalist rural community goats are among the most valuable of animals, but they become less so with increased specialisation and with the rise in the ratio of land area under cultivation to the proportion of the population in agrarian employment.'

'We used to have goats,' Thomasina commented.

None of the girls answered, each lost in her own thoughts for a long moment. Finally Thomasina spoke.

'It's a big place.'

'Which,' Aileve answered her, 'is why Lily is at their camp. So what's it to be, Elune?'

'Trussed and stuffed,' Elune answered.

'Nude, or torn and dishevelled?' Juliana asked.

'Oh, torn and dishevelled,' Elune said immediately.

'I still say he won't believe it,' Thomasina stated. 'You've been caught, tied up, your clothes ripped off, but you haven't been had? I don't think he'll even do it.'

'He will,' Elune said confidently. 'He's a man.'

'A modern man,' Aileve pointed out. 'I say he'll untie you and try to take you down to the police station. You'll have to run.'

'He'll fuck me,' Elune said with confidence.

'A stick of Torquay rock says he doesn't,' Thomasina put in.

'Taken,' Elune answered immediately. 'Give any man an opportunity to stick his cock in you without any consequences and he'll take it.'

'I agree with Thomasina,' Aileve replied. 'He'll want to fuck you, certainly, but his conscience will get the better of him.'

'I think he'll fuck her,' Juliana said as she opened an evil-looking barrel knife. 'I'm going to blindfold her, so he'll think she won't even know who did it. In fact, I'll predict exactly what he'll do.'

'What?' Thomasina demanded.

'He'll find her,' Juliana continued, 'start to untie her, hesitate while he wrestles with his conscience for a bit, drag her somewhere he's sure he'll be safe, fuck her well and good, go away, and come back ten minutes later to pretend he's just found her.'

'No,' Aileve said with certainty. 'You're forgetting DNA testing.'

'So he uses a sheath,' Juliana pointed out.

'I don't think he carries them. He prefers to leave protection to the woman,' Elune put in, 'but I still say he fucks me.'

'I'll put a kilogram jar of Mrs Stewer's set honey against anything you care to mention that I'm right, Juliana,' Aileve offered. 'He'll find her, untie her and take her straight to the police, or try to.'

'You're on,' Juliana answered. 'I'll buy the honey, and if he fucks her first you get to eat it out of me. Fair?'

'Fair,' Aileve agreed.

'Can I watch?' Elune asked.

'Me too, please,' Thomasina put in, 'but no turning on me. That thing with the Pietrain was just not fair.'

'You loved every second of it!' Juliana laughed.

'I did not!'

'Oh yes you did!'

'Oh no –'

'Girls, please,' Aileve interrupted, 'do stop squabbling.'

'You're right,' Juliana agreed, 'let's get Elune trussed and stuffed.'

'Lily hasn't phoned yet,' Elune pointed out, 'it might not even be today.'

Juliana merely shrugged as she pulled a hank of rough cord from her rucksack.

Six

Blinking the sleep from his eyes, Peter threw one leg out of bed, then the other. It had been a long night. First there had been getting to the police station in Dunstable and trying to explain to an overinquisitive constable what the four of them had been doing in the car with a teenage girl they'd only just met in the first place. Then there had been the police procedure for reporting a stolen car and finally the cab back from Dunstable to Milton Keynes.

Jack had been against reporting the incident at all, arguing that if the police caught up with Sally she was quite likely to defend herself by claiming they had abducted her. Baz had been determined, almost leading to blows, while Zen had point blank refused to abandon his stash of cannabis. In the end Peter and Baz had gone to the station while Jack and Zen had called a cab. It had gone three in the morning when Peter had finally collapsed into bed, and the temptation to turn the alarm off had been close to irresistible.

He was running on automatic as he washed, shaved and pulled his clothes on. The team-building exercise meant a lot of equipment, but he had put it together before going out on the Thursday evening, something for which he was heartily glad as he lugged his rucksack and suitcase into the boot of the Mondeo.

Both seemed excessively heavy, as did the car, power-steering notwithstanding. Despite everything he was at work by eight, after Phil but before Roger and Dex. To his relief a minibus had been arranged for the trip to Devon and, after loading up, he was asleep before they'd hit the motorway.

His second awakening was little more pleasant than the first, stiff and dry-mouthed against the window of the minibus. Rolling chalk downland was passing outside the window, which he recognised as Salisbury Plain. Behind them, to the east, the sky was clear, but heavy grey clouds were rolling in from the west, suggesting rain. He stifled a yawn and, as he began to dig in his rucksack for water, the first spots began to appear on the windscreen.

By the time they reached Exeter it had been raining steadily for two hours, with low cloud blanketing the countryside and obscuring the hills. As they left the A38 and began to climb on to Dartmoor it grew quickly worse, driving rain with clouds tumbling across the bleak landscape so that he was quickly dreading the prospect of going anywhere other than the interior of a warm pub.

What he got was a converted farmhouse, with the barn made into a Spartan dormitory and the main buildings given over to what was called the Command and Logistics Centre. After stowing their kit and an all too brief break for coffee, they were shepherded in by a tall, retentive-looking man in khakis who introduced himself as Ken McMahon. Three others were present, two men, both of whom gave earnest greetings, and a girl, slim, with long black hair and exceptionally pale skin, also so shy that she could hardly bear to meet their eyes as they greeted her. The room had desks set out as if it were a classroom, an image strengthened by the maps and posters on the walls. As they sat down, McMahon went to the front, and peered at his clipboard before addressing them.

'OK, as you all know, I'm Ken McMahon, the manager here at Team Confidence. What we're doing this weekend is all about just that, team, team, team.'

Peter nodded, along with all the other men. The girl merely looked shy. McMahon went on.

'OK, think group, think squad, think team! When I say team, you answer me, come on now, give it some energy, team, team, team!'

The men solemnly echoed, some even managing to sound enthusiastic. Only the girl stayed silent. McMahon nodded.

'OK, better, except for Linda. One more time, Linda too, team, team, team!'

Peter's heart had jumped at the name Linda, despite the fact that the black-haired girl bore no resemblance whatsoever to the con-artist of the same name. Once more they repeated the mantra, the men louder, the girl in a tiny voice barely audible to Peter although she was just two seats away. McMahon sighed.

'OK,' he continued, 'but by the end of this, Linda, I'm going to have you calling out just as loud and just as proud as anyone else. OK?'

Her answer was a murmur. McMahon withdrew a pencil from behind his ear and tapped his clipboard with it.

'OK, who've we got? Bob and Mike from Sellforce, Linda from Exeter Uni, and Phil, Peter, Roger and Dex from Truwood. As you know, over the weekend we're going to complete a series of exercises, all of which focus on what we're all about here at Team Confidence, which is?'

'Team, team, team!' Bob, Mike and Roger echoed, Peter and the other men joining in on the second 'team'.

Linda remained silent, but as Peter turned to glance out at the rain-swept moor he caught her eyes for just a second, long enough to see that they were a vivid green before she quickly turned her head away. McMahon had begun to talk again, but Peter was no longer paying attention. He was thinking of beautiful green eyes twinkling with mischief and lust, Linnet as she had been when they first met, teasing and dirty, full of lewd promises. Patty had had green eyes too, and Sally, gazing wickedly at him as she bounced her gorgeous boobs in her hands . . .

His erotic daydream broke to puzzlement. How many girls with bright green eyes had he met in his life? The answer was none, or none that he could remember, right up until Linnet. Since meeting Linnet the total was four. It seemed a remarkable coincidence, and for all that he was quickly telling himself not to be paranoid it was impossible not to cast another, suspicious, glance at Linda. She was looking out of the window, paying no more attention than he was.

'. . . two teams, each member with an assigned task judged to get the best out of him . . . or her. First off, our team leaders. OK, who do we have? Phil, big man at the company, a natural boss, no. You know how to lead a team, Phil, I don't suppose there's much I could teach you, eh?'

He winked, a gesture Peter found particularly irritating for no reason he could put a finger on. Phil was looking slightly disappointed. McMahon went on.

'OK, so who's not a team player, let alone a leader? Linda, you're on the spot, Team Leader for Team Energy, and with you are Phil, and Bob, and . . . Roger. I know it's a tough call, but that's what we're all about, team, team, team!'

Peter managed to come in on time, and to hide the urge to sigh.

'OK, so who do we have for Leader on Team Go?' McMahon stated. 'Dex, Mike and Peter. How about Dex? Young, ambitious, speaks six foreign languages. Or Mike, head recruiting officer for Sellforce? Or Peter, Truwood's ace salesman, good guy all round, but not a team player.'

Peter glanced at Phil, who returned a smug smile.

'You're the Team Go Leader, Peter,' McMahon announced. 'OK now, break for lunch in the canteen, and the afternoon's lecture is "Understanding the Team".'

The meeting broke up, the men quickly coming together to size each other up, Linda walking over to the big wall map of Dartmoor. Peter spoke briefly to both Mike and Bob as they walked through to the canteen. He was hungry, and looking forward to lunch, so less than pleased to discover that they had to prepare it themselves from whatever they could find in the giant fridge-freezer against one wall. There was a single Calor ring to cook on, one saucepan, one frying pan and one set of cutlery.

'Initiative test,' McMahon stated smugly. 'Think as a team.'

Leaving the others to work it out, Peter went outside. The rain had slackened to a thin drizzle, but the clouds were thicker than ever and so low that wisps were breaking around the roof of the old farmhouse. The hills were invisible, but he could see down into a valley from the open end of the farmyard, the shiny black road snaking down to a cluster of big old trees beneath which a group of white painted houses seemed to huddle for shelter. One had cars parked outside it and a sign hanging over the front door, too small to make out by far, but

no less significant for that. Turning back to the
canteen, he clapped his hands for attention and gave
a deliberate imitation of McMahon's enthusiastic
voice as he spoke.

'OK, Team Go! Leadership decision: initiative.
We're going down the pub.'

Saturday morning found Peter in a far better mood
than at any point during the day before. By repeatedly showing genuine initiative rather than slavishly
tagging along he had managed to make an enemy of
McMahon, who was now determined to see him fall.
It was funny and, for all Phil's brief lecture before
they had turned in to their dormitory, which proved
to be one bed short of their needs, he had no
intention of mending his ways. Besides, he was
certain his attitude had drawn appreciation and
possibly even admiration from the shy but undoubtedly attractive Linda. To solve the bed problem
he had even considered attempting to sleep with her
in the girls' dormitory. After trying to chat with her
for a while he'd decided that she might be game, but
definitely not then and there, and had contented
himself with dismantling one of the spare beds,
carrying it across to the men's dorm piece by piece
and reassembling. The solution was supposed to have
been to put one man on watch while the others slept,
but only McMahon seemed to prefer it to Peter's
idea.

The rain had stopped, but the sky was still a sullen
grey. For breakfast there were porridge oats, and a
cow. To everybody's surprise Linda milked her
without turning a hair, while Peter managed to find
some sugar in McMahon's private cubby-hole. The
result was the best porridge he'd ever tasted, and
better still for Linda's surprisingly open gratitude for

the sugar. It left him well set up for the day, and as they came into the lecture room he was actually looking forward to the day. McMahon had a huge map of Dartmoor pinned up on the board, and had exchanged an officer's swagger stick for his pencil. He was rubbing his hands, and launched straight in the moment they had sat down.

'OK Teams, up until now, we've just been feeling our way with a few basic Teamwork and Initiative tests. I've been getting to know the way you all work too, and I can see we've got a bit of a maverick problem. Mavericks do not make good team players.'

He glanced pointedly at Peter, who returned a bland smile, then went on.

'Today, it gets serious; it gets tough. Go out on your own, and you're sunk; work as a team and you'll get through. What do we say?'

'Team, team, team!' the men, including Peter, chorused, Linda managing only an embarrassed croak.

McMahon fixed her with a look and tapped his swagger stick against the map, indicating where a red circle had been marked to show the location of the centre at the heart of the moor. 'We are here, at Rundlestone. Ten miles north across open moorland is the highest peak between here and the Appalachians, Yes Tor, six hundred and nineteen metres . . .'

Linda raised a diffident hand. 'Excuse me, but High Willhays is six hundred and twenty-one metres.'

McMahon looked irritated for just an instant before recovering himself.

'OK, whatever. Yes Tor is our Exercise Target . . . one of our Exercise Targets. This is how it works. On Yes Tor are five ordinary yellow tennis balls concealed among the rocks. Each has been cut, and within it you will find a slip of paper on which I've written three figures of a grid reference, one set in red, one in blue, one in green. Team Energy, your colour is red. Team Go, your colour is blue. The –'

'Excuse me,' Phil interrupted, 'will it be clear which way around the co-ordinates go?'

'Good question, that man,' McMahon answered. 'Yes, it will, because all the exercise locations are on Dartmoor, so the grid references will only make sense the right way around. Each team must secure their own set of grid references, and the green set of grid references. How you go about that is down to you, but I imagine you'll already be beginning to figure out the sort of skills that will be required: physical fitness, negotiation, initiative and, above all, teamwork!'

'Team, team, team!'

'You're getting there. OK, you've got your grid references. At each one you'll find another tennis ball, and inside it there will be a key, and a red or blue marble, like this one. The keys open a box, which you'll find at the green grid reference. Inside the box is a single green marble, and plenty of chocolate, which you'll be needing by then, believe you me. Secure that green marble and you're the winning team. You get steak for dinner. Your other marble gets you chips and peas. Bring back nothing, you get nothing. One other thing, I'm telling you now that you need to work together. All clear? Then pick up your gear from the table and go, go, go!'

He left the lecture room at a trot, the others collecting maps and compasses from a table by the door and following. The moor was as gloomy as ever, with a warm but damp wind blowing in from the west. Mike and Dex gathered around Peter as he opened the map, the others moving off to the side.

Peter considered the area between Rundlestone and Yes Tor. There was not a single road, or building, and the great majority of it was marked as bog and the contours were depressingly twisted and close together.

'So what do you reckon?' Dex asked.

'It's obvious how it's supposed to work,' Peter answered. 'We bust a gut getting to Yes Tor, but Roger, and you, Mike, are a lot younger and fitter than anyone else. You'll get there first . . .'

'We're supposed to stick together, aren't we?' Mike queried. 'To work as a team.'

'The guy's a prat,' Peter answered. 'He's probably got the tennis balls wedged in cracks halfway up a cliff or something, so we can only get them by standing on each other's shoulders. There'll be some trick anyway. It doesn't matter. The way I see it, whoever gets to Yes Tor first will win.'

'Sure,' Mike answered, jerking his thumb at the other team, who were already moving out across the moor, 'so let's go!'

'Relax,' Peter answered him. 'It's ten miles to Yes Tor, across heavy ground. Two miles an hour would be good going for any of us, and Phil's no spring chicken. This is the way we work it. The blue grid reference must be somewhere between here and Yes Tor, probably halfway, give or take. So I walk out on to the moor, while you two take a bus to Okehampton, here on the map. It's about two miles from Okehampton to Yes Tor, so I reckon you'll have between one and two hours to find all six tennis balls. You get the blue and green grid references, and phone them through to me. With any luck I'll be close to the blue one by then, and if you want a laugh you can buy a red biro in Okehampton and change their grid reference. Now we go.'

'Are we allowed to do that?' Mike queried.

'There's a bus stop down by the pub,' Peter answered, and set off after the others.

Dex and Mike hesitated only a moment, then set off down the track. Peter didn't hurry, keeping his distance behind the others and hoping they'd split up and give him a chance to get Linda alone. She might be shy, but she had definitely been showing interest, and he was sure that with just a little skill and just a little persuasion he would have her knickers off before the weekend was through. Shy girls were no different from any others; it just meant the man had more work to do.

A shy girl was also just what he wanted, having had his fill of outgoing ones. Linda was obviously highly intelligent, and also meek. It was a combination he was sure would be particularly satisfying in bed. The thought put a smile on this face as he strode out across the moor. He filled his lungs with air and picked up his pace a little, aiming for where a great stack of grey rocks showed through a rift in the clouds.

Half an hour later he had reached the rocks and was panting slightly. They had proved to be a great deal further than he had expected, seeming to recede even as he walked. They were also bigger than he had imagined, piles of coarse granite some four or five times his height and occupying the entire crest of a good-sized hill. He was high too, with clouds drifting over to plunge everything into a thick grey fog every so often. When they broke he could see for miles, miles of grey-green bog broken by the occasional rock-strewn summit. One, in the extreme distance, he identified from the map as Yes Tor, making him extremely glad he'd chosen not to try for it.

The other team had turned aside, into a valley which cut into the heart of the moor. They were well

117

below him, a little ahead, and still together. He moved forwards, postponing his plans for the seduction of Linda and wondering how much she would appreciate a share of the steak he would be eating that evening. It seemed a good move, and with luck one that would lead towards him bedding her.

It was an appealing prospect. She'd been in a heavy and shapeless coat the day before, but had changed to jeans for the morning. They'd been tight, showing off her slender figure and nicely cheeky bottom. She didn't have a great deal of tit, but on her knees she was going to look great. Just thinking about it was making his cock go hard, and he deliberately turned his mind to the exercise, only to stop dead as he rounded the corner of a vast boulder.

There was a girl on the ground in front of him, lying on her side, near naked, her clothes sorry tatters, jeans and jumper cut to ribbons, bra torn and pulled up over big pink breasts and knotted around her head as a blindfold. Her pink panties had been slashed and stuffed in her mouth as a makeshift gag. Her beautiful golden hair was a bedraggled mess, her body scratched and smeared with mud. Her hands were strapped high behind her back, her ankles and knees lashed together and tied off around her waist, forcing her to keep her legs high, her bottom open, the pink slit of her pussy vulnerable, and virgin. It was Sally, and as a final degradation a large parsnip had been stuffed up her bottomhole, her anal ring straining pink around it.

Peter dashed forwards, sympathy and anger and horror welling up in him at what had been done to her. Quickly he jerked the bra away from her face, only to stop dead. Something was wrong. Everything was wrong. Her presence could not possibly be coincidence. His heart hammering, he stood back with fists clenched, expecting grinning figures to emerge from behind the rocks at any moment, youths bent on mugging him, on revenge for what he and the boys had done to her, her boyfriend, intent on beating him up out of jealousy. Whatever, it was not going to be good for him.

Sally had seen him, and her big green eyes met his, pleading and desperate. He shook his head, his teeth bared in a manic grin, and moved away, putting his back to a rock, ready to fight. Nothing happened. Still he waited. Sally began to make muffled mewing noises through her panties, and to wriggle in her bonds, making her boobs quiver, along with the parsnip up her bottom. Still Peter held back.

Somewhere off among the rocks he caught a movement. His heart jumped and his fists clenched tighter still as he steeled himself to fight. A sheep trotted out from behind the rocks, cast him a single, incurious glance and went on its way. He let his breath out slowly and moved cautiously forwards again, to twitch the ruined panties out of Sally's mouth.

'Thank you . . . oh, thank –' she gasped.

'What's happening?' he demanded. 'And no bull-shit.'

'My . . . my boyfriend . . .' she panted.

'He did this?' Peter demanded. 'I don't buy it. Why leave you here? How did he know I'd be here?'

'He didn't, I swear!' she answered. 'Untie me, please, Peter. You are going to untie me, aren't you? You wouldn't fuck me, would you, not like this?'

'No, of course not,' Peter answered, telling himself that the note of pleading in her voice had to be for her to be untied and not fucked on the spot. 'Relax. I'm going to untie you, in just a moment.'

The rock pile behind him was an easy climb, deep cracks in the granite providing footholds. In seconds he was pulling himself on to the top, his heart still in his mouth as he quickly scanned the area around. It was empty, save for sheep and the occasional pony. Phil and the other team were still visible, well up the valley, and another walker standing alone on the hillside opposite, a woman to judge by the length of her dark hair and her slender build. He called out for Phil, knowing his voice would simply be blown away on the wind, and, sure enough, there was no reaction from the distant figures.

He clambered down again. Sally lay as he had left her, patient in her bondage with no say in the matter. Peter ducked down beside her, feeling a touch cowardly and a touch mean now that his suspicions had proved false. As he caught the scent of her pussy his cock twitched in his trousers and he felt meaner still, wishing his body wouldn't respond with quite such primitive instincts. Still, it seemed only sensible to start by withdrawing the parsnip from her bottom-hole.

'This may hurt a little,' he said, and Sally nodded as he took hold of the protruding end of the vegetable.

She winced as he pulled, but the parsnip came easily enough, exiting her body with a sticky sound to leave her anus a gaping red hole into her body. The thought of replacing the parsnip with his now erect cock rose up in Peter's head, but he bit it down, once more cursing his own instincts. He could think of nothing to say that could possibly do justice to what had happened to her, or compensate for his guilt at his initial assumption that it was some sort of trap. As he began to work on her bonds he realised that he was growing paranoid.

Sally's arms came loose from the bind around her body and she winced in pain as she moved them. Peter tried her wrists, but the binding was tight and

120

wet, impossible to get a purchase on. He went for the knot that held her legs to her body instead, forcing him to move close. Immediately his cock was pressing to her bottom, sending a jolt of need through him so strong that he had to grit his teeth to hold back. Sally closed her eyes, made a little whimpering noise in her throat, and then she was speaking.

'Oh, Lord . . . you're going to fuck me, aren't you? You are, aren't you? You are –'

'No!' Peter snapped. 'I'm not . . . I'm sorry, I . . . I just can't help myself . . . I'm so sorry . . .'

'Just . . . Just get it over with, I beg you!' Sally whined. 'Do it, if you have to . . . do it now!'

Peter closed his eyes in a frantic attempt to keep out the image of the naked, helpless girl. It didn't work, her scent, the feel of her trembling flesh, the knowledge that just two thin layers of clothing separated his cock from her virgin pussy all made it impossible. The knot was stubborn, and his fingers were shaking so hard he couldn't get a grip, Sally still babbling as he wrestled with it.

'Please, Peter, stop tormenting me . . . just do it . . . I know you're going to, so just fuck me . . . fuck me, you bastard, and get it over with! I can feel your cock, sod you, you pig, bastard, pervert!'

'No!' Peter repeated.

He was fighting the knot even as he fought his own temptation. What he wanted to do was wrong, utterly wrong, but his body was telling him otherwise, reacting by pure instinct to her body, and to her helplessness. She thought he was going to do it too, to fuck her where she lay, to pull out his erect cock and force it into her body. It would be so easy. Out it would come, between her sex lips, one good push, her hymen would burst and he'd be up to his balls in ripe teenage cunt, her first time ever . . .

Peter screamed in frustration as he wrenched at the knot, then gasped in pain as a fingernail bent back. Suddenly anger had joined his lust and frustration and confusion. His hands went to his fly, jerking his trousers open, and Sally was screaming.

'That's right, fuck me, you pig, you bastard . . . take me . . . use me . . . fuck my hole, you dirty piece of –'

'No!' Peter gasped, pulling his hands up, completely horrified at what he'd been about to do.

Again he put his hands to the big knot, determined to make his strength tell. Sally moaned, shaking her head in misery and despair. Peter swallowed hard, forcing his lust down, and began to talk to her, softly.

'Don't worry, Sally, it's OK . . . it's OK . . . I'm not going to hurt you . . . I'm going to help you –'

She groaned, a sound of weary resignation, and she was speaking. 'No, you stupid man! You're not supposed to help me; you're not supposed to untie me; you're not even supposed to take my panties out of my mouth unless you want to make me suck your cock! You're supposed to fuck me, you moron!'

For maybe two seconds Peter was just staring, frozen in astonishment. Then he was tearing at his fly, jerking the zip loose, wrenching his aching cock from inside his boxer shorts, to hold it to the slippery valley between Sally's bottom cheeks. He'd had enough of being used, tormented, ripped off, by Linnet, by Linda, by Patty, and now Sally, but even as he put his cock to her virgin hole he knew she was getting exactly what she wanted, just like the others. It was not going to stop him, his lust and sudden anger far too strong to hold back. He pushed.

His cock slipped, on to her bottomhole, the tight ring opening a little to the press before he pulled back once more. Sally gave a low moan, her voice low and strained as she began to speak once before.

'Yes, like that ... fuck my bumhole first ... right up ... really bugger me ... then use my cunt ... yes.'

'Dirty bitch!' Peter spat, and pushed once more, this time holding his cock to her pussy hole.

He felt the slippery mouth of her vagina, the tight constriction of her hymen, taut on his cock-head, tauter still, painfully tight, then loose as Sally screamed and he plunged the full length of his cock into her hole. He snatched at her ropes, clinging on as he began to fuck her, furiously hard, his front slapping on the meaty cheeks of her bottom, her huge boobs bouncing and quivering to the motion. She was screaming and gasping, her body jerking against the ropes as her muscles began to go into agonised convulsions. He kept fucking, jamming himself in again and again, nearly at orgasm, her virgin blood warm on his balls, her newly fucked cunt a slippery sheaf for his erection, so, so tight, so, so perfect ...

Peter's cry of ecstasy rang out across the moor as he began to pump spunk into Sally's body. She took it, jerking and shaking, her muscles twitching, her mouth agape with spit running from the corner, her soiled breasts heaving to her gasps. Peter just kept fucking, draining himself into her until at last he was spent. He sank back, his blood-smeared cock slipping from her deflowered hole, a great wave of guilt rising up to engulf him as his orgasm faded. Sally spoke.

'You really can't take a hint, can you?'

Interlogue

Elune watched with a slight smile on her face as Aileve stripped. Juliana was already nude, and Thomasina, who had the honey, topless. She and Lily alone were dressed, and standing at the door of Aileve's bathroom, watching with interest.

'I still say he wouldn't have done it if Elune hadn't egged him on,' Aileve insisted as she removed her panties, 'and you didn't say anything about the lavatory.'

'Nonsense,' Juliana answered her as she settled herself on the loo, 'he'd have just taken a little longer. You've never quite got the concepts of chivalry and courtly love out of your head, have you? As for the lavatory, I'm quite happy to go on your bed, or the sofa, if you prefer?'

'Here will do,' Aileve answered moodily, 'and a typical knight would have fucked her without giving it a second thought. I simply didn't realise he was such a primitive.'

Stark naked, she kneeled on the floor, her pale, boyish bottom stuck out as she got into position, her tight pink anus on show, her neat little pussy already beading with moisture. Juliana slid her body forwards, her thighs well spread, to show off the ready slit of her own sex. Thomasina made a face as she scooped out a

*large spoonful of the thick honey for Juliana, who took
it in her fingers and pushed it up into the mouth of her
sex. A second followed, and a third, until the mouth of
Juliana's vagina was gaping wide around a thick clot of
golden-white honey. It had already begun to melt as
Thomasina extracted a fourth spoonful, thick gold
liquid oozing slowly from Juliana's pussy as it melted
to her body heat and trickled down over her anus.*

*'Come on, Aileve, darling, feeding time,' she teased
as she pushed more honey in. 'You can lick my
bottomhole first.'*

*Aileve nodded and went forwards, pressing her face
to Juliana's sex, planting a single kiss on the swollen
lips, then starting to lap as she'd been instructed. Elune
moved closer, watching as Aileve's little pink tongue
flicked in and out, taking up the melted honey right
from the dimple of Juliana's anal ring. Juliana sighed
in pleasure and took a handful of Aileve's long black
hair, twisting it hard into her fist. Aileve gave a little
squeak of pain, but began to lick harder, burrowing her
tongue into Juliana's anus.*

*'Good girl,' Juliana sighed, 'that's right, deep in.
More honey, Thomasina, just over my pussy to get me
good and sticky for when I rub her face in it.'*

*Thomasina quickly obeyed, scooping out more honey
and using a finger to pile it on to the shaved bulge of
Juliana's pussy mound. It quickly began to melt,
running slowly down Juliana's skin to wedge against
Aileve's nose. Elune giggled at the sight and reached
out to take Lily's hand, pressing it to the bulge of her
own sex. Lily began to rub.*

*'If your students could see you now, eh, Dr Alice,'
Juliana crowed, 'eating honey out of another woman's
bottomhole. What would they think?'*

*Aileve gave a muffled sob but kept licking. Juliana
laughed and tugged on her handful of hair, forcing*

Aileve's face against her sex and rubbing it well in before once more relaxing her grip. Aileve came up with most of her face smeared with a sticky mixture of honey and pussy juice, causing all three of the watching girls to laugh.

'Now eat what's in my pussy,' Juliana demanded, 'and make me come, but first, I really think we ought to wash your face.'

Aileve made to protest, at exactly the wrong moment, so that she caught the full force of Juliana's pee in her mouth. All four of the other girls dissolved into laughter as Aileve went into a choking fit, struggling to swallow her dirty mouthful with pee still splashing directly into her face.

Seven

Peter cut into his steak. After all the fuss it was only an indifferent piece of rump, but in the circumstances he would not have tasted the finest sirloin. Nor were McMahon's comments on the boundaries between taking initiative and cheating registering as anything more than background noise. His mind was on the events of the day and his head was swimming with emotions he was struggling to keep in check.

When he had realised that the entire episode with Sally had been set up, his anger had exploded. She had manipulated him body and mind, with an ease that left him humiliated as well as bitter. Never before had he experienced the intensity of emotion as his conscience fought against his native sexual urges, nor the blend of agony and ecstasy as he finally gave in. He had been fighting to hold back his anger as he untied her, anger that drew partly on his bewilderment. Once loose, she had simply spent a moment rubbing her wrists and legs, and afterwards she had been laughing and joking, teasing him for his behaviour, apparently unfazed by being bound nude on the moor, and by having her virginity taken by him. Finally he had been forced to accept that to her the whole episode had been a joke, something she had done for a thrill. It had been more than he could take, but, when his anger had finally flared and he had demanded an explanation, she had stuck out her tongue at him and run, disappearing over the moor with astonishing agility. He had tried to follow, but found himself totally unable to keep pace, with her derisive laughter still floating back as she disappeared into the mist.

Yet it did not make sense. He had taken her virginity, surely a moment of great significance for any woman, or any man for that matter? She had been stripped, bound and gagged, a parsnip forced into her anus, left helpless and naked, at the mercy of any passer-by. It was not an experience he would have expected anyone to find amusing, just the opposite, especially an eighteen-year-old girl.

Once she had gone he had been left standing in the mist, seething with anger, guilt, frustration, bewilderment and more. Only when his mobile phone had gone off had he been brought back to earth, or at least some of the way. It had been Dex, to say that he and Mike were on Yes Tor and had found five of the six tennis balls. After what had happened the statement had been so mundane, so normal, that he had laughed aloud.

There had been nothing to do but carry on as before, ridiculous though it had seemed. He could hardly report the incident to the police, and could only pray Sally wouldn't. Nor could he really speak about it to anyone else. So he had done what is always the easiest thing when faced with the inexplicable and untenable, pushed it to the back of his mind and carried on.

McMahon's exercise had proved absurdly easy. The blue grid reference had taken him to one of the rocky outcrops, Rough Tor. It had been a tough walk, with bog, tussock grass and fast-flowing streams, but a fraction of the distance to Yes Tor. As he had suspected, the tennis ball was wedged into a crevice about two feet higher than he could reach, but he had solved the problem by simply asking the next hiker who passed to give him a leg up.

With the blue marble safely in his pocket, he had moved on towards the green grid reference, at Great Mis Tor, the rocks he had passed just before meeting Sally. The weather had begun to clear and Dex had told him that the rival team had not even reached Yes Tor, so he had taken his time and what he judged as the driest route, all the while trying to find an explanation for Sally's behaviour. Nothing had fitted, and as he had rounded the edge of a gully in which erosion had taken the peat down to bare granite he had received his second shock of the day.

There, in an area of flat grass sheltered by high banks of peat, had been four girls. One had been Sally, now with a coat on, but carelessly open to show that she was nude beneath. The others were all taller, and all dark haired, one buxom with a gentle, easy face, one athletic with cruel eyes and a sneer of amusement, one slender and lithe with a look of cool intelligence. All four shared the same brilliant green eyes, and all four had been eating chocolate.

His initial reaction had been surprise, and anger, but even as he had begun to bluster out a question the athletic one had very casually produced a barrel knife, and smiled as the blade flicked out. He had beaten a hasty retreat, and they had not followed, leaving him more angry and bewildered than ever. Still there had been nothing he could do but continue on his way by a different route. When he had found the box on Great Mis Tor it had been open, the lock forced and the chocolate missing, also the green marble. He had taken it back, blaming hooligans, which seemed entirely apt. He had made no mention of the girls.

Events had made McMahon's exercise seem utterly trivial, the lengthy and speculative conclusions he had drawn from it yet more so. Linda had not returned from the moor, leaving the others some way short of Yes Tor after getting a phone call and saying she had to hurry back to Exeter. McMahon put her behaviour down to low self-esteem. Peter was sure he knew otherwise, and a quick conversation with Phil revealed that she had made and received several other private calls.

He had accepted the steak, too drained to do more than eat it in a mechanical fashion, while the others chatted and poked fun at each other over the events of the day. McMahon had appointed a social hour, but Peter went to bed, exhausted, but still unable to sleep for the whirl of thoughts in his head.

Sunday morning was no better, his feelings sharply at odds. The bleak Dartmoor hills had taken on an air of menace they had entirely lacked the day before, but he was also affected with a strong sense of longing. He wanted to understand, more than anything, certainly more than he wanted to participate in McMahon's second team-building exercise, which involved building a makeshift bridge over the river at the bottom of the valley. His team failed miserably, earning some smug remarks from McMahon over lunch. Aware that McMahon would be sending a report on the entire farce to the directors at Truwood, he did his best in the afternoon, successfully winning a Support and Logistics Exercise that involved getting supposedly injured team members off the moor. Despite his effort, he was expecting to stumble across Sally gagged and bound at every turn, that or the cruel-eyed girl with the knife. Nothing happened.

130

They got together in the pub that evening, several pints of strong local ale going some way towards helping Peter recover his humour. He was still starting at shadows as they walked back up the darkened track, and even in bed was staring out at the sullen, moonlit hills until he fell asleep.

Not until he was back at home on the Monday evening, bathed and refreshed with a cold beer in his hand and a plate of curry on his lap, did he manage to think at all clearly. After eating he determined to make what sense he could out of the situation and sat down with his pad to cross names off the list and make fresh notes.

A few facts were clear. There was a group of girls, five at least, probably six with shy Linda as opposed to Linda the con artist, maybe seven with Patty. All had green eyes, and not just green, but a vivid green. It was an extraordinary feature, and they could hardly all be sisters, yet it had to be in some way significant.

As he pondered the question he remembered reading a Sherlock Holmes story, *The Red-Headed League*. In it, a character had been offered a membership of a philanthropic society open only to men with strikingly red hair. Possibly the green-eyed girls were some similar group? As he remembered more of the story a new thought occurred to him. The fact of a man having brilliant red hair had been a blind to get him to leave his shop so that it could be used for criminal purposes. There had been no society. Things were not always as they seemed, and perhaps the girls' green eyes were simply the result of coloured contact lenses, perhaps to allow them to change their appearance easily, more likely as some sort of gang mark.

It made sense. They certainly behaved like a gang, although it seemed bizarre that they should dedicate themselves to his sexual humiliation. Had he somehow offended one of their members? If so, why play such an elaborate game? The girl with the knife had not looked the sort to go in for subtle or abstract revenge. Yet it made more sense than any other solution he could think of.

If there were as many as seven of them, and if they were sufficiently determined, it was easy to see how they could always have somebody near him. At the realisation that he might have missed far more staged encounters than he had run into a cold shiver went down his spine. There also had to be a link, some way of explaining how they had known where he would be, and when. It also accounted for the effort they put into it, if they were being paid, and the rent-boy, who would also have been paid. Everything pointed at somebody from work being involved, and probably Phil. Phil had the means, the money and just possibly the motive.

How had Phil behaved on Dartmoor? For one thing he had been on Linda's team, apparently by coincidence, but he booked the weekend and could well have nobbled McMahon, if only by explaining Peter's supposed need for a better team spirit. There was also the question of how the girls had known where the box was on Great Mis Tor. Possibly one of them had seen McMahon hide it, more likely they had been told, but not by Linda, who had left before their team had the green co-ordinates. That left Phil, who could have planted Linda on the Teamwork course in the first place. In fact, now he thought about it, it seemed likely that the entire Teamwork farce had been designed to get him in the right place at the right time. Phil had set it up. Roger seemed a lot less likely, Dex still less so, unless all three were involved.

He remembered an old maxim from the police soaps – follow the money. Who gained from fucking him over? Roger or Dex might want his patch, by far the most lucrative of the three sales areas. Phil's gain seemed less obvious, and then it hit him. His contract had been signed long before either Roger's or Dex's. It gave him the full commission on his sales; theirs gave 70 per cent, and the rest went to Phil. If he quit, whether Roger or Dex got his patch or a new man was brought in, Phil would get 30 per cent of every sales commission in the UK outside the London area. On last year's figures that would mean twenty to thirty thousand pounds on top of Phil's salary.

There was a wicked grin on Peter's face as he poured himself a large Scotch. It made sense, all of it. By hiring the green-eyed girls Phil intended to drive him out, maybe by racking up the stress until he quit, maybe by having him arrested for some sexual crime. It even explained Sally's behaviour. If he hadn't fucked her there would have been no evidence to link him with the event. As it was . . .

The thought left him suddenly cold, the glass of whisky clutched tight in his hand. It was too late. He might have worked it out, but it was too late. Sally only needed to go to the police and tell them he'd accosted her on the moor, tied her and raped her. She had proof, his DNA, and undoubtedly her friends would add weight to her story. He remembered the girl he'd seen across the hill after finding Sally – tall, slim, dark haired, undoubtedly one of the green-eyed girls. Then there was the fact that he hadn't said anything when he got back to the centre, which was bound to be considered suspicious. He cursed and swallowed the whisky at a gulp. What to do?

A solution hit him with the kick from the Scotch. The girls didn't care what happened to him. They were paid and, if they'd take Phil's money, they'd take his. He had to outbid Phil, and he could do it. As he poured a second Scotch he was already taking a mental inventory of his assets. He'd cleared the mortgage with his last bonus; the car and credit card were no big deal. There was thirty-seven thousand plus in the bank and he could raise more if he had to. It had to be enough. The big problem was that, if Sally hadn't gone to the police already, she was sure to do so soon. He had to act, but how?

The girls were in Devon, presumably. How to find them was a different matter. He had no way whatever of tracing Sally, nor the others he had met on the moor. Patty quite evidently had no link whatsoever with Retro Records or any other music business. Linda had claimed to be associated with Exeter University, but that might be false, and to attempt to follow the trail would be likely to alert Phil. There was Linnet's car, but short of getting a police trace it was hard to know how that helped. There was the photo of Linnet on the book cover, and that was a lead.

Peter was on his way out even as he reached his conclusion. The big service station in Newport Pagnell sold dirty books, and would still be open. Twenty minutes later he was there, an hour and he was back in the house. The photographer was Luke Richter, a name he remembered Linnet using when she'd explained how he'd made her suck him off. Another five minutes on the Internet and he had the address of Richter's studio in Coventry, just a short blast up the M1. A minor bit of rescheduling and he could be there in the morning.

He took the book to bed, hoping to get lost in it, but still found himself straining his ears for the sounds of distant sirens and expecting the crash of a size-twelve regulation boot on his front door at any instant. Only after half an hour did he think to look at the picture on the front cover and the final piece of proof fell into place. Linnet's eyes were not green, but brown.

His luck held in the morning. Deciding to phone Richter first rather than cold call, he discovered that Linnet modelled under the name Rosy Parker and worked through a studio agency in Birmingham, Dolls and Guys. There was a sour grin on his face as he called them, sourer still when he discovered she was not only available, but working there that very morning. He gave his name as Ronald Davis and said he would call later in the morning.

A quick change to his schedule, swapping Harry Trent at Splash! for Jim Wheeler at Bayou Bathrooms and he had made up his time. There was no call to go into the office, and he was in Birmingham by eleven. The call went easily enough, Jim keen to buy, and after a hurried lunch he made for Dolls and Guys. It was on a trading estate no more than a mile from Bayou Bathrooms, a square breezeblock box built with only function in mind. Within was a tiny office and a corridor from which doors opened into a blank wall.

Peter gave out the cover story he had worked out on the drive up and was not only accepted, but told that he could wait in an upstairs gallery overlooking the studios. He went, at last hoping he might be in time. A big enough offer of money, a few phone calls from Linnet and he could breathe again, and start thinking about how to revenge himself on the bastard Phil.

The gallery was a long whitewashed room with dark orange carpet tiles, pictures of various models from the agency's books, chairs and a long window overlooking the studios. There was a coppery gleam to the window, and Peter realised it was one-way glass as he peered through and the people below took not the slightest notice of him. Whatever was going on, it didn't look as though they were modelling clothes. There were two girls, both thin and blonde, both with large and heavily enhanced breasts. One was on her knees, her face set in mock ecstasy, the other crouched over, her tongue an inch from her colleague's anus, pretending she was about to lick it. Powerful spotlights and no less than seven men surrounded the couple, every one with a camera.

Peter moved on, eager to find Linnet. She was in the next studio, and one glance at her made the blonde models in the first seem nothing more than mannequins, essentially fake. Her exquisite little body was not naked, but what she was wearing made the fact that she was showing every detail that mattered far more striking. It was completely ordinary, a well-cut woman's suit in a conservative dark blue, a crisp white blouse beneath, smart shoes, the dress of a successful businesswoman or a female politician. It was also somewhat disarranged. The blouse had been pulled wide, her bra up, perfect little titties sticking out, perky and proud. The jacket had been tugged down her back, trapping her arms and enhancing the exposure of her breasts. The skirt was rucked up around her waist, the plain white panties pulled well down, her bottom stuck well out, exposing the rear purse of her sex and the tight brown knot of her anus in a pose as lewd as the clothes were decent. His cock was instantly stiff in his trousers.

He watched as she posed, unable to break away even to get himself a coffee. The clothes never came off, but her positions grew ever more revealing and ever more lewd, as did her behaviour. Peter couldn't hear, but it became clear that she'd been told to masturbate, rubbing at her breasts, bottom and pussy with ever greater intimacy. Eventually she was spread out on the floor, thighs wide, one hand on a tit and the other on her pussy, her face set in an ecstasy that he was sure was real. By then his cock was a rigid pole in his trousers and he was wondering if he might not manage to fuck her after all, or at the least squeeze a blow job out of her for the way she'd behaved.

She was smiling as she began to adjust her clothes, and chatting to the photographer, a spectacularly ugly man with wild brown hair. Peter hurried downstairs, composing himself for what was sure to be a confrontation. He had to be calm, he knew, calm and businesslike, at the very least until his payoff had been accepted. Then he would see what could be done about getting her into bed. Even if it meant paying, it was sure to be a trifling sum compared with what it was going to take to pay them off for Phil.

Her studio door was opening even as he reached the bottom of the stairs. The photographer emerged, case in hand, still talking back through the door. Peter paused, not wanting to add his presence to a situation already complicated enough. The man nodded to him, leaving the door wide. Linnet stepped out, still fastening the buttons of her blouse, smiled sweetly and walked straight past him.

'Linnet,' he stated firmly. 'Stop, I need to talk to you, now.'

'Eh? Who are you?' she demanded, her accent thick Birmingham. 'I think you've got the wrong person.'

'No more games,' Peter went on, putting an arm out to block the corridor. 'Believe me, Linnet . . . or Rosy, or whatever you want to call yourself, I have a better offer for you.'

She stopped, looking puzzled and somewhat annoyed. 'What offer? What are you talking about? Are you the guy I'm supposed to be with next?'

Peter drew a sigh. 'You know perfectly well who I am, Linnet. I'm Peter Williams, who Phil Brewster paid you to stitch up. Yes, ring any bells?'

'No. Look, I just have to shout and security'll be here.'

'How much did Phil pay? I'll double it.'

'Look, mate, I don't know who you are or what you're on about, but –'

'Come on,' Peter urged. 'You just have to tell Sally to back off and I'll pay whatever it takes!'

'Sally? Who's Sally? Look –'

'I know what's been going on!' Peter snapped, now struggling to hold himself in. 'I know about you and the other girls. I know about Sally, and Linda, and the rest, and I want to make you a better offer. At least listen! Ten grand, twenty grand, whatever, it's yours . . .'

She had turned to walk away, but stopped. 'Twenty grand? What are you on? I'm a model, OK? I don't know anything about this shit.'

'Linnet, I –' Peter began, and stopped. Something was wrong, something that had been nagging at his mind since the girl had stepped into the corridor.

'How tall are you?' he demanded.

'Five-three,' she answered, 'not that –'

'Hang on,' he urged, 'bear with me just a second. I'm sorry if I seem angry. This is you, yes?'

He had pulled out the book from his pocket. She took a single glance and answered. 'Sure, one from a shoot I did with Luke Richter.'

'And you are five foot three inches tall?'

'Yes.'

'What car do you drive? Is it outside?'

'Yeah, it's an Uno.'

'Do you mind showing me?'

'If you think I'm going outside with you, mate, you've got another think coming! We get enough weirdos in here.'

'I'm not a weirdo,' he answered, 'just ... just confused. Please could you show me your car, just open it so that I can see it's yours.'

'What, and have you push me in it? I'm calling security.'

'Don't bother, forget it,' Peter answered hastily. 'There's been a mistake. I did book you, yes, but I thought you were somebody else. I can see you're not, so there's no need to be alarmed, OK?'

She looked doubtful, and defensive. A door opened further down the corridor and the men who had been photographing the two blondes began to stream out, chatting excitedly about their experience as they made for the gallery stairs.

'I'd just like to talk to you for a second,' Peter went on, 'perhaps upstairs in the gallery.'

'Look,' she stated, 'are you booking me, or not?'

'Not now, no,' he answered, 'but –'

'Then fuck off,' she answered. 'I haven't got time for this shit.'

'OK, OK, I'll book you, whatever it takes,' Peter answered. 'How much would it be?'

'Eighty an hour.'

'Fine,' he answered, digging for his wallet. 'Here's a hundred, just to come and have a coffee.'

'No, you don't pay me, you pay at reception, I –'

'Just take the money, OK?'

She shrugged and took the two fifty-pound notes Peter had extracted from his wallet. He led her upstairs to the gallery, where the men he had seen before were clustered together, talking and comparing cameras and their results. As Peter went to the coffee machine, he was trying to work out where he had gone wrong. Rosy Parker was clearly not Linnet. She was too tall, and there were other differences, in the way she held herself, in her accent and manner, but, most importantly, her personality was completely different. Rosy looked life in the eye. Linnet laughed at it.

He took two coffees from the machine, wincing as he tasted it. She had waited, her arms folded, sullen and defensive. He took a chair and gestured to another, not too close, but close enough for their conversation to be private.

'So?' she demanded as she sat down.

'I need some facts,' Peter answered, watching her closely. 'First off, do you have a sister, perhaps younger, but very like you? Or know anybody who looks strikingly similar to you, just a little smaller?'

'No,' she answered. 'I've a sister, but she's a lot older than me.'

'Does she have striking green eyes, or ever wear green contact lenses? About thirty, perhaps, quite curvy?'

'No. Her hair's blonde, dyed, and her eyes are brown.'

Peter nodded. She was telling the truth, he was sure, yet if her resemblance to Linnet, and to Patty, was a coincidence it was a pretty extraordinary one. Besides, Linnet had not only claimed to be the model on the cover, but seemed to have known Luke Richter. Then again, Richter's name was on the back of the book as cover photographer.

'Luke Richter,' he went on. 'Is he good to work with? Does he give you a hard time, try to pressure you into sex maybe?'

'Luke!? He's gay, and he's a really nice guy too, if you –'

'OK, OK, there's no need to get defensive. Have you been to Mapley's recently?'

It was perfectly delivered, he knew, the crucial question dropped in unexpectedly and casually, an old sales technique to see if the client had been talking with any competitors. She just shrugged, not betraying the slightest flicker of recognition, surprise, guilt, anything that might have betrayed her. Clearly she knew nothing. Peter stood up.

'Sorry to have wasted your time then.'

'Is that it?' she asked.

'Yes.'

'You don't want me to model?'

'I don't even have a camera with me.'

'Oh.'

She smiled as he turned away, her beauty showing through for just an instant, an instant in which Peter once more felt the sense of longing he had before. Then it was gone, his problems clouding out everything else. She was not Linnet, so her appeal did not matter, merely a distraction. He put her out of his head as he left the building, forcing himself to focus on the task in hand. A new element might have been added to what was already a confusing situation, but what mattered was getting in touch with the green-eyed girls.

As he had suspected, there was no Le Mans Green MG Roadster among the cars outside, but there was a Fiat Uno. He was shaking his head as he climbed into the Mondeo, conscious of time wasted and what might happen if he didn't act fast. He drove back to Milton Keynes on autopilot and at a furious pace. There was a sick feeling in the pit of his stomach as he turned into his road, expecting to find a police car pulled up outside his house, but there was nothing. For whatever reason, Sally had not acted.

It occurred to him that Phil might have tried to cheat her, holding back the money until she was in too deep to back out, or that, once in control, she might have demanded more. Whatever the case, he was more than grateful for the delay. Indoors, he moved on to his second choice, the link with Exeter. An Internet search revealed several Lindas associated with the university, but nothing he could be sure of. Then it struck him. He called, imitating McMahon's mealy voice as he asked for the accounts department, then enquired to whom a partial refund cheque for the teamwork course should be sent. The answer was a Dr Alice Chaswell. Another Internet search revealed that she was a highly respected expert on medieval archaeology, which didn't seem to fit, and a picture, which did. Alice Chaswell was the tallest of the girls he had run into on Dartmoor.

His breathing was deep and hard as he clicked off the Internet connection. This time he had done it; there could be no mistake. Wednesday could be rearranged, it had to be rearranged. He would be in Exeter first thing and, if Sally had waited so long, there had to be a fair chance she would wait longer.

For an hour he forced himself to behave as he usually did, making jokes and wry remarks as he called his clients to adjust his schedule. As he put the phone down for the last time a car pulled up outside, sending his heart into his mouth until he saw that it was simply a van making a delivery to his neighbours. He went for the Scotch bottle, but changed his mind with it in his hand. He needed to be out of the house, distracted, and perhaps to at least put off disaster.

The Pig and Whistle was too obvious. If the police had information from Phil it would be the second place they searched. He had to get away from his normal haunts, somewhere anonymous, maybe even stay the night. That made sense, because even if Sally had been to the police there would be a chance he could persuade the girls to change their story.

To think was to act. He threw some things together and went back out to the car, trying to behave as casually as possible in front of his neighbour and the delivery man, who were still talking on the pavement. He left, and as he moved down the main road a police car passed in the opposite direction, towards his house. More nervous than ever, unsure if the car had been meant for him, he turned south for London, full into the worst of the rush hour.

By the time he was clear of the traffic the strains of the day were telling on him. Tired and hungry, he pulled off at Swindon and made for Midlander's, a place as anonymous as he could possibly have wished for. A quick meal and he retired to bed, only to wake just two hours later and find it impossible to get back to sleep. Finally he gave up and dressed once more, making his way to Fat Sam's for the solace of music and Scotch.

The bar was much as it had been the night he met Linda the con artist, and his first act was to scan the faces for her. She wasn't there, hardly surprisingly, and he took a double Scotch to a seat in the corner, listening to the piano as at least some of his tension began to drain away. His thoughts had quickly turned back to Linnet, and to Rosy. Even when late in the evening a woman came to sit with him it was impossible to give her any real attention, and he returned to the hotel alone and boiling with frustration.

Interlogue

Elune placed her hands on her head, displaying her naked body for inspection. Her huge breasts felt unpleasantly heavy, and yet there was a strange comfort in their weight and size that had little to do with sexual pleasure. The same was true of her bottom, the size of her cheeks awkward yet satisfying, while there was no denying that having it so big increased her desire to be spanked.

'Is this enough, do you think?' she asked.

'Another couple of inches on your boobies and your botty and you'll be there,' Thomasina suggested.

'No,' Juliana put in, 'I think she's already overshot.'

'You should go to Portsmouth again,' Aileve suggested.

'I very much doubt he'll notice the difference,' Lily countered, 'but I have to agree with Thomasina, you still need a little on your breasts and bottom, your tummy too.'

'Dye your hair again, too,' Aileve added, 'and remember to keep your pussy bare.'

'I will,' Elune assured her. 'Thomasina, you're usually quite plump, do you constantly feel as if you need your bottom smacked? I do, and it's getting worse.'

'Any more of that and you'll get it!' Thomasina answered. 'I suppose I do, at least when I'm feeling

rude, or guilty over something, but I don't think it has anything to do with the size of my bottom.'

'I imagine the extra weight of your cheeks makes you more conscious of them, and therefore more likely to think of having them smacked,' Aileve suggested.

'If that were true,' Juliana said thoughtfully, 'you would expect that the frequency with which girls got spanked would be in direct proportion to how fat their bottoms were, especially nowadays, when most men have to be made to do it. Do you think that's true?'

'If it is,' Thomasina answered her, 'then it could just as well be because men prefer to spank girls with fatter bottoms. How could you tell the difference?'

'It wouldn't necessarily work that way,' Aileve insisted. 'There are too many factors involved. For one thing, I suspect you'd only be more aware of your bottom while your weight was increasing. For another, with being thin so much in fashion, I imagine that for most ordinary women embarrassment of having a fat bottom would counteract any added desire they might have to get it smacked. As with any aspect of human behaviour, it would be very hard to produce reliable statistics, although it might be possible to apply a multiple regression if you had sufficient data, and thus –'

'Shut up, Aileve,' Elune interrupted, 'none of us have the faintest idea what you're talking about. All I know is that it works for me. Pass me round, will you? Lily first, and do it hard.'

'Fair enough,' Aileve answered, reaching for the long-handled hairbrush on her bedside table as Elune draped herself, bottom up, across Lily's knee.

Eight

After leaving Swindon the moment he had swallowed a cup of coffee, Peter made Exeter well before nine, and was at the university when the first of the students were just drifting in towards lectures. Even knowing what he did, it was hard to accept that nearby might be the source of all his troubles. The place held a studious atmosphere, implying nothing more sinister than the occasional student prank, and an environment as far from the one in which he'd been imagining the green-eyed girls as it was possible to be.

The number of Dr Chaswell's room was advertised on a board in the foyer of the Department of Archaeology, and he found it without difficulty, beyond a museum displaying artefacts from every period of British History. Telling himself that he would be firm but strictly businesslike, he knocked on the door. A female voice answered, soft, with just a touch of hauteur. He pushed in at the door, to find a room cluttered with paper and artefacts much like those in the museum, the walls lined with maps and diagrams and charts. She sat behind a desk directly opposite him, her expression cool, certain, deeply intelligent, and with an air of slight amusement.

'Mr Williams, I presume?' she asked. 'I've been wondering when you'd turn up.'

146

'You were expecting me?' Peter demanded.

'Of course,' she answered, 'I hardly imagine it was difficult to work out?'

'No,' Peter answered, 'not that difficult, and so here I am. I expect you know more or less what I have to say as well?'

'Let me guess,' she said, 'you want to know why you're being led on a goose chase around England by a series of girls with deep-green eyes and a somewhat peculiar sense of humour.'

'That one I've already worked out. What has Phil paid you? I'll double it if you back off.'

Her look of cool amusement changed to open surprise.

'I'm sorry, you've lost me. Who's Phil? Not the man who was on the teamwork course with Lil – Linda?'

'Don't you start, I've had enough of that bollocks already. Phil is my boss, as you damn well know, the man who paid you to set me up with Sally. I saw you on the moor with her, and you've already admitted you know who I am, so there's no good in denying it.'

'I'm not denying it,' she answered, stifling a smile, 'at least, I'm not denying that I met you on the moor after your little escapade with my friend, but I assure you that otherwise I have no idea what you are talking about. Why should your boss have paid us? You don't think he put her up to it, do you?'

'Yes! Of course I do. I don't just think it, I know it!'

'You do? Well, in that case you know a great deal more than I do!'

She was trying not to laugh, her mouth curved up into a smile and her chest quivering. Peter felt hot anger start to rise up inside him, but before he could speak she went on.

'I am sorry, Mr Williams, and I shouldn't really laugh. Are you saying that you think your boss is attempting to blackmail you in some way, by putting you in a compromising position?'

'Yes!'

'Then please let me assure you that he isn't, or at least not to my knowledge. I have never met him, nor have any of my friends, with the exception of Lily, whom you know as Linda. Why would he want to do so in any case?'

'Never mind that. I want to know what's going on, and I want to know now. If Phil isn't setting me up, who is, and why?'

'I wonder,' she remarked, 'whether, if I refused to tell you, would you give me the same treatment as you gave Sally?'

'No, I would not,' he snapped. 'That was . . . that was stupid of me, I realise now.'

'A shame,' she remarked, 'it might be quite fun to be ravished across my desk, but never mind, I can see you're not in the mood. I suppose I had better put you out of your misery, then. Don't worry about Phil, or blackmail. Sally was merely . . . amusing herself . . .'

'Amusing herself! Do you seriously expect me to believe that?'

'It's the truth. She is capricious by nature, and she takes particular pleasure in driving people to extremes of emotion, men generally.'

'She certainly does that! But why? What does she get out of it? And what about Linnet, and Patty? What about my mate's car? What are you people after, Dr Chaswell?'

'Amusement.' she answered. 'At least in their cases. Personally, I rather sympathise with you, though of course what you should have done is to give her a good spanking.'

148

'What!?'

'You should have spanked her, at first . . . Linnet.'

'Spanked her? Why would I want to do that? Well, I can see –'

'Exactly, her behaviour does rather cry out for it. A good spanking and she's as meek as a lamb, at least for a while. As to your other questions, I believe Sally left the car in Watford. Don't worry about Patty, as you're highly unlikely to see her again, or Sally for that matter. If you do, my advice is to give them the same treatment, find somewhere private and spank them until they howl.'

She was smiling, and still holding back her amusement, with a gleam in her eyes not so very different from Linnet. Peter drew in his breath.

'Fine, so you're telling me that I've been put through hell for the amusement of some group of spoiled-brat rich girls, to egg me on to spank them?'

'That's a reasonable summary, yes.'

'But why? And why me!?'

'Why, Mr Williams? If you are asking me why some women like to be spanked, or indulge in any other behaviour generally considered to be degrading, then I would have to point out that this is the Department of Archaeology. Psychology is on the far side of the campus, the Washington Singer Laboratories to be exact. Take it from me that Linnet, Patty and Sally all enjoy it, but that, to get the most out of it, they have to feel they deserve it and, more importantly, know that the man, or woman, really means it. It's difficult nowadays, you know, when so few men will respond in the right way. Linnet hoped you would, when she first met you –'

'What, in the middle of a service station?'

'That would have delighted her.'

'And got me arrested!'

149

'That would also have delighted her. But weren't you tempted at Mapley's? Not to spank her, maybe, but to take your feelings out on her in some way?'

'I never saw her at Mapley's!'

'She was there, but she rather got caught up in her own game. As I said, caprice is very much her nature. Now, of course, if your response hadn't been sexual, but merely aggressive, she would have run and, believe me, Linnet can run.'

Peter drew in his breath.

'Fair enough, so, if what you're saying is true, prove it.'

'Prove it, you say? That's an interesting proposition. You're welcome to borrow my phone if you wish to ring the local constabulary and check whether any voluptuous blondes have reported being raped on Dartmoor over the weekend, but I imagine it might take a little explaining away when you find they haven't. Unless you have a better suggestion?'

'Dead right I do. That's a speaker phone on your desk. Ring Sally now, and when she answers say, "It's all off" – just that and nothing else. Let's see what she says, shall we?'

'How ingenious you are,' Dr Chaswell replied, reaching for her phone. 'Very well.'

Peter watched carefully as she flicked the speaker to on and dialled the number. A moment later Sally answered, her soft tones unmistakable.

'Hello?'

'It's all off,' Dr Chaswell stated.

'What?' Sally demanded. 'Is that you, Aileve? What's off?'

'Our evil plot to blackmail Peter Williams,' Dr Chaswell went on, 'who happens to be sitting in my office with me.'

'He's there, in Exeter? What's he doing there? And what are you talking about, "blackmail him"?'

'He came to offer us money not to report him to the police,' Dr Chaswell explained.

'What!?'

'It's all rather complicated, but basically he thinks his boss paid us to pretend you were raped by him –'

She stopped as Sally burst into laugher, a peal of glee-filled, mischievous delight. Dr Chaswell put the phone down and turned back to Peter.

'Convinced, Mr Williams?'

Peter could find no answer. His cheeks were flaming red in hideous embarrassment at the derision in Sally's laughter, at Dr Chaswell's supercilious little smile, at the realisation that he had been comprehensively used, and that it was simply for the girls' amusement.

'Bitches!' he spat.

'Don't be too hard on them,' Dr Chaswell responded. 'After all, you must admit, you do rather rise to the bait. Next time, I suggest you simply accept your good fortune.'

'Next time? You mean there's going to be a next time?'

'Quite possibly. Now, if you will excuse me, I have a lecture to deliver.'

She indicated the door. Peter rose, struggling for words to do justice to his feelings. None came, and he found himself being politely but firmly shepherded from the room. Dr Chaswell gave him a bright smile as she locked her door and walked away. He watched her go, the rotation of her neat buttocks beneath the material of her trouser suit as taunting as Linnet. She herself had advised punishing girls who behaved that way, and for an instant he considered just grabbing her, whipping her across his knee, jerking her trousers and panties low and dishing out the mother of all spankings.

It was impossible, the idea of reducing the calm, intelligent young scientist to a squalling, tear-stained brat immensely appealing, yet utterly against everything he had come to believe about how women should be treated, about how women wanted to be treated. Then she had turned the corner; the moment was past, and he was left standing, at once bitterly frustrated and heartily glad he had not reacted on his instincts. One simply could not go around spanking respectable university lecturers, let alone bare-bottom and in public. Perhaps in referring to Linnet she had been talking about herself as well, as women so often did, so she might want it, she certainly needed it, but he was not the one to do it. As she had said herself, if he'd done Linnet at the J49 services she would have revelled in the spanking and laughed as the police dragged him away.

As he walked back to the Mondeo he reflected on their conversation. For all his embarrassment and anger it was an immense relief to discover that he was not about to be arrested. Not that it excused the girls' behaviour, and one thing Alice Chaswell had said stuck out – he was highly unlikely ever to see Sally or Patty, yet that there might be a next time. That could only mean Linnet, a prospect that filled him with longing and anger, and lust and a burning to assuage his feelings on her body. She had started it, deliberately egging him on, and the next time she would get what she wanted, in detail. For initiating the whole thing and for sheer impudence he would spank her. For tricking him into allowing the rent-boy to suck him off he would bugger her. For pissing over him in Portsmouth he would give her just the same treatment, in her mouth.

Just thinking about it felt wonderful and, if there was more than a little guilt for his intentions at the back of his mind, it was assuaged by the conviction that she would enjoy every second of her degradation. How, he could not understand, but, from what Alice Chaswell had said, it was clearly the case. Guilt or no guilt, it was satisfying to think about, and there was a grim smile on his face as he started his day's work.

That evening, seated in front of the TV with a large Scotch in his hand, he resolved to get back to the things that really mattered. Work came first, as one of the most irksome things about the green-eyed girls' interference with his life was that it had caused him to rearrange his schedule, twice. True, he had managed to create the entire conspiracy theory in his own head, and fortunately he hadn't done anything really stupid, like confront Phil, but he still knew squarely where the blame lay.

Second, but not by so very much, was the try-out for Retro Records. It was a point in his life he had been working patiently towards for years, and he did not intend to blow it because some self-centred rich bitch had decided to play games with him. He would explain to the boys what had happened, or at least give them a version of what had happened that showed him in a better light, and then get down to some solid practice, starting at the weekend.

Third was the question of his sex life. He was not going to be a toy for any women, however attractive. If Linnet did put in an appearance he would know what to do about it but, once he'd thoroughly indulged himself, that would be that. He would be kind about it, a great deal kinder than she had been to him, but that would be that. However beautiful she was, a long-term relationship with her was clearly madness. His nerves simply wouldn't stand it. The same went for Sally, and he knew he could never feel right with Patty knowing that Baz, Zen and most of all Jack had fucked her too. What he needed was a calm, sensible girl, sexy but not perverted, fun, but with a sense of responsibility. One possibility intrigued – Rosy Parker.

It was, after all, she who had originally attracted him, and after the green-eyed girls she was refreshingly normal. They could hardly be said to have got off to a good start, and it was notoriously difficult to try and start a proper relationship with a woman when their first contact had been a commercial transaction, even if it had been a ruse on his part. To stand a realistic chance he would have to meet her outside the context of her modelling work, while for all he knew she already had a boyfriend, even a husband. For all the difficulties, she appealed, and it was not something he intended simply to let pass. What to do about it was a different matter.

For the rest of the week he threw himself into his work, turning in some impressive sales figures. It proved impossible not to keep an eye out for girls with startling green eyes, and also for Linnet's car. There were no girls, and no car, so by the time he drew the Mondeo to a stop outside his house on the Friday afternoon he was at last feeling in control of his life once more. A letter was waiting for him, from George Marks at Retro Records, giving the details of when they would be playing for the try-out, and telling him that they would be expected to play three numbers. He immediately turned his mind to the task of finding out all he could about George Marks.

The band was due to play at The Pig and Whistle that evening, and all four of them had agreed to turn up early and get an hour's practice before the pub started to fill up. Zen was supposed to have everything set up and ready, while Peter expected to be the last to arrive. Sure enough, when he strolled over, Strat in hand, the others' cars were already there, including Baz's Astra, slightly dented. He had his version of events ready for public consumption, and was grinning as he pushed through the pub doors. Immediately he caught Baz's voice and stopped between the two doors, waiting for the best moment to make his entrance.

'. . . in Watford, the next street to Benji's!' Baz was saying. 'The local traffic cops picked it up because it was parked on a red route, half on the pavement and all!'

'Dumped in a hurry?' Jack suggested.

'That's weird,' Zen stated. 'She said she lived in Exeter.'

'She's not going to tell us where she really lives, is she?' Jack put in. 'Not if she's going to fuck off with the car.'

'I don't think she did steal it,' Baz put in.

'Of course she fucking stole it!' Jack exclaimed.

'You saw her, man,' Zen added.

'Oh she did steal it, sure,' Baz went on, 'but I don't think she meant to, not at first. I think we scared her.'

'Scared her!' Jack laughed. 'You have to be joking! She didn't have the brains to be scared, that one, and you were the one jumping up and down and calling her a mad bitch and all!'

'Yeah, right, and what about that thing with her bra?' Zen put in. 'Didn't look scared to me.'

'Trying to make herself feel better about what she'd done?' Baz suggested. 'Try to see it this way. She's had an argument with her boyfriend. Called her a tart. She's well pissed off, and she wants to get back at him. In the heat of the moment she decides to go with another man, and lose her virginity to him, just to get back at the boyfriend. She meets us, picks Peter as the man for the job, but we push her into blow

155

jobs. She puts out, but then loses her cool, decides she can't go through with it. But what's she to do? She's on her own with four blokes, who're likely to fuck her whether she likes it or not –'

'No way!' Zen cut in.

'I know that,' Baz went on, 'and you know that, but Sally didn't. All she knew was we were capable of demanding blow jobs in return for a lift and a place to sleep. So she pinches the car, and drives back to her boyfriend in Watford for a tearful reunion.'

'You're fucking soft, you are,' Jack retorted.

'It makes sense,' Baz asserted.

'It does make sense,' Peter said, stepping out, 'only it didn't work out that way.'

'Eh?' Jack queried.

'She did it to wind us up,' Peter explained, 'for a laugh. I know this because I met her last weekend, and had the pleasure of accepting her virginity. Pints all round, boys?'

He moved casually on to the bar, leaving the three of them open-mouthed behind him. As he ordered the lager they found their voices, Jack first.

'You jammy bastard!'

'Nah.' Baz laughed, his voice full of doubt and envy. 'He's joking. He has to be joking.'

'For real, Peter?' Zen demanded.

'For real,' Peter confirmed, turning to lean on the bar as John began to pull their pints. 'She does come from Exeter, and I happened to run into her while I was on that teamwork training course I told you about, on Dartmoor.'

'Yeah?' Baz breathed.

'She was a bit embarrassed at first, naturally,' Peter went on, 'but I soon calmed her nerves. We got talking over a bar of chocolate, and it came out that she'd rowed with her boyfriend because he was getting pushy about not having full sex. She was scared, but she didn't feel she could tell him that, so it ended in a shouting match. He'd had other girls too, and she didn't feel right about that, so she'd decided to go with somebody older and more experienced, like Baz guessed, and, like Baz guessed, you prats scared her off.'

He took the first two pints, passing them to Baz and Jack, then turned back for the others as he continued.

'So, to cut a long story short, I persuaded her that it was a good idea, took her behind some rocks, popped her panties down, and whoops!'

'Just like that?' Baz demanded.

'Well, no,' Peter answered, 'but you shouldn't give away all a lady's secrets.'

'Fuck that,' Jack answered him. 'I want the dirty bits, and she's no lady, not the way she sucks cock. What way did you have her, spread, arse up?'

'On her side,' Peter said. 'It's the gentlest way.'

'I'd have turned her arse up and watched my cock tear her cunt,' Jack said with relish.

'Which will be why she chose me and not you.' Peter laughed as he sat down.

'Nah,' Jack responded. 'You're just jammy, that's all.'

Peter merely smiled. Baz was staring at him in wide-mouthed envy, Zen with deep respect. He sipped his lager, trying not to smirk too openly. For all that he had been through, he had coped, even come out well, or at least in a position from which he could make it look good. Now it was behind him, and he could turn his energy to securing the recording contract. He took out the letter from Retro Records.

'This is from George Marks,' he stated, tapping the page. 'They want three numbers, our choice, and I reckon that's a part of the test as well. At the

Snappin' Squirrel he liked the way I put Faithful Copy down without being blatant. That's the way he plays, and if there's one thing I've learned as a salesman it's that people respond better if they think you're on the same wavelength. So we ask ourselves – what's going to impress? What's he really into, and I don't just mean music? What will make him know we're the right choice?'

'He said he was into the fifties,' Baz suggested.

'No,' Peter corrected him, 'he said the cover albums would be focused on the fifties, that's not the same thing. How old do you think he was?'

'Fifty-five?' Baz suggested.

'Sixty, easy,' Jack put in.

'No way,' Zen disagreed. 'Fifty, if that. White hair don't mean you're old.'

'He's fifty-three,' Peter told them. 'That means he was born in 51. Jack, what's the best feel-good number for you?'

'You know that, mate, "My Way", the Sex Pistols' version. Shagged my first tart to that, I did.'

'Exactly,' Peter went on, 'and that's what we need to find, the songs George would have been into when he was sixteen or so, which is always the most important time of anyone's life, emotionally.'

'Yeah, I get that,' Zen agreed.

'So we're looking at maybe 65 to 70,' Peter stated, 'and I also know he was big in the hippie scene and spent five years in California after quitting school when he was just fifteen. We play "California Dreaming", and any money says it hits the spot.'

'I say that works,' Jack agreed.

'How d'you find all this stuff out, man?' Zen queried.

'Contacts, the net, some from music books,' Peter answered. 'For someone who doesn't play, George Marks has made a fair impression.'

'And the other two songs?' Baz asked.

'We kick off with "Hound Dog", Big Mama Thornton-style, the way we opened when Patty was here,' Peter told them. 'At first he'll be listening out for mistakes, and we know we're good there. Second –'

He stopped. Early customers were beginning to drift in, all regulars up until that point. A girl had walked in, small, pretty, plump, with two of the largest breasts he had ever set eyes on, straining out from her thin T-shirt like a pair of inadequately wrapped melons, with her huge nipples as the stalks. She was also familiar, boobs and face both – Katie from Portsmouth.

'Fuck me, I bet you don't get many of those to the pound!' Jack remarked, even as Peter stood up.

'Katie?' he queried.

She smiled as she saw him, a nervous, uncertain smile, and began to speak.

'Peter! Oh I am so glad you're here! I . . . I had to find you. You're the only person I can turn to, and . . . and –'

'What's the matter?' he answered her, placing an arm around her shoulders as she buried her face in her hands and burst into hysterical sobbing. 'Here, come and sit down, tell me about it.'

He put his arm around her shoulder, guiding her towards the table, her huge breasts quivering with her sobbing as she began to babble.

'It was awful . . . it was horrible . . . she . . . she . . . made me do it, in front of all those people, and . . . and –'

'Do what, love?' Jack queried. 'Who?'

'Annie,' she sobbed. 'She . . . she was always so nice to me, but . . . but she said this gentleman had paid ever so much to see an . . . an enema, and he

159

wanted me specially . . . and I had to . . . with everyone watching . . . three pints . . . of best bitter. It felt so awful, and . . . and it all came out my bum . . . in my knickers and everywhere, and then . . . then they . . . they took turns with me, up my bottom!'

'Bastards! You lead me to 'em, love, and –' Jack threatened.

'Just relax,' Peter urged, 'come and sit down. I'll get you a drink. A breezer, yeah?'

She turned to him, her plump lower lip trembling, her soft, pretty face a picture of dejection, her huge eyes wet with tears, and green, a brilliant, sparkling green. Katie's eyes had been baby blue.

Peter's sympathy vanished, his voice harsh as his fingers locked in the material of her T-shirt.

'Not this time, you scheming little bitch!'

He threw himself down into a chair, dragging her with him, full across his knee. She gasped in surprise and shock, then again, in pain, as he snatched one chubby arm and twisted it hard into the small of her back. Still she struggled, her legs kicking, her arms flailing wildly about, her whole body quivering like an oversized jelly. The boys were staring in amazement, and so was everybody else in the pub, but he took no notice whatsoever and finally she found her voice.

'What . . . what . . . what! Why! Why are you –'

'Going to spank you?' Peter grated, clinging on to her struggling body as he took a firm grip on the hem of her tight denim skirt. 'Let's just say it was what the doctored recommended for you, and for me.'

He yanked her skirt high and her squeals of horror doubled in volume as her panties came on show, pink and taut around her ample bottom. Peter took a handful of the seat but she snatched back, holding on to her waistband in a desperate effort to prevent any further exposure. He tried to improve his own grip, but she was fighting crazily and squealing like a stuck pig as she fought to keep her panties up, with her big bottom wobbling crazily within the confines of the overtight pink cotton. For a moment it was all he could do to keep her on his lap, but in her desperation she succeeded in pulling the panties up into her slit. Twin slices of fat, creamy white bottom flesh spilled out to either side. She screamed in shame and frustration, then again as her panties gave in and tore, exposing the full, fat peach of her bottom, her chubby pussy lips peeping out behind. He kicked a knee up to get her into the right position for spanking and the rude brown dimple of her anus was showing too.

Being bare didn't stop her fighting, but only increased her outrage and the volume of her howls of rage and frustration. Her fists were beating on his legs, her own legs pumping frantically, her fat breasts bouncing, her golden curls flying in every direction, a baby cyclone of flesh and hair and clothing. Peter simply laid in, clinging on to her for all he was worth as he began to spank, hard and fast, slap after slap delivered to her meaty cheeks with every ounce of his strength. She went crazy, a ball of insensate fury, clawing and biting, one leg jerking back and forth in an effort to kick him as futile as it was absurd. He just spanked faster, and no less hard, setting her cheeks squashing and spreading as the slaps fell, her bottomhole winking between.

Slowly but surely the fight began to go out of her, still wriggling and kicking, but with her fury giving way to pain. Her angry demands and curses changed to sobs and pleas, then to apologies and she was whimpering over his lap, choking her words out between squeaks and gasps, contrite and miserable,

161

heedless of her nude bottom. Peter kept on spanking, now slow and methodical, making sure her cheeks got an even roasting from hip to hip and between the top of her slit and the chubby overhangs to either side of her sex, until finally his anger began to subside.

'Peter? Peter? What are you doing, man?' Zen's voice penetrated, then John's angry demands for him to stop from behind the bar.

'What I should have done a long time ago,' Peter answered, and stopped.

She stayed were she was, sobbing miserably, her big bottom up and open, anus on blatant show, pussy too, and with white fluid dribbling from the hole. Peter gave her a moment to think about the position she was in, then pulled her panties up and smoothed her skirt down over her bum.

'Up,' he ordered.

Immediately she rose, showing a face wet with tears in a frame of bedraggled gold curls. Peter took her by the hand to pull her towards the back and she came, stumbling meekly behind him. In the storeroom he pushed the door closed, locked it and sat down on a pile of beer cases. She got to her knees without having to be told, mouth open even as he pulled his cock from his fly. In it went, and she was sucking, the tears still rolling down her cheeks as she mouthed on his cock, looking up at him out of her big green eyes. He reached down, to jerk her T-shirt up and spill out her fat breasts, then off, leaving her topless as she immediately took him back in her mouth.

Like her friends, she was good, and had the same trick, using her tongue to tickle the underside of his foreskin. Peter watched, admiring her huge boobs and pretty, tear-stained face as she worked on his erection. After a while he paused to adjust her skirt and panties, leaving her with her spanked bottom stuck out behind as she sucked his cock. She didn't complain, sucking all the harder, and as he felt himself start to come he took her firmly by her hair.

She gave a little mewl of complaint, nothing more, as he took his cock in hand and she realised what he was going to do. Then she closed her eyes and opened her mouth, waiting for it, and getting it, as his cock erupted in her face, spraying come into her hair and one eye, into her mouth, then over her nose and the other eye. The last blob he squeezed out on to her nose and let go, grinning savagely as he watched his muck start to roll slowly down her face.

'Was that good?' he demanded. 'Is that how you like to be treated?'

Her response was a weak nod.

'Good,' he went on, 'and, if you see Linnet, or Sally, you can tell them to expect the same treatment when I catch up with them.'

Again she nodded. She rocked back on her heels, and only then did he realise that she had a hand down the front of her half-lowered panties, and had obviously been masturbating as she sucked him off. He pulled her to her feet.

'Tidy yourself up. Then you can watch us rehearse. Afterwards I'll take you home and you can expect more of what you've just had, plenty more. Got it?'

She nodded once more, no less meek than immediately after her spanking, and followed as he returned to the bar. Peter was bracing himself for an onslaught from John and possibly others, but it never came. Most were staring at him in amazement, and the band followed him on to the stage without a murmur. They began to play, kicking off with 'Hound Dog' as they intended at the try-out and working their way through a dozen other numbers before he called a break. The green-eyed girl who had pretended to be

Katie sat in silence, staring at Peter as if mesmerised, but had a pint ready for him the instant he stepped off stage. As he began to drink it he caught an envious 'Fuck me!' from Jack.

It was the same during the second part of their set. She sat as if in awe, sipping a drink and refusing to be drawn into conversation by any of the men who attempted it. Peter's response was to play as he seldom had before, high on pride and power as well as the music. They finished with 'Rebel, Rebel', Peter bringing the song to a crescendo that shook the windows and, while everybody else was clapping and calling for more, she was standing there patiently by the wall, a fresh pint of lager ready in her hand. He took it, the others clustering around, eager to talk or perhaps hopeful for a repeat of the incident with Patty. Peter took a deep draught, half-emptying his glass, and spoke.

'You'll excuse me, boys, I'm sure, but I think the lady is in need of some attention.'

'You're not joking, she is.' Jack put in, his eyes fixed firmly on her straining top. 'Let's rock her both ends, eh, Peter?'

'Sorry, mate, this one's mine,' Peter answered, and drained the rest of his pint.

'Ah, come on, Peter, mate,' Jack began, 'you can tell she's up for anything you say! Don't cut your friends out, yeah?'

Peter drained the rest of his pint, gave Jack a friendly slap on the back and clicked his fingers as he set off for the door. She came behind, as eager and faithful as any puppy dog, right at his heels, and he caught a last wistful 'Fuck me!' as they left. Outside the door he put his arm around her waist, steering her in the direction of his house.

'So, what's your real name?' he asked.

'You know, it's Katie,' she answered immediately. He stopped.

'Are you after another spanking, right here, in the street? I mean your real name, the name Linnet and Dr Chaswell and the others call you.'

'Katie, I promise. Don't spank me again, please! I'm still really sore.'

'Tell me the truth then.'

'It is the truth.'

'Katie had blue eyes, baby blue. I remember. Yours are bright green, like Linnet's, like Sally's, or do you girls wear green contact lenses as some sort of group thing, is that it?'

'No, I was wearing blue contact lenses that night.'

'Then your eyes would have been sea-green, surely?'

'No. I think they reflect or something. There's this optician near the Guildhall –'

'Fair enough,' Peter broke in, still sure she was lying. 'So you really did work for Annie?'

'Yes. Linnet got me the job, and I told her where we were.'

'Eh? How did . . . no, never mind.'

She was lying, he was certain. It showed in her voice, and what she was saying didn't add up. He wasn't even quite certain if she was Katie or not. For all that they looked similar, Katie had giggled incessantly, and had seemed the sort of girl who would have taken an enema in her stride. Not that it mattered. It was no time for interrogations. It was time to enjoy his revenge.

'What do you think you deserve for that?' he asked.

'What – whatever you want,' she answered.

'At the least you can expect to be spanked again,' he told her, 'as and when I see fit, that is if your behaviour isn't absolutely immaculate. For a start, as soon as we get in you can run a bath. I rather enjoyed that wash and massage in Portsmouth, until Linnet arrived.'

Interlogue

'Isn't it rather tempting fate to buy the syringe before you've won the bet?' Thomasina asked. 'You know how it is, that way it's bound to end up being your bottom it gets stuck up.'

'No,' Juliana answered, lifting the heavy brass garden syringe to make a critical inspection of the nozzle, 'because there is no chance whatsoever of my losing. Elune is Elune, and he won't be able to put up with her behaviour for a day, never mind a month.'

'She stayed with that old man on Inishmaan for longer than a month.'

'He was mad. He thought she was a pixie. He was also old and grateful and lonely. So he put up with her. It's not every day a man like that can hope to find a girl who's willing to wet her panties in front of him. This Peter man won't put up with her, not for a month. I'm safe.'

Thomasina made a doubtful face. Juliana went on.

'Anyway, if I don't buy the syringe and I do lose, she will, and, being Elune, it's sure to be huge.'

'That one looks quite big enough to me!'

'Two litres, it says.'

'That's what, four pints?'

'Near enough.'

'Well I'm glad it won't be me!'

'Aren't you going to help me test it then?'

'No!'

'I'll use water.'

'No!'

'Elune's getting chilli sauce.'

'Well, I'm not getting anything!'

'Oh, come on, Thomasina. I'll butter your bottom for you.'

'No!'

'There's ice-cream in the fridge.'

'No, I . . . what flavour?'

'English Toffee.'

'Oh.'

'It's made with full-cream Jersey milk.'

'Maybe . . . maybe just a bit then, not the whole syringe, and you're not to make me expel in my panties.'

'Strip nude if you like, but I'm afraid it has to be the whole syringe.'

'No!'

'I've got clotted cream, and treacle.'

Thomasina made a face, but her hands had already gone to the button of her jeans. Turning her back to Juliana, she pushed them down, taking her panties with them to show off the full, meaty globe of her bottom. As she stuck it out and her cheeks spread to expose the rude pink star between, Juliana began to fill the syringe.

Nine

Peter awoke to the sight of Katie's tumbled gold curls on the pillow beside him. He smiled. It had been a good night. She had bathed him, given him a leisurely massage until his cock had been a rigid bar, and allowed him to enjoy her in every position he could think of, and in every way. Throughout it she had seemed to appreciate his commands, responding better the more stern he was. He had not even had to spank her again.

Tugging the bedclothes down, he exposed her naked body and planted a smack on one chubby bottom cheek. She squeaked and briefly reached back to rub her bottom, then quickly scrambled out of bed, still rubbing her eyes.

'Bring my breakfast,' he ordered. 'Coffee the same way you made it last night, two pieces of toast, fried eggs and bacon. Chop, chop.'

She responded with a nod and hurried to go about her task. Peter propped himself up on the pillows. Spanked or otherwise, it was impossible to imagine Linnet, Patty or even Sally being so pliable. Katie knew how a man should be served and, if he was still finding it hard to accept that she could really be so meek and obedient, nothing in her behaviour had given him cause to think otherwise.

Presently he caught the smells of frying bacon, coffee and toast, and before long she appeared with a tray, still nude except for a pinny, and that worn to leave her breasts bare. He lifted his knees and she put the tray down on his lap. Her eyes immediately flicked to between his legs. Already his cock was beginning to fill with morning blood, and with a click of his fingers he indicated that she should go down on him. She obeyed immediately, and he began to butter a piece of toast as she climbed on to the bed, to kneel between his legs, then on all fours, her bottom high as she buried her face in his crotch.

As he began to feed, so did she, on his cock, sucking him with all the skill and attention he had come to associate with the green-eyed girls. All four he'd enjoyed had been excellent cock-suckers, so good that it set him wondering how they got the practice and if some, or all, were in fact high-class hookers. It certainly made sense for Linnet, with her car and no visible means of supporting herself.

Soon he was hard in Katie's mouth, pushing away all thoughts of anything besides sex. She let him free and took him in her hand as he set his tray to one side, taking his balls in her mouth. He closed his eyes in bliss and set his legs further apart, allowing her complete access. Her response was to pull off, give him one long, lingering look, poke her tongue out and go down on him again, lower still.

His mouth came open in shock and pleasure as she began to lick between his buttocks, not just under his balls, but right on his anus, then inside, holding his cock and wanking him gently as her tongue burrowed in. It felt exquisite, and also gave a wonderful rush of power, to have a beautiful young girl willing to lick his bottomhole, just for the pleasure it gave him, a girl in nothing but a pinny with her breasts pulled

170

out to either side for his pleasure, her bottom bare behind . . .

She stopped, leaving him an instant short of orgasm, only to quickly gulp his cock into her mouth, jamming the head into the tight cavity of her throat. He came on the spot, gasping as he pumped spunk down her throat with her struggling to stay on, and to swallow, then immediately rushing off to the loo with her cheeks bulging, to be sick. He remembered Katie doing the same and allowed himself a nod of self-appreciation. It was the same girl.

He stretched in satisfaction, trying to remember the last time a girl had attended to his morning erection, let alone brought him breakfast in bed as well. The answer was never, and as he got up to wash he was wondering if his determination not to start a relationship with one of the green-eyed girls wasn't misplaced after all. Perhaps the others weren't so bad either? After all, Katie had put up a hell of a fight to stop herself getting her spanking, especially when it came to taking her panties down, but once it had been done she'd been as meek as a lamb. Perhaps Dr Chaswell was right, and he should have spanked Linnet that first day at the service station, not actually in the restaurant perhaps, but somewhere nearby with a bit of privacy.

She waited patiently for him to finish with the bathroom, then went in herself, not making the slightest effort to hide her nudity. He began to dress, but she didn't, just slipping the pinny on again, boobs still showing, and going about the housework. Thoroughly enjoying the sense of being served, he let her get on with it, putting his feet up with the paper as she put the dishwasher and washing machine on, tidied the kitchen and made the bed. All the while she was bare front and back, until by the time she came in to ask if he'd like another coffee his cock was once more beginning to harden. He told her to suck him and once more she went down without hesitation, bringing him to one more exquisite orgasm in her throat.

It was the same when Pizazz practised that afternoon, Katie hurrying to help when she could and staying out of the way when she wasn't wanted. To the others she was polite, and he was sure that if he only chose to give the word she would suck any or all of them, maybe even let them fuck her, and not for her pleasure, but because he ordered it. He resisted the temptation, keen to keep her for himself, but the realisation brought him one step closer to deciding not to show her the door when the weekend was over.

By the evening his decision was firm. Her behaviour had been immaculate, obedient yet playful, never pushy but ever willing. Twice more he had felt the need to come, and had done it, once between her glorious tits in the storeroom of The Pig and Whistle, once with her bent across the kitchen table as she prepared dinner, her naked bottom stuck out for entry. As he ate he was wondering just how far he could take her before she began to protest. It was tempting to try, for all that he was promising himself he would stop just as soon as she no longer seemed to be enjoying it.

She had cooked dinner, steaks with fried onions, mash and peas, then a strawberry cheesecake she had insisted on buying with her own money on the way home. Despite having only the clothes she stood up in, she seemed to have plenty of money, and he found himself wondering if she hadn't stolen from Annie and was being so good because she was scared of being reported or taken back. It made some sense, but he was less eager than ever to force the issue and so ruin his pleasure.

The meal over, she poured him a generous Scotch and busied herself with tidying up. He sat back, enjoying watching her work and in particular the way her bottom and boobs moved. She was plump, verging on fat, no question, but her flesh was extraordinarily firm, also smooth, creamy in both colour and texture. By the time he'd drunk half his Scotch his cock was beginning to harden once more. He beckoned her to him.

'Stand by the chair, Katie,' he instructed, 'with your back to me. Yes, like that. Now put your hands on your head.'

She obeyed immediately. He put his hand to her bottom, stroking her ripe cheeks as he sipped his Scotch. Despite the severity of her spanking, she had hardly bruised at all, but it seemed to have taught her a lesson, as she was trembling ever so slightly, presumably through fear of getting the same treatment. He made a resolve to do it when she seemed to deserve it, hoping that if she knew she could trust him not to abuse his power, then she would continue her good behaviour. Meanwhile, his cock was beginning to stiffen in his trousers and he was considering that there were other things a man could do with a girl's bottom.

'Stick it out a little,' he instructed.

Again she obeyed without demur, sticking her bottom out to open her cheeks a little. Peter began to tickle her between them, making her giggle, then sigh. Chuckling to himself, he swallowed the last of his Scotch and unzipped, pulling out his cock as his fingers found the little puckered hole between her bottom cheeks. She gave a little squeak of surprise and just perhaps of consternation too, but giggled again as he began to tickle her anus. Her flesh was damp, tempting him to penetrate her. Sure enough, a

173

gentle push and the tip of his finger slid into her ring, and beyond, up into the hot, moist cavity of her rectum.

She moaned, now trembling hard enough to make her big cheeks quiver against his hand. He pushed his finger deeper in, wondering how his cock would feel sheathed in the same hot tube of flesh. Her bottom was still out, her hands still on her head, apparently surrendered to whatever he pleased, but he had to be sure, while never for a moment seeming weak.

'You do know I might well bugger you, don't you?' he asked, pushing his now erect cock forwards to make a stiff pole above his fly.

'Yes,' she answered. 'I know.'

'Do you want to be buggered?' he went on.

'Do whatever you like with me,' she said meekly.

'OK. Sit on my cock, with your cheeks held apart.'

He pulled his finger out and Katie hastened to obey, squatting on his lap with her plump bottom held well apart, her now thoroughly moistened anus right over his erect cock. Every detail showed, the little brown star open in the middle to reveal a pink interior, her ring twitching slightly, wet and ready. He took hold of her hips and eased her gently down, putting the head of his cock to her hole. She gave a little gasp, then another as he began to pull her down and her ring started to spread over the tip of his erection, tight and wet and hot. He watched her flesh stretch and push in, Katie gasping and shaking as she was penetrated, her ring gaping wider and wider still, until suddenly he was in, her anus open around the neck of his cock.

She was whimpering softly to herself as he began to push, still with her bottom held wide to let him see as inch after inch of thick, hard cock was pushed up into her bottomhole. Only when the full length of his erection was engulfed in tight, hot rectal flesh and her empty pussy sat on his balls did she let go, wiggling her bottom down with a sigh of satisfaction. He took hold of her by the curve of her cheeks and began to bounce her on himself, delighting as much in the very fact that it was a girl's bottom his erection was embedded in as the feel of doing it.

For a moment she took it with no reaction other than a soft panting, and then her legs had come apart, her hands had gone down between her legs, and he realised that she was masturbating. He slowed, already on the edge of orgasm, waiting as her breathing grew deeper and faster, her shaking harder, until at last her bottom cheeks began to tighten in his hands, her anus to contract on his cock and she was coming. Immediately he jammed himself in deep. Katie screamed, her straining ring went into violent spasms and he too was coming, his cock milked into her rectum and she squirmed and bounced on top of him, on and on until he felt faint with ecstasy and her hole was slippery with spunk.

She finished long after he was spent, took a moment to recover, then began to lift herself slowly up, pulling off his cock to leave her anus dribbling spunk. He stretched for some nearby tissues, but to his utter astonishment she turned around, went down on her knees and took his cock deep into her mouth. Her eyes were closed in bliss as she sucked, sucked and swallowed and swallowed once again, and as he caught the fleshy sound of her fingers working in her pussy he realised that she was masturbating. He let it happen, watching half in disgust and half in delight as she licked and sucked his cock clean, the cock that a moment before had been jammed to the hilt up her bottom. When she came it was with no more than a little mewling noise as her body went tight, and then she had rocked back on her heels, her face set in sleepy bliss.

'Thank you,' she said softly, 'that was good, really good.'

Peter found himself unable to find any answer that even came close to doing justice to her behaviour, so he nodded calmly and indicated the Scotch bottle. She immediately scurried off to fetch it, poured him a glass still more generous than the first and made for the bathroom only when he had begun to drink it. Peter sat back, shaking his head in wonder. He had buggered her, just about the dirtiest thing you could do to a girl, and reputedly painful as well. She had not only submitted to the experience, but thoroughly enjoyed it, then done something he would never have dreamed of demanding. Lifting the whisky tumbler to his lips, he drank a silent toast to the world's dirty girls.

Her behaviour was no different on the Sunday, submissive, compliant, obedient, ever willing and ever helpful. She made his breakfast and sucked his cock in the morning. She did his ironing and kneeled to be fucked from the rear on the kitchen floor. She cooked the finest roast beef dinner he had ever eaten and went down on him once more as he sipped an after-lunch brandy. She sat attentively through band practice and offered to take him in her mouth again afterwards. He refused, his cock painfully sore, his balls aching, and she responded with a sweet smile and went to buy him another drink. That night it took all his will power and a great deal of teasing from her before he could rouse himself to fuck her.

Monday was due to open with a sales meeting at the office, following which he had to drive up to see Dave Pickering of Interiors, Interiors in Norwich, who was apparently now being targeted by two rival firms. Katie was up before him, with his breakfast ready, so that for the first time in years he awoke to the smell of frying bacon. She wanted to attend to him with her tongue while he ate, but took it well when he explained he had no time, and saw him off with an affectionate kiss. He was still feeling somewhat uneasy as he left. She was just too perfect, and during the meeting he was suffering from disturbing thoughts of the entire gang of green-eyed girls looting his house in his absence, or attempting to get the neighbouring housewives together for an orgy, or simply burning the place to the ground on an idle whim. By the time it was finished he had decided to take Katie with him.

She was keen to go, and chatted happily from the moment they left his house to the moment they arrived outside the Interiors, Interiors warehouse, making it impossible for Peter to focus on the task ahead. As he gathered his things together he was feeling irritable and ill prepared, wishing he'd trusted her after all. Not only had she distracted him, but in her short denim skirt and overtight top she looked exactly what she was, a prostitute. Over the weekend it hadn't mattered, but now it did. He drove past the warehouse, parking at the far end of the industrial estate, where bulldozers had pushed up a great mound of rubble from a demolished factory.

'Stay here,' he instructed as he climbed from the car.

'Couldn't I help?' she offered. 'I'm sure he'd stick with you if I gave him a nice suck with every order. He can even fuck me, I don't mind.'

'No!' Peter answered. 'For goodness sake, Katie, you can't do that sort of thing!'

'Why not?'

'Well, he's married for a start, and it's in an open-plan office!'

'So? His wife needn't know, and we can take him out for lunch and go somewhere lonely afterwards. You could even share me, one in each end the way you did with Patty. I'd bet he'd be loyal after that.'

'I bet he would,' Peter answered, 'but you just cannot go about business that way. It's tantamount to blackmail.'

'No it's not! It's just giving perks, that's all.'

'Katie, this is my job. You stick to what you know best and let me handle the sales. OK?'

'If you say so, Peter. See you in a while then.'

He was struggling to get his head together as he made for Interiors, Interiors, but an hour later he had managed to bring Dave Pickering back into the fold with some witty repartee at the expense of Ipswich Town Football Club and a hefty discount. Feeling somewhat happier, he returned to the Mondeo to find it unlocked and Katie gone. Annoyed, and somewhat puzzled, he looked around, only to catch her laughter from beyond the great pile of rubble. More puzzled than ever, he climbed the rubble, to find himself staring down at her, on her knees, her top up over her boobs, with one man's cock in her mouth while she kept another erect in her hand. Both men were rough, burly types but he had called out without a second thought.

'Katie!'

She came off the cock she was sucking, leaving a string of saliva dangling from her lower lip as she turned, smiling.

'Oh, hi, Peter, with you in a minute,' she greeted him, and went back to sucking.

Furious, Peter started down the rubble, only to come up short as he realised that there were two more men sitting to one side, both as heavily muscled as the first two, and both with their cocks out and ready to be sucked.

'You leave it, mate,' one warned.

As Peter realised that there was absolutely nothing he could do, bitter, helpless frustration welled up inside him. There was only one choice.

'OK, I'm going,' he stated, starting back up the rubble.

Katie immediately came off the man's cock, her voice more than a little hurt as she spoke. 'Don't go, Peter! I won't be a moment.'

He simply raised his hand in a gesture of wordless exasperation and continued to climb. One of the men laughed, but a moment later Katie was scrambling after him.

'Hey, what about our blow jobs?' the man demanded, his fellows immediately echoing the question.

'And our money!' one added, louder.

Sensing the menace in their voices, Peter moved fast, pulling open the door of the Mondeo and twisting the key in the ignition even as Katie threw herself down in the passenger seat. Angry voices followed, and a lump of concrete sailed past the window as he let the clutch in, and as the Mondeo tore forwards Katie burst out laughing. Peter drove on, tight lipped with anger, until he was well clear of the industrial estate and on the A11. Pulling off into a lay-by, he found his hands were shaking as he let go of the steering wheel.

'What the hell do you think you were doing!?' he demanded. 'God in Heaven, you are a stupid cow! I mean, why do that!?'

'What's the matter?' she answered, her amusement changing instantly to hurt. 'I just wanted some money to get some clothes. I thought you'd like me to have some new clothes?'

179

She burst into tears. Peter opened his mouth to release the stream of invective that had been building up since leaving the estate, but it never came out. Instead he put his forehead to the steering wheel, knocking it gently against the leather.

'Jesus, why me?' he managed after a while. 'Why me? Are you mad, Katie? If you wanted some money for clothes, you only had to ask. You do not need to go sucking men off, damn it!'

His anger gave way to guilt as he turned to see her miserable, tear-streaked face, and realised that what she had done was probably all she knew. He put an arm around her shoulders and began to stroke her hair.

'There, there, Katie,' he soothed. 'I understand. Don't cry. It doesn't have to be like that any more. You're with me now. Don't cry.'

She swallowed and sniffed, then pulled back.

'Aren't you going to spank me then?'

'No,' he answered, 'don't worry. Those days are over.'

'But –'

'No, Katie, don't say a word. You don't need that stuff, and it was wrong of me to do it before, but everything's going to be different now. No more spankings, no more sex for money, no more –'

'But, Peter –'

'No buts, Katie.'

'Yes, but you've got to spank me, surely? For that! I thought you might use one of the brushes from your samples cases, a Series 4 maybe?'

'What?'

'Come on, Peter, don't get all mealy on me. Spank my bottom for me, hard.'

'Katie –'

'Oh, for goodness sake, Peter, be a man, won't you? That was awful, what I just did to you. You ought to leave me so that I can't sit for a week, then bugger me and leave me in the ditch with the brush handle stuck up my bum.'

'Katie!'

'Well, it's what you want to do, isn't it?'

'No! What is it with you . . . and Sally, and Linnet, and . . . and even Patty. You're all fucking mental!'

'No, we just like it hard and rude. We thought you'd be good for it, but you're not, are you? For my Lord's sake, I want to be spanked! I want to be spanked! I want to be spanked!'

She was shouting, her face pink with emotion, her chest heaving. Peter could find nothing to say, and didn't answer her, merely staring as he tried to find the words to do justice to his feelings. She stopped and went on, suddenly calmer.

'Let me explain. That first time, when you met Linnet, who is, it must be said, a little brat, you should have stayed put. Her car was there, and so was she. Mapley's is a pretty lonely place too, so you would have plenty of time to deal with her. You could have taken her by the scruff of her neck, dragged her into the loos and stuck her head down one while you gave her a good spanking, fucked her and spunked all over her bottom at the same moment you pulled the chain on her head. She would have appreciated that, although it's true it would only have led to her doing something even more horrid back.'

She paused to adjust her top, spent an instant examining the bulge of one of her oversized nipples, then went on.

'Now with Patty, you behaved quite well. That Jack, now he is a pig, a real boar of a man, four like him and she'd really have had a good time. He lacks style though. Then there was Sally. You should have treated Sally like you treated Patty, all four at once, and taken her virginity with a cock in her mouth, then done it up her bum too for good measure. She only pinched the car because she got bored. Even on Dartmoor you really took your time getting the hint. Then there was me. That first spanking was good, great in fact, but now you go all soft on me, and when I've been so nice to you all weekend! What is it with you? Oh, and you could have given Aileve a good seeing to as well ... that's Alice Chaswell to you. She wouldn't have minded ... not too much anyway.'

Finally Peter found his voice. 'I can't go around behaving like that! They'd lock me up and throw away the key!'

'No,' she insisted, 'you can't go around behaving like that to women who don't want you to. What do you want – a big green light on the top of my head? I mean, you want to do it, don't you?'

'No I do not!' Peter answered angrily, then remembered his plans for Linnet and Sally after he'd found out they'd been tormenting him. It was still true.

'What I want,' he explained, 'is a nice, normal girl, a girl who likes sex and isn't ashamed to enjoy her body, a girl who can share, who doesn't see everything as some sort of contest! OK, so I would dearly like to get even with Linnet, and I dare say Sally could use a spanking, but –'

'Well if Sally deserves it, I certainly do!' she interrupted. 'Come on, get one of those big heavy bath brushes out. Whack me until I howl then make me go down on your lovely cock!'

'No! That's not how it should be between a man and his woman! Katie, love, I know ... or at least I think I have some idea of what you must have been through in your life –'

'You do not, believe me.'

'OK, so I probably don't, but I'm not completely unimaginative. I know how I'd feel if I had to sell my body for men's sexual gratification, and, yes, I know I go to pros, but ... but ... but never mind that. What I'm trying to say is that it doesn't have to be like that, always a question of trying to get the best of each other ...'

'It's not like that at all, Peter. We just like our bottoms smacked occasionally, that's all, and maybe a little more. Believe me, it is simply not possible for me to have what you would think of as a normal relationship.'

'I sincerely hope that's not true, Katie. I don't know what you've been through, but you can build self-respect, regain your self-esteem. You don't need to do these things –'

Katie was laughing.

'What's so funny?' he demanded.

'You!' she answered. 'You really have no idea at all, do you? You're a man of your times, Peter, and I suppose you're not really to blame for that, and I do appreciate that you are trying to be nice, but, please, just get over yourself.'

'I don't know what you're talking about.'

'No, you don't, do you? Oh well, bye then.'

'Where are you going?' Peter asked as she made to get out of the car.

'Back to finish off those four builders,' she answered. 'I bet they'll spank me, maybe rough me up a bit too.'

'Katie!'

He had grabbed her door handle, and jerked it shut, pulling her back into her seat. The central locking clicked into place even as he let the clutch in, the Mondeo hitting seventy before they'd joined the main road.

'Very masterful,' Katie said sweetly, 'so how about that spanking then?'

Peter shook his head.

On Tuesday he left her at home, Wednesday also. Nothing awful happened, and she had returned to her model behaviour, keeping house and providing sex on tap, with no more unusual requests. By the Thursday he was beginning to think he might have been a bit unfair to attempt to stamp his own ideas on her. After all, there was Alice Chaswell, a respected academic, who seemed to have made not dissimilar sexual choices. After a dinner of pasta in some delicious sauce he decided that perhaps if he knew a little more he might be able to try and fulfil what was evidently a strong need in her without having to be teased or tricked into it. It still didn't feel right, but there was no denying the satisfaction it would give him, just so long as he felt it was for something. After the incident with the four builders, that was not a problem.

'So, Katie,' he said as he accepted his after-dinner glass of Scotch. 'Tell me about your friends with the green eyes.'

She hesitated a moment before answering. 'Think of us as a club of women with a common interest.'

'Kinky sex?'

'Rather more than that.'

'But you all like to be spanked and stuff?'

'Yes, that's true enough.'

'And this is something you joined of your own accord?'

'Yes.'

'So, just let me get this absolutely clear. You, of your own choice, with no pressure from Annie, or Alice Chaswell or the evil-looking one –'

184

'Juliana.'

'– or her, you joined a society in which the girls get spanked, because they want to be spanked?'

'Yes. I was involved long before Aileve for a start. Annie has nothing to do with it.'

'And membership is restricted to girls with vivid green eyes? That seems a bit fussy. I mean, what if a girl wanted to join, and was very into being spanked, but she had blue eyes?'

Katie shrugged.

'Never mind. Fetch me a Series 4 from my samples case, and that's an order.'

She went, scampering out of the room, bare boobs and bum cheeks bouncing, to return a moment later with the big Series 4 bath brush, a heavy, two-foot-long implement in faux mahogany with a smooth, rounded end. He took it, feeling the weight, and smacked it against his hand. It stung, producing guilt and a savage pleasure at the same time as he thought of how it was going to feel across her bottom.

'I've decided you're right,' he stated. 'You do need to be punished for offering blow jobs to those builders. I'm going to beat you, fifty strokes with this brush, on the firm understanding that you never, ever do anything of the sort again.'

'Yes, Peter,' she answered meekly, waiting with her head bowed and her hands folded in front of her.

'Good,' he told her, 'now off with your pinny, I think you should be in the nude for this.'

She reached behind her back to tug open the bows of her pinny, letting it fall to the ground. He nodded, admiring her heavy breasts, the curves of her soft midriff, her full hips and plump pussy.

'Come over my lap.'

Without hesitation she laid herself down across the armchair and his knees, her big bottom lifted, the full cheeks well parted. He laid a hand on her flesh, feeling a slight trembling and running through her cool, smooth skin.

'Fifty spanks,' he reminded her, tapped the brush to her bottom, liftedit and brought it down with a firm, meaty smack.

Katie squealed and jerked, her legs kicking in pain, but Peter already had a grip on her waist and held her firmly in place as he began to beat her, smack after smack, to a steady rhythm. She struggled, unable to hold herself for the pain, wriggling in his grip, kicking and flailing with her arms. By ten her whole bottom was a rich pink and she had started to sob between smacks; by twenty her skin was prickling with goose bumps and she was snivelling; by thirty she was glossy with sweat and crying freely. Still Peter spanked, hard and even, ignoring her blubbering, her shrieks of pain, her feeble protests. It hurt, a lot, there could be no question, but as he laid in the final few smacks she had begun to push her bottom up and a new and eager note had entered her notice.

'Fifty,' he stated, 'and I hope that's taught you a lesson.'

'No,' she panted, 'more . . . give me more . . . hard and fast, like you were . . . beat me, Peter . . . beat me 'til I come.'

He hesitated only a second, then laid in again with the same heavy rhythm. She was wriggling and kicking in pain again with the first stroke, but her bottom was still up, and the note of pleasure had quickly returned to her mewling. He kept the pace, his cock now stiffening against her belly, the scent of her sex strong in the air. Her whimpering changed to panting, to gasps, to a heavy, uncontrolled moaning, and at last to an ecstatic shriek as she began to buck on his lap, her whole body quivering, her legs jerking back and forth, her hands locked tight on the arm of the chair. He kept on beating, until at last she went limp and she slid to the floor, only to twist around immediately, scrabbling at his fly.

In seconds she had freed his cock and was sucking urgently, and masturbating as she did it. He felt her come before he was even fully hard, and again as she mouthed on him, before she suddenly jammed his cock down into her own throat and he too was there, pumping spunk down her throat with his hand locked in her curls. His eyes were shut in bliss as he came, then abruptly open as clapping burst out just a few feet away. He looked up to find Jack, Baz and Zen staring in through his living-room window.

Interlogue

'One week, this evening, Juliana,' Aileve stated as she began to paint the honey on to the skin of the goose she was preparing, 'that's pretty good for Elune.'

'I'm amazed,' Juliana admitted. 'How does he put up with her? Make sure to put plenty of pepper on, Aileve.'

'I have been trying to teach her how to behave,' Lily stated.

'So have we, for years!' Juliana answered. 'It doesn't work. She's not the same as us. That wild streak of pre-Celtic mischief isn't something that can be changed, it's part of her. She's never been able to control it, and never will.'

'Four pints of chilli sauce, Juliana,' Thomasina taunted, 'right up your pretty bottom! And, talking of stuffing, what are you going to use?'

'No,' Juliana answered, 'she'll never make it. She'll give him a pint of pee instead of lager, or try and seduce his boss, or his boss's wife, something. How about a redcurrant and Demerara suet?'

'When she was Mistress to the Vicomte de Saulnier,' Aileve reflected, 'she got bored one afternoon and burned his house down, the townhouse in Paris, not the chateau, but still. I was going to use up the rest of the honey with breadcrumbs, lemon juice and maybe a few herbs.'

'Exactly!' Juliana responded. 'And how long had she been with him, six days! If you're going to do breadcrumbs, let's have sultanas too.'

'Five days, if I remember rightly,' Aileve said, 'but then she was never all that interested in him in the first place. This Peter seems to inspire her.'

'Is it because he wants to control her?' Lily asked. 'How about candied peel?'

'In a sense,' Juliana answered. 'Controlling men certainly bring out the worst in her, because they always rise to the bait so easily. Candied peel is a good idea.'

'Maybe Peter has taken Aileve's advice and learned to spank her properly?' Thomasina suggested. 'I vote for suet, but, if you must use breadcrumbs, I'll go and get some sweet sherry to bind it.'

'It won't work even if he has,' Juliana went on, 'not unless he does her on the hour every hour. What do you say, Lily, suet or breadcrumbs?'

'Suet please,' Lily answered. 'From what I saw of him, I don't think he's the sort to spank, not properly.'

'Shame,' Thomasina responded, 'because I really hope she makes it. Do you know what Juliana did? She said she wanted to test the syringe, and she promised not to make me do it in my panties, then when she'd put all four pints in me she hauled them up just as I let go. It was such a mess! That's three to one for a suet, Aileve.'

'OK,' Aileve sighed, 'I'll make a suet.'

Ten

For Peter, Friday meant Coventry, Birmingham and Walsall, and just about getting his schedule back on course. He left in mixed humour, the result of the night before. It had been impossible to be angry with the boys, not when they had shown so much admiration for the way he had treated Katie, and her response. There had been jealousy too, particularly from Jack, which had been impossible for Peter not to enjoy. The band practice had also gone well, with the three of them following his calls without once taking issue.

On the downside he was wishing that Katie's reaction had been just a little less ebullient. Most women, he was sure, even those deeply into spanking, would have been absolutely mortified to have their partner's friends watch as it was done. Not Katie. She had not even made a pretence of embarrassment, but dropped the three of them a mocking curtsey and bounced off to the bathroom, still with a curtain of his come hanging from her lower lip. Having a dirty girlfriend was great, but he would have preferred her to make herself exclusive to him.

He knew it was unlikely to happen. At heart she was a slut, hence her giggling acceptance of a job that the majority of women would not countenance, and which often left those who did hard and bitter. All in all, however sweet she was, however good in bed, he knew it would not last between them. He needed a woman who would regard herself as his, and his alone.

Then there was her weight. She was all tit and bum, and turned him on physically in a way very few other women ever had, but he could see it would be a social problem. Telling himself he would rise above it was all very well, but the simple fact remained, men who went out with fat girls lost respect, and it might affect his prospects at work. Nor was Katie discreet about her figure, anything but. He could already imagine the faint sneers from the wives of some of the directors and senior management.

Yet, despite everything, he had begun to feel responsible for her. For all her bravado she was evidently vulnerable, and he could not simply dump her. His mind was on the problem as he gunned the Mondeo out from the J14 slip road and on to the M1, and by the time the speedo needle had crept over the ninety mark he had the solution. It was perfect, solving the problem in its entirety.

Coventry was easy, Ben Mahoney of Tile Kingdom always a sure fire bet for a few hundred units if never more. Both appointments in Birmingham went equally well, and fast, leaving him at a loose end, with three hours to kill, while the last call had been Bayou Bathrooms. It was impossible not to think of Rosy Parker, in all probability just a few minutes' drive away, and with that thought came the old familiar longing.

Like Katie, Rosy filled him with desire but, unlike Katie, he was sure she would make an excellent partner. She was down to earth, for one thing, as well as being strikingly pretty in a way that was entirely socially acceptable. There would be no sneering wives with Rosy at the dinner table, and nobody need ever know she had been a glamour model. Assuming she was interested.

Telling himself that there was nothing to be lost by making the attempt, he set off for the Dolls and Guys studio. She was there, standing by her car in conversation with another girl, a blonde whose eyes Peter was relieved to note were deep brown as he approached. Rosy noticed his approach and turned him a doubtful look.

'If you're after a booking I'm busy all day.'

'No, no,' Peter assured her, laughing, 'I was just passing and wanted to apologise for the other day. I know I was out of order –'

'Yeah, you were.'

'Absolutely, and, as I say, I'm sorry. I want to explain too, if you have a moment?'

She shrugged. 'I suppose so. So you're not after hiring me?'

'No, I'm afraid not ... Not that you're not beautiful, but –'

'Right, right, OK.'

The blonde girl, who had been looking at him curiously, suddenly spoke up. 'You're the bloke out of that band, ain't you? The one that plays covers and stuff.'

'That's right,' Peter answered, 'Peter and Pizazz.'

'I saw you at Ike's Place in Northampton. I was stripping before you went on.'

'I remember! There was crazy foam all over the stage.'

'Yeah. That was a great night, that.'

She smiled, and so did Rosy.

'Come and see us some time,' he went on, 'we're on at The Pig and Whistle in Milton Keynes most weekends, not this Saturday though, we're going down to London to try out for Retro Records. There'll be one hell of a party when we come back afterwards though, that or we'll all be drowning our sorrows.'

'A try-out? Cool!' the blonde girl answered. 'You don't need a female vocalist, do you?'

'We could do. I'd like to hear you, anyway. May I ask your name?'

'Tina.'

'Look, Tina, I'm stuck for three hours before my next appointment, and I passed a decent-looking bistro a bit up the road. Why don't I give you lunch and we'll talk it over? You'd be very welcome too, Rosy.'

'Emma,' she answered, 'Rosy is strictly for the punters.'

Peter was singing as he eased the Mondeo to a stop outside his house. It was all going to work, or at least he had a fighting chance of making it work, and that was all he had ever asked. Lunch had been great, a masterpiece of play. Tina had hung on to his every word as he spoke of the band, gigs he'd played, people he'd met. She was heavily into Retro, but only twenty-two, which meant that he had attended events she thought of as legendary. Rosy/Emma had been less interested, but he had been careful not to play favours, and by the end it was clear she regarded him at least as somebody interesting. He had also been very careful to call her Emma when it had become clear that the girls divided males into two categories: punters and real men. A relationship with a punter was unthinkable, with a real man something to aspire to. Tina had a boyfriend, but Emma didn't. By the time he'd dropped them back at Dolls and Guys they had agreed to come down to The Pig and Whistle for the party after the try-out.

He had a night and a day to make everything work and, if it was possible, it was not going to be easy. First there was Katie, who was sprawled on the bed, naked and reading a book on the sinking of the *Lusitania*. He gave her a playful slap on the rump as he came in, at which she purred and rolled over, arms and thighs wide to accept him.

'Later, darling,' he promised her, 'just now there's only time to grab a snack and then it's off down to The Pig and Whistle. It's the try-out tomorrow.'

'Not even a little suck?' she urged, sticking her tongue out and wiggling the tip.

Peter hesitated, his hands already on the fly of his suit trousers. Naked and willing, Katie was just too tempting; having her naked while he was in his suit also appealed. He unzipped and pulled out his cock and balls. Katie immediately scrambled over, crawling on all fours, to nuzzle him, then take him in her mouth. Peter looked down, admiring the contrast between her pretty face framed in golden curls and the thick cock in her mouth with a touch of regret. She was good, so good, and at the least he could have a last proper go.

He took her firmly by the hair, pulling her head on to his cock so that he could fuck her mouth. She immediately grew more eager at the rough treatment, reaching back to play with her pussy. Peter reached for his case, drew out a Series 4 and showed it to her. She gave a little whimper, sucking all the harder and sticking her bottom up. He patted the heavy bath brush to one fleshy cheek, and began to beat her.

It felt good, no question, a beautiful, naked girl sucking willingly on his cock while he spanked her bottom, and he found himself wondering if Rosy would enjoy the same treatment. Regret for his intentions hit him, but it didn't stop him, the bath brush still smacking down on Katie's flesh, his cock now rock solid in her mouth.

'Turn around,' he ordered. 'I'm going to fuck you.'

She obeyed immediately, coming off his cock to twist around on the bed and present him with her meaty bottom, the cheeks red from the spanking, her pussy wet and open where she'd been playing with herself. He put his cock to her hole and slid deep in, his body arched back to leave her bottom showing, and vulnerable. Taking up the bath brush once more, he carried on with her spanking, only now with his cock sunk deep in her pussy.

Her hand went back, rubbing at her sex even as she was beaten and fucked, masturbating with her bottom bouncing and her huge boobs wobbling beneath her. Peter slowed his pace, easing himself in and out and pacing the smacks, slow and hard. Katie began to gasp, her pussy started to contract on his cock, her anus began to pulse, and she was coming, panting out her orgasm on his cock. He stayed in, even when she was done, thoroughly enjoying her and not too far from his own climax. She stayed put too, and made no complaint as the beating continued, Peter now timing the smacks to the pushes of his cock, faster and faster, until she had begun to whimper, then scream. He gave in, and came, dropping the brush at the last second to whip his cock out and ejaculate all over her beaten bottom, splashing the angry red skin with streaks and splashes of come.

Katie was moaning deep in her throat as she sank down on the bed, reaching back to rub the come into her bottom, on her hurt skin and between the cheeks, then inserting one slippery finger into her bottom hole. Her legs came wide, and he saw that her other hand was still on her pussy, rubbing in among the plump pink folds as she soothed her bottom. He gave a chuckle and went back to undressing, watching from the side of his eye as she once more brought herself off, and speaking only when she had sunk down in satisfied bliss.

'Come on, girl, there'll be more of that later, plenty more. I'm thinking of giving you to the band tonight, if they play well. For now, run along and get dinner ready.'

She gave him a big smile and a kiss before scampering off to the bathroom. Peter's mouth was twitching up into a wry smile as he went back to undressing. It would be a shame to lose Katie, though it had to be done, but their brief time together was certainly going to be a happy memory.

He showered, dried, put on his denims and brought the Strat out, all the time with the scent of frying onions growing stronger. By the time he was ready Katie had his dinner on the table, steak with onions, peas and chips. She was nude but for her pinny, as usual, and made sure he was seated comfortably with his dinner and a glass of beer before sorting herself out. She also dressed quickly, putting on panties, a short black dress and no more than a touch of make-up. Again he felt a touch of regret that he would be passing up a woman so devoted to his pleasure, but to look at her in the dress made his decision absolutely firm. She had everything covered, and yet her appearance still verged on the obscene.

They set off, walking the short distance to The Pig and Whistle, where Zen already had everything set up. All of them were there, Jack greeting Katie's appearance with a low whistle. In response she smiled and bounced her tits in her hands, leaving Baz goggle-eyed and John the barman shaking his head.

'You lot watch your behaviour,' John warned, 'and none of that hanky-panky this evening. Near as touch got yourself banned for that, you did, Peter Williams.'

'Sorry, John ... I, er ... got a bit carried away,' Peter answered as Jack favoured him with a lewd wink. 'We'll keep it clean this evening.'

John answered with a sceptical grunt and went back to polishing glasses. Peter went up to the stage to check on the equipment, leaving Katie to accept a drink from Jack and take her customary place in the corner. In addition to 'Hound Dog' and 'California Dreaming' he had decided to work on several other numbers, including The Velvet Underground's 'The Black Angel's Death Song', just in case George Marks's tastes proved a little less straight. It needed a lot of practice, and Peter was determined to get it exactly right, instructing Baz and Zen as they took their places.

'Not that again,' Jack stated as he sauntered over with the beers. 'I tell you, it's too weird for Retro.'

'It's not for the album,' Peter answered him, 'just to show what we can do. Now come on.'

Jack shrugged and started towards his drumkit, only to glance back as the door banged. A girl had come in, and she was unmistakable, her athletic build, the cruel certainty of her expression, her fierce green eyes, and he now knew her name – Juliana. Katie went to her immediately, hugging and kissing her on the mouth with open passion.

'Whoa!' Jack exclaimed. 'Nice.'

'Nice is right,' Zen put in.

Jack gave a lewd chuckle. Peter stepped towards the girls, smiling, his hand extended, only for Jack to put out an arm, blocking his path. Peter gave his friend a puzzled glance.

197

'No, no,' Jack said, 'you've had more than your fair share of cunt recently, Peter, you greedy bastard. This one's mine.'

'She's a friend of Katie's,' Peter explained, 'but I don't think –'

'Yeah, I figured that one out,' Jack answered, 'and any friend of your Katie's, well, I reckon I know how to handle her, and with old Jack there won't be quite such a ruckus before the panties come down. Look and learn, boys.'

He stepped confidently forwards. Juliana saw him coming and turned on a small, cool smile.

'Did I catch that correctly?' she asked, her voice sweet and soft. 'Something about my panties coming down?'

'That's the way it goes, girl,' Jack answered her, and reached out for her arm. 'Spankies time!'

Juliana's reaction was too fast to follow. Before Jack realised she had a grip on him he was being twisted backwards, and even as his body crashed to the ground she was on top of him, kneeling on his arms, her bottom poised over his face, her hand down the front of his trousers. For an instant he merely looked dazed, then tried to lurch aside, only to gasp and his face contort in pain. Juliana chuckled.

'What were you planning to do?' she enquired. 'You were thinking of giving me a spanking, were you?'

'I think he was,' Katie supplied.

'No, no, just joking around, that's all,' Jack stammered. 'Let go of my balls, yeah, that fucking hurts!'

'No doubt it does,' Juliana answered him, but stayed just as she was. 'So you thought it might be fun to spank me, did you? With my panties down? In front of all these people? Go on then, do it.'

'I . . . I was joking, yeah?' Jack pleaded.

'That is a pity,' she went on, 'because I do like a really good spanking, always bare, of course, and nice and hard. Unfortunately it takes a real man to spank me. You, Jack, just get to kiss my arse.'

'No way!'

His face immediately contorted in pain once more. Juliana wiggled her bottom, the taut seat of her skirt just inches from his face. He grimaced, but pulled his head up, to plant the slightest of pecks on one firm bottom cheek.

'That's not how you kiss a girl's bottom.' Juliana laughed. 'Don't you know anything?'

She reached back with her free hand, tugging her skirt up to expose a pair of silk black French knickers, stretched taut over her upper cheeks, but with twin crescents of smooth, pale flesh showing below the lacy fringe and the tops of her stockings.

'Again,' she ordered, 'on my knicks.'

Jack obeyed, planting one more reluctant kiss on the curve of her bottom.

'Good boy,' Juliana said. 'Now, you wanted to pull my panties down, so now's your chance. Down they come, and then you can give me a proper kiss.'

She lifted one leg to let his arm free, but he immediately lurched to one side. Juliana's leg jerked, slammed his arm to the floor, and as the muscles in her arm tensed he sank back with a gasp. Again she wiggled her bottom.

'You're not strong enough, Jack. Come on, panties down and kissy, kissy. What's the problem, never kissed a girl's bum before?'

His answer was an angry grunt, but as she once more lifted a leg he put his hand to her knickers, tugging the back down to bare her neat, muscular bottom, her cheeks open enough to show the tight pucker of her anus and a puff of pussy hair. His head came up; he kissed one cheek and sank down again.

'OK, it's done. Now let me up, yeah?'

'No,' Juliana answered, 'I'm enjoying this far too much. Now, Jack, you're going to say sorry, properly.'

'Sorry,' he answered instantly, 'I'm sorry . . . I'm sorry . . . I didn't understand . . . I –'

'No, Jack,' Juliana answered him, 'that's not what I meant at all. Perhaps I should have said you're going to show me that you're sorry, the way a bad boy like you ought to apologise to a lady, by kissing her bottomhole. Come on, pucker up.'

Jack didn't answer, his face contorted in humiliation as she lowered her bottom, before stopping just inches above his face; his eyes fixed on the puckered brown ring he had been told to kiss.

'Kiss it, Jack,' Juliana said sweetly. 'Come on, now, it's not so bad. A lot of men would think themselves lucky, don't you?'

'No way!' he protested. 'Get the mad bitch off me, Peter –'

'None of my business,' Peter answered him, 'you started it, you finish it.'

'Help, sod you!' Jack demanded.

'Just kiss her arse, man!' Zen suggested.

'No fucking way!' Jack swore, and started to struggle, and swear, only for his protests to break off in a muffled grunting as Juliana sat squarely down on his face.

Katie immediately burst into giggles. Jack's legs were kicking frantically, his body jerking, but he seemed to be pinned helpless, while his face was smothered between her cheeks, his struggles only succeeding in rubbing his nose on her anus. Then he stopped fighting, suddenly, and Peter caught the faint, wet sound of a kiss.

'Good boy!' Juliana crowed in delight. 'One more then, so everyone can see.'

She lifted, once more displaying every detail of her naked bottom, her anus now wet. Jack's face was a mess, smeared with pussy juice, his expression set in sullen defeat. His head came up, and as his lips met Juliana's anal ring Katie cheered and began to clap, just as landlord John and his wife Jackie appeared from the back. She screamed, and he was immediately roaring.

'What the fuck is going on here!? Out, now, the bloody lot of you! This is a fucking pub, not a brothel! Get out!'

Peter moved to protest even though the look on John's face told him it was not going to work. He knew why too – whatever John might put up with, he would never dare cross Jackie, and her attitude was all too plain. She had fled.

'It was just a joke, John,' Peter started, moving forwards. 'We were just larking around, that's all, like the other night –'

'Out!' John yelled. 'And take your crap with you!'

Peter made to reply, but stopped. Juliana had stood up, quickly tugging up her knickers and smoothing down her skirt, and was facing John.

'Do you object to what I did?' she demanded. 'I hear it was OK for Peter to spank Katie, so is it just when the woman had the upper hand that you –'

'Juliana, don't,' Katie cut in, 'it won't help. Leave them to it.'

Juliana nodded and turned for the door without another word. Katie followed, and so did Peter, leaving the others to start gathering up their kit. The two girls were standing together a little way outside the door, and he caught a snatch of conversation before they realised he was there.

'... no fun at all,' Juliana was saying, 'and it's getting worse. A few years ago at least his mates might have set on me.'

'I know, it's pathetic,' Katie agreed. 'Oh, hi, Peter, sorry we got you thrown out.'

'Don't mention it,' he answered, 'it was Jack's fault, the moron! I'm really sorry, Juliana, he just –'

'Don't be,' she told him, and turned back to Katie. 'I've brought the car up for you.'

Peter followed Juliana's nod as she spoke. The Le Mans Green MG was in the car park.

'Isn't that Linnet's car?' he asked. 'Is she around?'

'Not so as you'd notice,' Katie answered him. 'So are you still up for giving me to the band, Peter? Can Juliana join in too?'

'Er ... I –' Peter answered, completely thrown off tack by the suddenness of her question. 'Would you want to, Juliana?'

'I'm not sure poor old Jack could perform with me around.' Juliana laughed. 'But we'll see. Maybe the four of you could just about manage to hold me down.'

Peter found himself swallowing, and letting his eyes run down her body. Her black skirt and skinny top did little to hide her lithe contours, most of which he'd seen anyway, and it was easy to imagine her stripped for action. Then there was the way she had kissed Katie, which suggested more than simple friendliness. She had to be joking about wanting to be held down and fucked, but if only Jack would see the funny side of being made to kiss her arse and behave himself ...

'It's easy.' Katie laughed. 'Get her a big bowl of ice-cream, then you can do as you like with her.'

Juliana merely laughed, then turned as Jack himself appeared in the doorway, the bass drum in his hand.

'You are a mad fucking cow, you know that?' he
began. 'It's just not –'

'Cool it, Jack,' Peter advised, 'you got what you
deserved.'

'Fucking right!' he stormed. 'I was only pissing
about –'

'No you weren't.' Katie giggled. 'You thought if
you gave Juliana a spanking she'd go down on you
the way I did for Peter.'

'Sounds fair,' Juliana admitted, 'shame he couldn't
manage it. You'll have to try harder than that, Jack.'

'Fucking psycho bitch,' he muttered, moving off
towards the van. 'Down the garage, yeah, Peter?'

'I don't think he'll rise to the bait,' Katie remarked.
'He's scared. Maybe if he caught you unawares?'

'Maybe,' Juliana admitted. 'The brash ones often
prefer it that way, four or five on one. Soldiers too.
Funny the way second-rate men feel the need for the
support of a group, isn't it?'

'We have to rehearse,' Peter cut in. 'This business
with the pub is not good, but I can't let it get in the
way. Why don't you two go back to my place, and
get a few drinks on the way. We'll see you there later,
OK?'

'Sure,' Katie answered, taking the fifty-pound note
Peter had extracted from his pocket, 'and don't let
Jack spoil the evening, will you?'

'I'll try,' Peter promised.

He was shaking his head as they walked away.
Before they reached the car they had joined hands,
and Katie's laughter floated back to him. Evidently
they didn't take what had happened very seriously,
but he had to. They were going to rehearse, pub or
no pub, and when they played in front of George
Marks there would be no mistakes.

* * *

As he opened his front door it came as no great surprise to Peter to find Katie waiting for him in her pinny, boobs out and quite obviously bare behind, with a tray of drinks. As he took a Scotch with a heavy sigh, she bobbed a curtsey, smiling sweetly, then giggling as Jack slapped her bottom. She had to go.

The practice had gone as well as could have been expected, but he needed a drink, and swallowed the Scotch at a gulp. Zen and Baz were laughing about getting thrown out of The Pig and Whistle, and ribbing Jack for what Juliana had done to him. He'd been trying to put a brave face on it and, if his pride was hurt, then it had brought a new aggression to his drumming, an aggression reflected in the force with which he gave Katie a second slap before following Peter.

Juliana was in the living room, and had made herself comfortable in the best armchair with a glass of the Cointreau he had been given as a Christmas present some years before. Unlike Katie, she was fully dressed, yet still provactive with her elegant legs crossed and her feet bare but for her stockings. She raised a hand in idle salute as the four of them filed in.

'There's more beer in the fridge, boys, champagne too, snacks, and plenty of ice-cream. Help yourselves.'

'Cheers, love,' Baz answered her, throwing himself down on the settee.

Zen joined him, both pulling the tabs open on their beers and taking long swallows. Peter took the remaining armchair, leaving Jack to get one from the kitchen and place it in the opposite corner of the room to Juliana.

'Not going to get your revenge then, Jack?' she asked immediately. 'Maybe with a bit of help from your friends?'

'No way,' Jack answered immediately. 'I'm not falling for that. What is that stuff you do, some Chinky shit?'

'Perhaps,' she answered, 'or perhaps you're just old and slow.'

'I am not old, and I am not slow,' he answered. 'You just caught me unawares with your Hong Kong Fuey business, that's all.'

'Relax, Jack,' Peter advised, 'she's just winding you up. Come on, Juliana, you've made your point. Let's just enjoy ourselves, yeah?'

'That's exactly what I want to do,' she went on. 'Now if it was all four of you, then maybe you could do it. You could sit on my arms and legs, strip me bare, maybe cut my clothes off me. Then you could do as you pleased with me, and really take your time. Let me see, a good spanking to start off with, that would do me good, or a belting, yes, that would be even better. Yes, you could take your belts to my bum, really hard, so I was screaming. There are lots of good things you could do too, to add a little spice and to humiliate me. Maybe you could stick my ruined knickers in my mouth, whip me while I sucked cock and not let up until you'd come in my mouth, and you, Jack, you'd have to make me kiss your arsehole after what I did to you.'

'Juliana –' Peter began, but she went on, her voice full of amusement for all that she was describing her own violation.

'Then you could tie my hands behind my back and make me crawl to each of you, to suck you off, maybe with beer bottles jammed up my bum and in my cunt. That would be funny, wouldn't it? And you could spunk in my mouth and make me swallow it, or do it over my face, in my eyes so I'd be blind. Or make me choke on your cocks so I was sick down my tits, or

205

do it in a bowl and make me lick it up like a dog. You wouldn't have to stop, either. You could take me into the bathroom and piss all over me, right in my mouth, Jack. I bet you'd like that, wouldn't you, Jack?'

'I'm not fucking going for it, lady,' he responded.

'You'd be into that stuff, for real?' Baz queried, staring slack-jawed in amazement.

'Nah, she's getting a rise out of us, man.' Zen laughed.

'No,' Juliana went on, 'I'm quite serious. That would just be the start, too, because you'd still have me tied up, and there would be nothing I could do about it. You could make me suck you all hard again, nice and slow while you sipped Scotch, or a nice brandy, the way Peter likes Katie to do him. Then it would be fucking time. You could take turns with me, any way you liked, doggie-style, so I'm showing everything while you do me. And why stick to my pussy? You could fuck my bottomhole. That would really teach me a lesson, wouldn't it? Sticking your great big cock up the little hole I made you kiss. Just think, you could pull it out and stick it in my mouth when you were ready to come –'

'Fucking shit!' Jack interrupted. 'You are one dirty bitch, you know that, don't you?'

Juliana laughed, rich and free. Jack was red in the face, Baz goggling and open mouthed, even Zen looking thoughtful. Katie had come in, with fresh drinks on her tray, and started offering them round, bending a little at the waist each time to make her bottom push out invitingly from the sides of her pinny.

'No, you wouldn't dare, would you?' Juliana continued. 'You'd rather molest Katie, sweet, soft Katie, who wouldn't hurt a fly. I think you'd better let them, Katie, before they all come in their pants.'

'OK,' Katie laughed. 'How would you like me, Peter?'

Peter bit down his instinctive annoyance at her sluttish behaviour, reminding himself that it was exactly what he wanted.

'If you're game,' he said with a shrug. 'Why don't you take Baz upstairs? He does look like he's about to burst.'

'Don't you want to watch?' Katie answered him. 'Or Juliana and I could give you a show, if you prefer.'

'Cool,' Zen put in, '– no offence meant, Juliana.'

'None taken,' she answered, 'if you lot are too cowardly to take me on, I'm more than happy to play with Katie.'

She had stood as she spoke, and Peter found a sudden lump in his throat. Katie giggled and put her tray down. One tug and her pinny was off, leaving her stark naked as she moved to the middle of the floor to kneel down, her knees wide, her lips slightly parted, her eyes raised to Juliana.

'Well, boys?' Juliana asked. 'What would you little perverts like to see first?'

'How about a sixty-nine?' Zen suggested.

'Do a striptease, please,' Baz put in, begging. 'I'd love to see that.'

Jack stayed silent. Juliana nodded, extended one stocking-clad foot and pushed Katie backwards on to the floor. Peter reached out, flicking the random switch on his stereo system. As the Rolling Stones' 'Brown Sugar' kicked in, Juliana began to dance, fast, but sensuous, her athletic body moving with a grace that had Peter instantly riveted. There was no hesitation, and no inhibition. She teased, but from the start he knew every single piece of her clothing would be coming off, and that she would conceal nothing. She used her hair, her breasts, her hips and legs, each perfectly timed motion so alluring that his cock had begun to swell before she had revealed so much as a hint of flesh, and the more so because it was done for Katie.

Nor was she slow. In moments her top was up, rested over full, braless breasts that quivered and shook to her motions, making him wish he could hold them, kiss them, slide his erect cock between them. Her skirt followed, pulled right off to leave her dancing in the pretty French knickers, the little round cheeks of her bum peeping out from under the hem, shaking in perfect time. Peter squeezed his cock, wondering if he dare hope to fuck her.

As the song changed, so did her dancing, moving into 'Don't Stop' as if she'd known it would come, picking up the jerky rhythm so that her top came off in three quick movements. Her stockings followed, each flicked aside as she moved forwards to straddle Katie's body. She was dancing in just her panties, then they were down, and off, leaving her bare, and achingly beautiful as she stopped with the song, to stand naked and proud, her hands on her hips, her feet planted astride Katie's chest.

She looked down, smiling, and when the music began once more she didn't start to dance but swung around and down, kneeling across Katie's body. Peter quickly turned the volume down, his cock painfully hard, his heart beating fast as she reached back to take hold of her bottom cheeks and at the same time looked over her shoulder. Katie's mouth came open and her sharp pink tongue poked out.

'Say hello,' Juliana purred, pulled open the cheeks of her bottom, and sat neatly down in Katie's face.

Peter swallowed hard as Juliana's bottom settled on to Katie's face, bumhole to mouth. There was no hesitation, Katie puckering up to kiss the little pink ring, then poking her tongue out once more, to lick at Juliana's bottomhole in his full view. Jack moved, scrambling around to get a better view, and Baz and Zen quickly followed, all four squatting down to stare as Katie's tongue worked between Juliana's spread bottom, around the hole and in it, pushed well up.

Juliana was purring like a contented cat as her bottom was licked, eyes closed in bliss, her nipples high and proud on her breasts. Only when Katie switched to pussy licking did she move, down into a sixty-nine, to lick urgently at her friend's plump, wet pussy, the men apparently forgotten, or just irrelevant. Katie returned the favour, taking hold of Juliana's hips and burying her face in pussy. Again Peter wondered if he dare intrude a cock, perhaps slipping it into Katie's hole as Juliana licked.

He didn't do it, despite the fact that his cock was so hard he knew he would come in his pants if he so much as squeezed himself. It would ruin the moment, he was sure, destroy the intimacy between the two girls . . .

'Fuck us, you idiots!' Juliana gasped, breaking for an instant from licking Katie's pussy.

Peter didn't wait to be told twice. His fly came down, his cock out, and between Katie's face and Juliana's sex. Juliana immediately reached back, to take hold of his erection and guide it into her pussy. As he slid deep, Katie took his balls in her mouth, sucking on them, and Juliana began to wriggle her bottom in his lap. It was too much, far too much. He came, spurting the full contents of his aching balls into Juliana, so much that on the instant he drove back up her it exploded out into Katie's face, and he was gasping out his ecstasy as he milked himself over them.

Jack had hesitated; Baz held back. Not Zen, who had moved the moment Juliana invited him to. As Peter came he was already in Juliana's mouth, his face set in dizzy pleasure as she sucked on his erection. Seeing just how willing the girls really were, Jack pulled out his cock, putting it in Katie's hand. She began to toss him, and as Peter dismounted she twisted around, to take him in her mouth, leaving her pussy spread open and wet.

'Go on, Baz,' Peter urged, 'do it. She's ready for you.'

Baz nodded, his eyes round in amazement and delight as he shuffled over to get between Katie's thighs. His cock came out, only half-stiff, but Juliana took him in hand, running long, sharp fingernails up the underside of his shaft, bringing him up even as she worked Zen in her mouth. Baz was quickly erect, but still he hesitated, only for Juliana to tighten her grip and force him to come forwards. His cock-head touched Katie's pussy and his reserve went, his hands reaching out to cup Juliana's breasts as he slid himself up into Katie's hole.

Peter had sat back, spent, watching his come dribble from Juliana's open pussy in delight and astonishment at just how dirty the girls were being. Both were nude, and revelling in sharing four men, and each other, heedless to what they showed, or what was done to them, just so long as they got their fun.

Juliana reached back, rubbing Peter's come into her pussy, over her clit, her fingers briefly probing her pussy to squeeze out more come, then her bumhole, using the slippery spunk to open herself before she went back to masturbating. Jack came, first in Katie's mouth to make her cheeks bulge and her eyes pop, then whipped it out to do the rest over her face and neck, splashing her fat boobs too, and Juliana's back.

An instant later and Zen had joined him, full in Juliana's mouth, to make her gag briefly before she managed to swallow. With that Juliana came, gulping down Zen's come as she rubbed at herself, her pussy awash with white juice, her breasts quivering beneath her to the shivers of her body.

The moment Juliana had come down from orgasm she rolled off Katie, leaving Baz to mount up. Katie took him in her arms, holding on as he fucked her, her thighs up and open, her body shaking to the thrusts. Jack began to clap, egging Baz on, then Peter and Zen, quickly picking up the pace. Baz got faster, and harder, pounding into Katie's body until she was gasping and clawing at his back in her ecstasy, then stopped abruptly as he came in her, held deep for a long moment, then subsided on top of her. Peter gave an indulgent smile.

Baz climbed off and gave a triumphant thumbs-up signal to Peter, who returned it. Katie stayed down, her legs still wide, her face set in sleepy bliss. Her hands were on her boobs, caressing her big nipples, which made plump red buds of flesh between her fingers, both proud and stiff. Then one hand had gone down between her legs and she was masturbating, wanton and free, indifferent to who was watching as she brought herself off with a few expert flicks to her clitoris, crying out in ecstasy just as Juliana came to kiss her.

The two girls cuddled together as Katie came slowly down from her orgasm, kissing and rubbing their faces together, then hugging, long and tight. Juliana's bottom was up, and pointing right towards Jack, who gave it a playful slap after a moment of hesitation.

'All friends, now, yeah?' he asked. 'I was out of order, all right, and you shouldn't have . . . have sat on my face like that, not in public anyway.'

He laughed and turned a meaningful look to the other men.

'Friends,' Juliana declared, disengaging herself from Katie and extending her hand to Jack, 'and sorry I got you thrown out of the pub.'

'Don't be, it's a dump,' Jack answered, as he swallowed the last of his beer. 'Now that little show was what I call nice. If you ever want to dance for us, Juliana, just say the word. Be a doll and fetch us another can, Katie.'

'Me too, love,' Baz put in.

Katie scrambled up and made for the kitchen. Seeing his chance, Peter followed, going to the sink to wash his hands as she began to pull beer cans from one of the six packs in the fridge. She looked at him, her pretty face radiating happiness, despite one eye being closed where Jack had come in her face. Her breasts were spattered with it too, and little beads of white fluid even showed in her hair. Peter offered her a piece of kitchen roll.

'Thanks,' she answered, taking it. 'That was good.'

'It was,' Peter agreed, 'and you and Baz, well –'

'Baz?' Katie queried, turning to a mirror as she began to dab the spunk out of her eye.

'Yeah,' Peter answered. 'The way you were with him, it just seemed more intimate. Don't take this the wrong way, but I thought ... maybe, you'd be happier with him?'

'With Baz?' Katie answered, spinning around. 'But –'

'He's a great guy,' Peter said quickly. 'He'll look after you far better than I can. I ... I'm not the man for you, Katie, you deserve better. I'm away all the time, sometimes for days on end –'

'I don't mind,' she assured him.

'Yes you do,' he insisted. 'I know you do. Baz is a regular, steady guy, Katie. I'm not. I'm bad news.

212

You know what I'm like. Look how we met! Do you really want to be with a guy who'll hire girls for sex the moment your back is turned?'

'Yes.'

'No, you don't, Katie, you're just saying that. Now with Baz –'

'Are you dumping her?' Juliana's voice sounded from behind him.

Peter swallowed and turned, expecting to face Juliana's anger, even a knife. She was smiling, and still naked, and, if there was more than a hint of wickedness in her expression, she didn't actually seem to be threatening him.

'I . . . er –' he managed, 'I was just saying to Katie that I really think she would be better off with Baz.'

'No, no, I'm fine with you, Peter!' Katie insisted, sounding more than a little desperate, but not really hurt.

'Baz sounds good to me,' Juliana put in. 'He's a nice guy, easy-going. Nice cock, too.'

'Not as big as Peter's,' Katie answered defiantly, 'or at least not so fat around, and that's what counts.'

'What counts,' Juliana stated, 'is what Peter decides. So, Peter, you think Katie would be better off with Baz, and so you're finishing your relationship with her?'

'No!' Katie squealed.

'I . . . I'm really sorry,' Peter stammered. 'I don't mean to be harsh, but it is for the best, really. You don't want me, Katie, you want someone steady, faithful –'

'Kinky,' Juliana added. 'There's no point in fighting it, Katie. If Peter doesn't want you, then Peter doesn't want you. Accept it.'

'It's not that I don't want you, Katie,' Peter supplied. 'It's more that I don't think I can really give

213

you what you need. Juliana's right too, I'm just not into this spanking stuff. I'm a pretty straight guy when it comes to sex –'

'So's Baz!' Katie insisted, her voice now taking on an edge of panic.

'No,' Juliana answered with a shake of her head. 'Baz is a dirty little boy at heart. He'll spank you, and snigger over it with his mates. I bet he'd like to watch you wet your panties too, and I don't suppose anything like that would even occur to Peter.'

'Wet her panties?' Peter demanded. 'Why would she want to do a thing like that?'

'You see,' Juliana went on. 'Baz is for you, but that's not really the point, is it, darling? If Peter doesn't want you –'

Katie drew a heavy sigh.

'Oh, all right!'

'You see, I told you so,' Juliana answered. 'Could Katie and I speak in private for a moment, please, Peter?'

'Sure,' he answered, 'of course.'

Peter blew out his breath as he left the kitchen. He'd done it, and with help from the most unexpected quarter. As he closed the door he caught the girls' voices, Juliana first, then Katie.

'Now let me see, this can of beer holds five hundred millilitres, so it would be four of these.'

'I can't take it, Juliana, not that much, not in one go –'

Juliana's laughter covered the rest of Katie's words as the door clicked shut.

Interlogue

Elune could feel herself shivering as her wrists were knotted together beneath her. She was on a thick pine log, strapped firmly in place by her hands, her ankles and around her middle, the bark rough against her skin, the air full of the scent of resin and the tang of chilli. Her knees were forward, cocked wide as if she were riding a horse at speed. The position left bottom and sex spread and completely vulnerable, her anus stretched wide with a plug of best butter melting slowly in the little hole. Above her, Juliana wore a faint smile as she carefully poured thick red chilli sauce from a bottle into the two-litre garden syringe. The others sat around, Lily and Aileve on other parts of the felled pine to which Elune was strapped, Thomasina on an old field gate, her legs dangling nonchalantly, a piece of grass in her mouth.

'Do you suppose I should try and make up for getting them thrown out of the pub?' Juliana asked thoughtfully as she tipped in the last of the sauce.

'I think you should,' Thomasina suggested. 'It would only be fair.'

'Perhaps we could help them with their try-out?' Lily suggested.

'Good idea,' Juliana answered. 'So, Elune, would you like to be whipped first, to warm your bum up a little?'

'Just do it!' Elune snapped suddenly. 'Give me my enema! Why do you always have to drag it out?'

'It wouldn't be torture if I didn't drag it out, would it, silly?' Juliana answered. 'You know that!'

Elune nodded miserably in response. The butter in her anus was making her skin tickle; the bark felt like sandpaper against the skin of her oversized breasts, and her pussy was beginning to stick to the log where her juice was drying in the hot sun. To cap it all, something with too many legs was crawling across her back and towards her bottom. Juliana continued to pour chilli sauce, slow and methodical.

'Someone?' Elune pleaded. 'Please could you remove the spider from my back?'

'It's a beetle,' Aileve answered.

'I don't care, could you get it off! It tickles like mad!' Elune answered her.

'Leave the poor thing alone,' Thomasina put in. 'It's probably just after the butter.'

'It's a Carabid, they're carnivorous,' Aileve corrected her.

Elune sighed in relief as Lily reached forwards to flick the beetle gently away.

'Last bottle,' Juliana stated, and Elune felt a new shiver run through her, her pain suddenly imminent.

Twisting her head around, she watched as Juliana poured out the last of the chilli sauce, a different brand, yellow-orange and full of pips, the label showing a caricature Mexican with flames erupting from his ears. Juliana was grinning now, her face full of malevolent delight, so broadly that as she screwed the brass nozzle back into place her teeth had started to show.

'Here we go, Elune, enema time!' she declared happily, as she rubbed butter on to the tip of the nozzle. 'And you're not to squirt until you absolutely have to. Hold it for one minute, or I'll nettle your pussy into the bargain.'

'That's not fair!' Elune wailed, then gasped as Juliana settled the syringe between her well-spread bottom cheeks.

She felt the cool, slippery metal touch her anal skin, and poke in, sliding up into her bottom. Her anus tightened on the intruding nozzle in a futile effort to keep it out, and the muscles of her bottom and belly began to twitch. Juliana spoke again, cool and amused.

'Be a darling and pick me some nettles, Thomasina.'

Thomasina immediately jumped down from the gate, wrapping her sleeve around one hand as she began to select choice nettles. Elune closed her eyes, her bottom-hole still pulsing on the thick nozzle, the butter now running down into her open pussy hole.

'Here goes,' Juliana stated, and Elune heard the squeak of the plunger as it was depressed.

For an instant there was nothing, and then she felt it, her rectum immediately starting to bloat as the sauce was forced into it. Her eyes came open again, and her mouth, in wordless dismay as her gut began to bulge, filling quickly, the pressure rising, wet sauce oozing out of her bottomhole around the nozzle, and starting to sting. Immediately she was gasping, her toes wriggling, her fingers locking in her pain. Her control started to slip as the hot agony quickly rose, her feet kicking pointlessly in her bonds, her head shaking to toss her hair about.

'All up, two litres,' Juliana said happily.

Elune let out a choking sob, but forced herself to clamp her ring tight as the nozzle was withdrawn. Her anus was a ring of pure fire, and she felt as if somebody had forced an entire football up her bottom, but she was determined to hold on. Her teeth were gritted and her fingers locked tight on the bark of the pine log as she fought not to let go, and Juliana began to count.

'One little second, two little seconds, three little seconds . . .'

217

The others joined in, chanting out the seconds as Elune writhed in her pain, a trickle of sauce already escaping from her anus for all her efforts, to run down over her pussy and set her sex flesh burning. She screamed out, overcome, and again, only to shut up as Lily quickly pulled off her panties and pushed them deep into Elune's mouth. Still the girls chanted, following Juliana's lead, twenty, and thirty, and forty, Elune's pain rising all the time, until the tears started from her eyes and the sweat began to prickle on her skin.

'. . . sixty little seconds.'

Elune gave in. Chilli sauce exploded from her rectum, spraying out behind her in a high arc to the sound of the girls' laughter and delighted clapping. She screamed as it came, spitting out Lily's panties, and again with the second spurt as her burning anus went into urgent and utterly involuntary contractions, spurt after spurt erupting from her tortured body on to the ground behind her.

Slowly it died, but there was no end to the stinging pain. Plenty had gone down her pussy, and she had come, her whole sex now a mass of inflamed flesh, yet as she went slowly limp she at least knew it would soon be over. Above her Juliana chuckled, then spoke.

'Nettles, please, Thomasina.'

'But . . . but . . .' Elune gasped. 'You . . . you said if I held it in for a minute! It was a minute!'

Juliana answered. 'No it wasn't.'

'Yes it was, you said!'

'I lied.'

Elune screamed as the bunch of nettles was thrust between her open thighs.

Eleven

As Peter pulled the front door open, his worst fears were realised. They were gone, both Katie and Juliana, taking the MG with them. It had backfired horribly. Instead of moving her neatly over to Baz, as he had intended, he had finally pushed her too far. Her words came back to him – 'I can't take it, Juliana, not that much.' He hadn't understood, because Juliana had said something about beer before. Now it was clear. He'd subjected her to the one thing she couldn't handle, rejection. He'd broken her.

She would go back to Portsmouth, to resume her life of selling herself for men's amusement, and all because he had had to play the control freak. It had been stupid, incredibly selfish, getting rid of her just because she was too plump to be socially acceptable among the cold, snobbish wives of men he had to fawn over. Had he been any sort of a man he would have stuck by her. She had come to him for protection, out of all the men she might have gone to, and he had turned her away.

The others were still asleep, but he paid no attention as he pulled on a random selection of clothes. He had to see her, at least to try and get her back, by going to Portsmouth. As he climbed into the Mondeo he found himself calculating the time it would take to get to the south coast and back in time to make the try-out. It was feasible, although the very fact that he could be so calculating at such a time added to his guilt.

He worried all the way, over whether she would be there, or would have gone off somewhere with Juliana, or alone. Would she be safe? Would she be safe from herself? What if she did go but Annie hadn't forgiven her and sent her away? As he pushed in at the door of the Green Dragon he was biting his lip, and praying she would be there. He entered the back bar, to find Annie, holding court with her girls, Cherry, Zoe, three others he didn't recognise and Katie, as large as life, sipping an alcopop and munching on a cheese roll. Annie had already seen him.

'Mr Williams? What a nice surprise, on a Saturday and everything. We're just having a bite of lunch –'

'May I have a word with Katie?' he interrupted. 'Katie?'

Katie looked up, giggling around her mouthful of roll, from big baby-blue eyes.

'Sure, what's up? Do you want me now, 'cause –'

'I –' Peter answered, and stopped, puzzled.

The girl in front of him was not Katie or, at least, not his Katie. She was very similar, certainly, with the same voluptuous figure and soft, sweet face, but not identical. Her boobs were just a touch less pneumatic, her skin not quite so milky-smooth, her hair a marginally less rich gold, and her eyes were baby-blue, quite definitely baby-blue.

'You all right, Mr Williams?' Annie asked.

'I . . . I don't know,' Peter answered. 'Annie, when did Katie get here?'

'Get here?' Annie queried. 'Why, she's been here since we came.'

'No ... I mean, was she here last night? In Portsmouth?'

'Why, sure she was.'

'Course I was,' Katie added, and there was no duplicity in her voice, no hint of a lie, while for his Katie it would have been an absurd claim.

'Excuse me,' Peter managed after a moment. 'There's been a mistake. Katie, do you ... No, forget it.'

He walked out. There was no point in asking if she knew a girl almost exactly like her but with green eyes. He'd been through the same with Emma and Linnet. The answer would be no.

He drove back in a state of utter bewilderment, and anger too, pushing the Mondeo to its limits on the A3. Linnet and Emma, the two Katies, Patty and Sally for that matter, all were linked, they had to be linked. To think of them together it was as if one girl, very like Emma, had chosen to become as close to Portsmouth Katie as possible, by styling her hair and putting on an immense amount of weight. It fitted, except in that it was not humanly possible to put on that much weight so fast. Just possibly, with extensive plastic surgery, but then his Katie would have been covered in scars, and her skin was as smooth as cream, without so much as a blemish.

The problem was still going round and round in his head when he got back into Milton Keynes, despite his best efforts to push it down and think about the try-out instead. The others were outside his house, the van ready to go. They watched as he climbed out of the car, Jack shaking his head as if in despair.

'Where've you been, Peter?' he demanded. 'We've got to get to London, yeah?'

'I know, I know, just –' Peter answered, and stopped as the girls emerged from the house, Katie limping slightly, but smiling happily too, hand in hand with Juliana. She waved as she saw him, and spoke as they reached him.

'There you are, Peter. We've been looking everywhere for you. You missed lunch, which is a pity, 'cause Juliana and I got some toffee fudge ice-cream with real –'

'Never mind that,' he cut in. 'Just tell me, please, who are you?'

'Who am I? You know who I am!'

'No I do not. You're not Katie from Portsmouth, that's for sure, because I've just been there and spoken to her. Now –'

'Peter?' Zen interrupted. 'Look, man, I don't know what you're on, but you need to come down.'

'I'm not high!' Peter snapped. 'You, Katie or whoever you are, just fuck off, out of my life –'

'Hey, Peter!' Baz interrupted. 'What's your problem?'

'My problem,' Peter began, indicating Katie, 'is that she . . . she . . . has been . . . been . . . and her friends . . . or –'

'Jesus, Peter, take a look at yourself, will you?' Jack cut in.

'Get him in the van,' Zen advised. 'Anyone got any downers?'

'Get your fucking head together, Peter,' Jack went on. 'You're the man, we can't do it without you!'

'Yeah, come on,' Baz added, taking Peter's arm.

'I'll help him,' Juliana offered.

'No . . . not you, n– no way,' Peter stammered, but she had taken his other arm in a steel-hard grip, and he found himself being helped into the van.

He went, allowing them to put him in a seat and strap him in, then push two pills into his mouth and the neck of a water bottle. The others climbed in,

Katie sitting with her arm around Baz and her head resting on his arm, Juliana in the front beside Zen, glittering green eyes turned to him with a look of concern that entirely failed to hide the amusement behind it. He was still talking, but nothing sensible seemed to be coming out, and then cars were passing, and trees, and buildings, in a kaleidoscope of colours so pretty that nothing else really mattered.

The others were talking, and he seemed to figure a lot in the conversation, particularly about whether or not he could play his guitar. It was silly. He knew he could play his guitar. He could play better than any man alive. They were already at the Retro Records studio, and he was going to play so well he would blow their minds, just as soon as he could find the door to the van.

It was very pretty inside Retro Records too, with lots of posters of Elvis Presley and Buddy Holly and other mediocre performers. Even Dan from Faithful Copy was there for some reason, and some man called George who kept slapping him on the back and talking about contracts and release dates. Contracts and release dates didn't matter, only the music, and he told George so, in no uncertain terms. George seemed a little surprised, but took him down to a really nice studio with lots of pretty lights and girls with clipboards and microphones and men doing things with wires, and his Strat.

His old friend Baz was there, and wanted him to play 'Hound Dog'. Somebody suggested 'The Black Angel's Death Song', and he played that too, and 'Hotel California', and 'Stairway to Heaven', and 'Johnny B. Goode'. When he played 'California Dreaming' the man called George was in tears, and then people were clapping and cheering and making him sign things and pressing tall, cool glasses into his hand. Juliana was there, helping him back into the van with people talking all around him, full of excitement. Lights were passing, to the beat of a song he'd had in his head since he was a child, then slower, and slower still, until they became simple street lights along the side of an urban motorway, and what people were saying once more began to grow clear.

'. . . such a prat,' Jack was saying, 'I mean a total and utter prat. OK, we had a few beers, and a couple of whiskys, but that was the lot. We were playing the next day, I knew we were playing the next day, and yeah, sometimes I get a bit pissed, but not this time, not when it matters. Not Ken though, oh no, not Ken. He has to take on a girl who says he can fuck her if he drinks a pint of Stoli first. Serious, that's what happened, Dan told me, 'cause he was well pissed off, and was trying to say we put her up to it. Gorgeous she was, so he says, boobs you could die between and an arse like a peach, some porno model, he reckons. So she comes down the Squirrel lunch-time and starts flirting with Ken, 'til eventually the thick bastard gets the hint and asks if she wants a portion of black pudding around the back. She says she does, but she wants to see him down a pint of vodka first. So what does he do? Does he tell her get her knicks off and stop farting around? No, he drinks the fucking vodka, straight down, and then he wonders why he can't play the fucking drums! What a prat!'

'You must meet Thomasina sometime,' Juliana told them.

'Thomasina? Who's Thomasina?' Jack asked.

'Your porno model with the arse like a peach,' she answered him, 'only she's not a porno model.'

'One of yours?' Peter managed.

'He's back from the land of the fairies!' Jack

laughed. 'Welcome to Earth, Peter, got your head straight yet?'

Peter didn't answer. He felt drained, and slightly sick. They'd played, and got the contract, that much he could remember, but only as if he was waking from a dream. The events of the morning still seemed distant, and made no more sense than they had before. Katie was in the front with Baz, drinking champagne from the bottle and chattering happily. Only she wasn't Katie, or she was, but not Katie the tart, in which case . . .

He sank back with a groan. Juliana promptly passed him a bottle of water and he drank greedily, his head clearing with every gulp of the cool liquid. She came to sit by him, putting an arm around his shoulders, her voice low and soothing as she began to speak.

'Don't worry, Peter, just let it be. Believe me, it is by far the most sensible thing you can do. Katie is Katie, Baz's new girlfriend, that's all. Like you said, she's not for you. Forget about her, find somebody more . . . more sensible maybe.'

'I just need to know –' Peter began, and stopped as Juliana's words brought back the full memory of what he'd been intending.

'Shit!' he swore. 'Zen, stop at The Pig and Whistle, will you? John'll let you in, for a minute anyway. There should be two girls there, one small and dark haired, the other taller and blonde. Emma and Tina, they're called. Tina wants to sing backing for us, and Emma –'

'Nice one, Peter!' Jack laughed. 'High as a kite, but he's still got us cunt on a plate all round. Nice are they, these two? I bet they are, you dirty bastard you!'

'You keep your paws off Emma,' Peter answered him, and glanced guiltily at Katie, who paid him not the slightest attention. 'If Tina's game, that's up to her.'

'Got you, mate,' Jack answered and raised his bottle in salute to Peter, who lay back in his seat.

'Emma,' he said quietly, 'is the girl who modelled for the cover of a book called *Tease*. She looks very like Linnet, uncannily like Linnet in fact, only her eyes are brown. I met her when I was trying to find Linnet, because –'

'That's nice for you,' Juliana said gently, 'now why don't you try and sleep for a few minutes?'

'I –' Peter began, but the determination and anger that had driven him before wasn't there, and as Juliana began to stroke his hair he felt his exhaustion rise up to engulf him.

His head was resting in Juliana's lap when he was woken by the van coming to a bumpy stop. He pulled himself up, accepting the water bottle from her and drinking deep. They were outside The Pig and Whistle, and if Emma was going to be inside then the last thing he wanted was for her to find him scruffy and half-asleep, never mind with his head in another woman's lap.

Zen had already got out of the van, and Peter made to follow, quickly brushing back his hair and smoothing out his clothes the moment he had hit the ground. John could say what he liked, he didn't care, and he was sure that getting banned would only add to his glamour in Tina's eyes, and hopefully Emma's. Sure enough, as Jack jumped down beside him, Zen and the girls came out. Tina was in a blue mini-dress, giggling and flushed, Emma wearing tight black jeans, a T-shirt and an excited smile. For a moment he caught the noise from within the pub, including Jack's voice, cut off as the door closed.

'How did it go?' Tina was asking. 'Did you get the contract?'

'Did we get the contract!' Jack answered her, his eyes running down her body appreciatively. 'Did we get the contract! Of course we got the fucking contract. We played a blinder, girl, and Peter, you should have seen Peter. He was the best.'

'Ace!' Tina answered, and there was no mistaking the quality of Emma's smile as she came to stand beside Peter.

'We played well, yeah,' he said. 'We deserved it.'

'Do I get to sing with you?' Tina asked.

'A babe like you and you can sing too!' Jack responded. 'Sure. You're in.'

Peter made to speak, meaning to qualify Jack's offer, but decided it was not the time. Tina was already standing close to him, and as his arm came around her waist she gave no resistance. Jack was grinning, and making no secret of his admiration.

'You look great,' he remarked, his eyes fixed firmly on where her mini-dress ended barely far enough down to cover her pussy and bottom. 'Nice legs, they go right up, they do, right up to –'

'Cheek!' she responded, and gave him a playful slap, giggling as he retaliated with a firm swat to her bottom.

'I hear you got banned!' Emma laughed. 'What for?'

'Long story,' Peter answered quickly, 'let's just say things got a bit frisky at a band practice.'

'So don't tell us we've come all this way for nothing?' Tina demanded. 'The party's on, yeah?'

'Sure,' Jack answered immediately. 'My place. We need to get some more booze in, that's all. You drive the girls round, Zen, we'll see you there, yeah?'

Peter hesitated, but Juliana was already helping Tina up into the back of the van, with Emma right behind her.

'Nice,' Jack remarked as the door of the van thumped shut. 'So you're after the little brunette? Cute, but I prefer mine.'

227

'Just as well then,' Peter joked. 'Seriously, Jack, I want to make something of this one, so no clowning around.'

'As if I would,' Jack answered, 'but we've got to have a decent party, and anyway, if she won't go, she's no fucking use anyway, is she? Better to find out now than later.'

'Just leave me to do things my way, yeah?'

'Sure. I know what you mean, you've got to make them feel they're the special one. Pain that, as it goes. I don't half fancy that Tina, but we're going to do Juliana.'

'Juliana? What do you mean "do" Juliana?'

'The way she said. You know, hold her down and fuck her and make her do dirty stuff with us.'

'Better not,' Peter advised.

'It's what she's into,' Jack answered him. 'She said so!'

'I'm not sure she was serious,' Peter cautioned.

'She was,' Jack insisted. 'Katie told us. Some girls like it rough, and she's one of them. I just don't reckon I can get in there and have Tina too. One or the other. Still, if Zen and Baz go for it, it's bound to turn ours on.'

'You reckon so?'

'I know so. Girls love a fight, makes then horny.'

'Maybe . . . just so long as they know Juliana's up for it.'

'Good thought.'

They reached the off-licence, and went inside. Jack began to load his arms with beers from the fridge, while Peter went to the display of champagnes, selecting several bottles without thought for price. It was hard to see Emma and Tina being able to handle the kind of free-for-all they'd had with Katie and Juliana the night before. Short of trying to get Emma alone before anything really bad happened he had no idea what to do. The boys were going to resent any attempt he made to tone it down, and Katie and Juliana would just laugh at him.

He said nothing as they walked back to Jack's, praying that the situation would take care of itself. The van was already outside Jack's house, in which the lights were on and the curtains drawn. Laughter could be heard from within, and they found Katie and Juliana wrestling playfully on the floor. Katie already had her boobs bare, with her top pulled up to trap her arms, and she was giggling so hard that she was completely helpless in Juliana's grip. Zen and Baz were watching, beers in their hands, the girls too, Tina giggling, Emma looking taken aback but happy enough.

'Leave it out, girls.' Peter laughed, quickly taking the place on the settee beside Emma. 'They're crazy, these two!'

'Submit?' Juliana demanded, twisting Katie's top and pulling back.

Katie didn't answer, her huge breasts and plump little tummy quivering with her laughter despite the painful position she was in, and being bare. Juliana tightened her grip still further. Katie squeaked and began to babble.

'I submit! I submit! I submit! Pick on somebody your own size, you big bully!'

Juliana laughed and let go, standing to place her hands on her hips. Katie stuck her tongue out as she scrambled away, to grab a beer and quickly curl up on Baz's lap.

'So who's next?' Juliana demanded, beckoning to all and sundry.

'Not me!' Emma giggled and moved closer to Peter.

His heart jumped, and without further thought he put his arm around her shoulder. She made no effort to pull away, but snuggled into him. Tina had stood up.

'I don't want to fight you, Juliana,' she said, 'but I'll go two on one with you against any man who's got the guts.'

'No way, man!' Zen answered promptly, Baz nodding vigorous agreement.

'Jack?' Juliana enquired, cocking her head to one side.

Jack hesitated, then glanced to Zen and to Baz.

'Come on, boys, we said we would.'

Baz scratched his ear. Zen had already begun the careful process of rolling a joint. Jack swore under his breath. As Tina sat down once more there was open scorn on her face. Jack promptly stood up.

'All right, all right, but no funny stuff, right?'

'Anything goes.' Juliana answered.

'Yeah, right,' Tina put in. 'She's going to make you kiss her arsehole again, Jack boy!'

Jack's face went abruptly pink, but he stayed up.

'Like you said, Jack,' Peter remarked. 'You're going to do Juliana. Well, now's your chance.'

Jack nodded, biting his lip, still hesitant but clearly aware that if he turned the girls down he might well lose his chance with Tina.

'Go for it, man,' Zen advised. 'I can think of worse things to do than kiss Juliana's bum.'

Again Jack nodded. Space had already been cleared, a good-sized rug marking the area Katie and Juliana had been wrestling on. His decision made, he stepped forwards, flexing his arms as he went into a crouch. Juliana sank down to face him, poised and ready, her eyes fixed on his, chuckling, and squeaking in surprise as her panties were abruptly snatched down from under her skirt from behind. Zen pulled hard on the panties, and she went down, into his lap, completely off-balance.

Jack was already moving, and grabbed her feet, hauling them high to flash her legs, bum, and her pussy peeping out from between her thighs. Zen snatched at her torso, but she was already twisting, wrenching herself free of his grip, and Jack's. She went over, sprawling across the arm of Zen's chair with her bare bottom stuck out towards the room and her panties stretched taut between her thighs. Jack fetched her one meaty smack, and then she had rolled free, bouncing to her feet even as she tugged her panties back into place. Tina had barely moved, but came beside Juliana as the men moved to face off.

Emma had her hand over her mouth in shock, but delight too, and she was clinging firmly to Peter's arm. Katie had been laughing so hard she'd spilled her beer down her front, plastering her top to her boobs. She pulled it off and tossed it casually aside

'You'd better help your friends, Baz,' she instructed. 'I think they're going to need it.'

Juliana nodded and shifted her position a little as Baz stood to join the other men. Jack nodded to Juliana.

'You ought to take those panties off.'

'Why?' she demanded.

'We got 'em down, they should stay down,' Zen put in.

'You want my panties off, come and take them off,' Juliana answered, and hurled herself forwards.

She went for Baz, catching him half on-guard and twisting his arm to send him stumbling into Jack, who fell, landing on the floor with Baz on top of him. Juliana immediately applied an armlock and twisted her free hand hard into Baz's collar, pinning both men on the ground, still fighting. Zen bent down, reached up under her skirt and quite casually pulled down her panties again.

'Tina!' Juliana complained as her skirt was hoisted up to show off her bare bum.

'I'm on it,' Tina answered even as Zen began to spank Juliana's bottom.

Tina grappled Zen, trying to pull him off, but he held on tight to the waistband of Juliana's skirt, still spanking even as Tina changed her tactic and began to wrench at his trousers. Katie was laughing hysterically, Emma also, as the trousers came loose, and down, Zen's boxer shorts with them, and as Tina grabbed him by the balls he finally released his grip on Juliana. He bent and staggered to one side so that Tina was riding on his back, her legs kicking wildly, her tiny panties on show to Peter as her skirt lifted.

Zen went down, Tina on top of him, just as Jack finally managed to writhe out from underneath Baz and Juliana. Tina's dress was right up, her panties well into her slit, twin egg-shaped bottom cheeks sticking out, a perfect target she could do nothing to hide as Zen clung on to her arms. Jack smacked it even as he pulled himself to his knees, just gently, then again, harder as Tina reacted with a squeak of consternation that was at least half feigned.

'Hold her, Zen!' Jack instructed, and began to spank properly, taking a tight grip on Tina's waist and slapping away a dozen times to the sound of Tina's squeals and giggles.

He stopped; his hand went to the top of her panties and they were hauled down. The note of her protests changed, becoming abruptly more urgent and very real, but it was too late. Her bare bum was on show, the little wrinkled hole between her cheeks, and her pussy, pink and wet and ready. Jack made to pull the panties back up, apologising hastily, even as Juliana got one foot to the middle of his back, and pushed.

Jack and Tina went down in a heap on top of Zen, her bottom still bare. She was complaining bitterly, and wriggling about in an effort to get free, so making an even ruder show of her pussy and anus. Katie was in hysterics, and Emma still giggling, amusement Peter was beginning to find infectious. As the pile broke apart Tina was immediately clutching for her panties, and covered herself as she rolled away, to sit down, panting and dishevelled, one tit sticking out over the top of her dress until she covered that too.

'You bastards!' she gasped, but there was no malice in her voice, and the next instant she had launched herself at Jack.

He went down, taken by surprise, sprawling on the rug with Tina on top of him. Zen had scrambled quickly out of the way, and pulled himself back into his chair, where he took a long draw on his joint. Baz was helpless in Juliana's grip, and she had turned her attention exclusively to him, pulling down his trousers and pants to set to work on his buttocks with a drumstick, drawing pained squeals from him and gales of laughter from Katie. Suddenly he was begging for it to stop, at which Juliana twisted the stick in her fingers, put it neatly between his buttocks and stuck it in. His mouth came open in wordless shock as he was penetrated, and Juliana rocked back on her heels, releasing him.

'That's mine dealt with, I think.' She laughed. 'Do you need a hand, Tina?'

'Please,' Tina grunted, even as Jack rolled under her, putting her on to her side on the carpet.

He swung a leg over, trying to pin her down, only to cry out in pain as Juliana twisted his foot, forcing him on to his back once more. Tina was on top of him in an instant, snatching his arms to pin him out on the carpet. He pushed back, lifting her easily, only to collapse back as Juliana added her weight.

'Oh, shit!' Jack swore, looking up at Juliana.

'This time,' she said softly, 'you take me all the way, until I come. Get his cock out, Tina.'

Emma gave a little gasp, Tina an excited giggle. Jack shut his eyes, his breathing deep and even as Tina's hands went to his fly. She drew it down, stuck her hand in to pull out his cock, half stiff.

'Wank him,' Juliana ordered, 'they always lick better if they're hard, and I want his tongue right up my bum.'

Tina gave a shy giggle, but she was already tugging on Jack's cock. He gave a low moan as his face disappeared beneath the hem of Juliana's skirt. She paused a moment to pull her top up over her breasts, and to cup them, tease her nipples quickly to erection, then wiggled her bottom in his face. Jack gave a muffled sob from beneath her, then lurched, Juliana only just regaining her grip in time.

'You were right,' she said, 'I should have taken my panties off. It would have made this easier. Zen, you seem to like pulling them down, so if you wouldn't mind?'

Zen didn't hesitate, coming down on to his knees and quickly tugging Juliana's skirt up to expose her panties, which he pulled down as far as they would go, leaving her bottom bare over Jack's face, her bottomhole showing, and her pussy.

'Kiss it,' she demanded, 'right on my hole, and put your tongue in this time.'

Jack pulled his head up, his lips puckered, to kiss her anus, and as she gave a sigh of pleasure he twisted violently to the side. Juliana went back, right into

234

Zen's arms. Tina rolled off with a squeak, landing on her back, and the next instant Jack was on top of her, between her open thighs, his erect cock pressing to the crotch of her tiny panties. One twitch of his fingers and they were aside, his cock-head at the mouth of her pussy, and in.

Tina gave a gasp of surprise as she was penetrated, but the next one was of ecstasy as Jack pushed himself deep up her. He began to fuck her, pumping away energetically between her legs, and the moment her shock and consternation had passed her thighs had come up and her arms were wrapped around his neck. A moment later they were kissing.

Peter had felt Emma's body shudder against his as Tina was entered, and he pulled her closer to him as they watched the fucking. His cock was hard, and the urge to give her the same treatment close to over-whelming, but he held back, uncertain. Katie had no such reservations, letting out a squeal of joy as Jack's cock pushed up into Tina's pussy and pulled Baz to her. Juliana was still in Zen's lap, but they stopped fighting, and as they watched his hands stole cau-tiously on to her boobs, cupping them. Her response was to purr, rubbing her naked bottom into his crotch. He took the hint, freeing his cock and slipping it into her from behind even as Katie took Baz's in her mouth. Again Emma gave a little shiver, but this time she reached out to take a tentative handful of Peter's erection through his clothes.

He reacted, turning to scoop her up in his arms and lifting her easily as he rose. She gave a delighted giggle and pulled herself close, kissing him as he carried her from the room. He made the stairs before he put her down, and she immediately scampered up, Peter following, and into Jack's bedroom. She sat down, looking up at him from her big brown eyes for one long moment before she began to very slowly lift her top.

Peter watched, his throat dry and his cock rock solid as the gentle curve of her tummy came bare, her ribs, and her little apple-sized breasts, firm and round, her upturned nipples perky with blood. She was smiling, her eyes bright and excited, and she gave a little laugh of pleasure as his tongue flicked out to wet his lips.

'More?' she asked.

'Please, yes,' Peter responded.

'My bum? Like on that cover shot?'

Peter nodded, lost for words. She turned over, on to her knees, and pushed out her bottom, making it a rounded ball in the seat of her jeans, the black denim stretched tight. He swallowed and made a quick adjustment to his cock, which felt as if it was going to burst. Emma looked back over her shoulder, her hands on the button of her jeans as she spoke.

'Do you like me?'

'Yes,' Peter croaked, 'a lot.'

'Do you want to see?'

'Please.'

'You first.'

Peter tugged his trousers open, fumbling the zip in his haste, and pulled out his cock and balls. Emma licked her lips.

'Oh, my!'

'Now you, slowly.'

She nodded. One quick tug and her jeans were open. Her thumbs went into the waistband and they were coming down, eased slowly lower, to expose the top of a pair of crisp white panties, and more, her panty seat, bulging with perfectly rounded bottom flesh. The panties were just a little tight, taut across her cheeks and cutting ever so slightly into her flesh at either side, with generous slices of pale skin sticking out to either side of the leg holes. With her jeans down around her knees, she put her thumbs in the waistband. Peter briefly closed his eyes, sure he would come if he didn't.

'More?' she asked.

'Please.'

'What, everything?'

'Yes, everything.'

'My bare bottom?'

'Yes.'

'My bottomhole?'

Peter nodded urgently.

'You'll see my pussy too, and I suppose you'll want to put that dirty big cock inside?'

'Yes . . . please . . . now. I'm going to come, Emma, I'm not sure if I can hold it.'

She giggled, and her panties began to come down. Peter gripped his cock, his eyes fixed as her waistband moved gently down, to reveal the full glory of her peach, and the slit between. Her flesh was pale and smooth and resilient, her cleft deep and hairless, her bottomhole a tiny pink star. She hesitated, the rim of her panties just below the tuck of her bottom cheeks, her bumhole showing but not her pussy, then everything as she quickly slipped the panties down around her thighs. Her pussy was a delight, pouting pink lips, shaved bare, her slit wet between, her clitoris showing among the moist folds, her hole ready for cock.

Immediately he was scrambling on to the bed behind her, to grab her bottom, settling his cock between the beautiful, bare cheeks. She giggled as he began to rut in her slit, then gave her bottom a teasing wiggle. Peter began to explore her, not daring to touch his cock, but rubbing it gently in her bum slit from time to time to keep himself rock hard.

It was the perfect moment, the same beautiful bottom he had first admired on the book cover, now his to touch, to stroke, to kiss, to fuck when he pleased. She gasped when his thumb brushed her anus, or when he slid a hand beneath her to cup her sex. He bent down, to kiss each perfect cheek, and after a moment's hesitation the little pink star between, sending her into delighted giggles. He spanked her, not hard, but just enough to put a little colour into her cheeks and make her squeak. He fingered her, slipping one, then two up into the sopping hole of her pussy and opening up her bottomhole with the top of his thumb. He masturbated her, holding her pussy in his hand and rubbing her clit while he smacked and stroked her bottom.

Finally, when he could hold back no more, he fucked her, mounting her from behind and taking her tits in his hands as he probed for her hole, found it, and slid his cock deep into her body. Her cool snapped immediately, and she was panting and moaning beneath him, her body jerking to his thrusts as he pounded into her, struggling not to come too soon as she began to masturbate herself.

He made it, Emma crying out in ecstasy and her pussy tightening on his cock as he reached the point of no return. His cock erupted and they were coming together, Peter pumping spunk into Emma's body as she shook and jerked beneath him. His whole being was focused on her body, the rounded balls of hot girl flesh in his lap, the feel of her pussy tightening over and over on his erection. Spurt after spurt of come went into her, until she was rubbing it in as it squashed out to his pumps, and snatching at his balls, smearing it over him, and herself, lost in wanton ecstasy.

Peter held himself in, letting her finish in her own time, still jiggling her tits in his hands despite the blood singing in his ears from the sheer vigour of the fucking he had given her. Only when she collapsed down on to the bed with a contented sigh did he let his cock slip free, and as he came down beside her they were kissing instantly, mouths open together to add a beautiful touch of intimacy to their ecstasy.

For a long while they lay side by side, talking and occasionally kissing, Emma with her head resting on his chest. They could hear the noises of the party from downstairs, bumps and groans and cries as the three girls were fucked, but only when the others had become quiet did they get up to wash. They were holding hands as they came down the stairs, to find the others also finished, drinking champagne from the bottle.

Katie was in one armchair, with Baz perched on the edge, smiling contentedly as he played with her hair. She was unashamedly nude, her neck and breasts still flushed from sex, her expression a sleepy smile. Jack and Tina were on the settee, curled together and kissing, both looking thoroughly content, and she with her knickers around one ankle. Juliana was sprawled in another chair, also naked, with Zen curled at her feet, both with freshly rolled joints in their hands.

Peter saluted them, grinning as he sat down, pulling Emma on to his lap and accepting a bottle of champagne from Baz. As he took a gulp he was suffused with a sense of well-being. It was perfect, his triumph complete. With the record contract he had achieved a goal he had set himself the day he gave up his hopes of becoming a pop star for a stable career, to at least make some solid mark on the world of music. He had Emma, now cuddled tight on his lap, a girl he now realised he had fallen in love with the moment he had seen her picture. It was her too, the real thing, not Linnet, not Patty, not Sally, not even

Katie, who looked thoroughly content with Baz. To add an extra touch, Jack seemed to have found a soulmate in Tina, and even Zen seemed to have found some common ground with Juliana.

He raised his champagne bottle.

'A toast, ladies and gentlemen,' he called. 'To Pizazz, and to us.'

'Pizazz,' the others echoed.

Peter took another swallow of champagne and passed the bottle up to Emma. Katie had been a little too enthusiastic, making the wine froth up in the bottle and spill out over her chest. She was giggling as she tried to mop it up, making her huge tits and chubby little belly quiver. Baz blew out his breath.

'Isn't she beautiful?' he said.

'Do you really think so?' Katie answered.

'You're the best, believe me!' Baz answered.

'Peter? Jack? Zen?' Katie queried.

'Hey, any girl with tits bigger than her head is just fine by me,' Jack answered, immediately getting a playful slap from Tina.

'You're cute,' Zen answered.

'Peter?' Katie repeated when he didn't answer. 'Be honest with me.'

'You are beautiful, yes,' Peter replied. 'You're certainly one of the prettiest girls I've ever met, and maybe you could lose a little weight, but you're still beautiful.'

'Do you think so?' Katie responded, taking a pinch of her belly.

'Nah, you're perfect just the way you are, darling,' Baz responded.

'You be yourself, Katie,' Tina put in.

'No,' Katie answered, 'Peter's right. I do like being this size, because it makes me feel rude, but I suspect that will wear off, and it does slow me down.'

'I saw this great diet –' Emma began, but stopped as Katie laughed.

'I don't need to diet, not me,' she said. 'Watch.'

'Elune, no!' Juliana shouted, but Katie paid no attention.

Her flesh had begun to quiver, ripples spreading over the smooth pink surface. She closed her eyes and her mouth came open, her tongue protruding. Drool began to run from the sides, thickening quickly to a yellow-white mucus. The rippling of her skin grew stronger, and the surface began to wrinkle. Her legs came apart, showing off her pussy, with white fluid oozing from the mouth of her sex. Pee erupted from her, squirting out in a high yellow arc to spatter on the carpet. Her anus opened, extruding a fat sausage of some gelatinous substance.

Tina was screaming; Baz flattened against the wall in horror; Emma had fled. Jack and Zen were staring, and Peter, all three transfixed as Katie's body began to slump down into the chair, viscous fluid running from every orifice, her skin now a great loose sack. What was left of her chest heaved and she was violently sick, spewing thick, lumpy yellow material over breasts and belly and on to the floor. A rich, buttery scent caught Peter, making him want to be sick in turn, yet still he stared.

Again Katie puked, and again, thick yellow grease splashing over her front with each eruption. Folds of slack flesh hung down over her sex and mercifully hid the matter oozing from her pussy and anus. It was coming though, running out by the gallon, into the chair and on to the floor, so that the grotesque mound of shapeless blubber that had been her body seemed to swim in the glistening muck.

It stopped, abruptly, leaving her body a wrinkled mass of folds and tucks, barely recognisable as human, and all the more hideous for Katie's head on the top, smiling. For a moment the horrible thing was still, and then it had begun to contract, the reams of skin pulling in, tightening, while, beneath the chair and on the carpet before it, a thick puddle of grease was still expanding slowly outwards.

Juliana had covered her eyes with her hands and was slowly shaking her head. The others had fled, Tina's screams still echoing back from the road outside, but Peter could only stare, unable to move a single muscle as the thing in front of him tightened up, once more taking on human contours, but slim, petite, a form uncomfortably like Emma, but smaller. Finally a new girl sat where Katie had been, naked, glistening with grease, but perfectly formed, her only similarity the green, green eyes, glittering with mischief – Linnet.

'Better?' she asked.

Peter didn't answer. He had fainted.

Epilogue

Elune hung helpless from the rusting derrick, her hands tied above her head, her legs spread wide and each lashed securely to the rusting iron rails of the ship-wreck. She was naked, her hair a black, bedraggled mess around her face, her skin glistening with sweat. Aileve sat opposite, her chin in her hand, considering, as Juliana concluded her remarks.

'. . . so I feel it is only right that we make a full restitution on Peter's behalf, taking into consideration not only obvious torments, but more subtle factors such as what he must have suffered while thinking his boss was attempting to blackmail him –'

'That was not my fault!' Elune squealed.

'Irrelevant,' Aileve stated calmly.

'– also,' Juliana went on, 'for becoming a boy specifically to play on his abhorrence for being involved in homosexual behaviour.'

Thomasina giggled.

'I wasn't a boy!' Elune protested. 'I just made myself look like a boy! I didn't even give myself a cock! Anyway, how was I to know he couldn't handle boys –'

'It was a reasonable assumption, and proved to be correct,' Aileve answered her, 'and do stop sniggering, Thomasina. We're supposed to be helping Elune correct her behaviour.'

'Fat chance!' Thomasina laughed. 'How long have you been trying? Six hundred years?'

'Don't spoil the game, Thomasina, or we'll string you up next to her,' Juliana threatened. 'I'm sure those fat titties would benefit from a touch of the Lion's Mane.'

Thomasina stuck her tongue out but went silent. Lily, seated next to Thomasina on the gunwale, leaned over to peer dubiously into the bucket in which two large brown jellyfish were swimming.

'Do you have anything to say in Elune's defence, Lily?' Aileve asked.

'A little, maybe,' Lily answered shyly. 'After all, if it hadn't been for Elune he would never have met Emma, and I'm not sure he'd have got the recording contract either.'

'Pure speculation,' Aileve answered, 'in the case of the contract that is. You are right about Emma, but . . . let me see . . . no, it doesn't balance against everything else. I find in favour of Juliana.'

Elune began to squirm.

'Titties first!' Juliana said happily. 'Then your bum, and if you come when I do your cunt, Elune, I may just have to start all over again.'

Thomasina and Lily cuddled together, their hands going straight to each other's bottom. Aileve opened her legs and slipped a finger into her sex. As Juliana began to pull on a pair of elbow-length rubber gloves, she turned towards the distant line of the North Devon cliffs and England.

'I'm going to enjoy this. Thank you, Mr Peter Williams.'

NEXUS NEW BOOKS

To be published in June 2004

PRIZE OF PAIN
Wendy Swanscombe

Britain is to host the most bizarre TV game show ever, as hopeful submissive males enter a lottery to appear on 'Prize of Pain'. One day soon discreetly perfumed black envelopes will slip through the letterboxes of five lucky men and they will receive their instructions from the Domina de Fouette. Public humiliation awaits, and attempts to cheat will be detected and cruelly punished. Four men are unworthy and will fail the ordeals She sets them: one only will win through to the ultimate prize. The prize of pleasure . . . and of pain. Who wants to enter Mistress's Lair? And no coughing!

£6.99   ISBN 0 352 33890 3

DOMINATION DOLLS
Lindsay Gordon

Is it a beauty treatment? A fashion statement? Or the costume of a sinister cult? How do these masks of transparent latex transform ordinary women into beautiful vamps, dominant mistresses and ruthless femme fatales? A timid socialite and her shy maid suddenly become merciless exploiters of male weakness; a suburban mother changes into a cruel mistress who takes an assertive interest in a prospective son-in-law; a mysterious female traveller leaves a trail of bound, disciplined and thoroughly used men behind. These are some of the stories of the Domination Dolls and the men they walk upon. Confessions collected by the librarian chosen to work in London's secret fetish archive, a woman who turns detective but soon succumbs to the temptations of female domination.

£6.99   ISBN 0 352 33891 1

LESSONS IN OBEDIENCE
Lucy Golden

What would you do if a young woman arrived unannounced on your doorstep one day to make amends for someone else's sins? And what if you detected, beneath her innocent exterior, a talent and a willingness to submit you'd be a fool not to nurture? Faced with that challenge, Alex Mortensen starts carefully to introduce his pupil to the increasingly perverse pleasures that have always featured in his own life. But what should he do when she learns so fast, catches up with him and threatens to overtake? A Nexus Classic.

£6.99   ISBN 0 352 33892 X

To be published in July 2004

THE PLAYER
Cat Scarlett

Carter, manager of an exclusive all-female pool tour, discovers Roz in a backstreet pool hall. When he sees her bending to take her shot, he can't resist putting his marker down to play her. But, when he signs Roz up to his tour, she discovers that the dominant Carter has a taste for the perverse, enforces a strict training regime, and that an exhibition match is just that.

£6.99   ISBN 0 352 33894 6

THE ART OF CORRECTION
Tara Black

The fourth instalment of Tara's series of novels chronicling the kinky activities of Judith Wilson and the Nemesis Archive, a global network of Sapphic corporal punishment lovers dedicated to chronicling the history of perverse female desire.

£6.99   ISBN 0 352 33895 4

SERVING TIME
Sarah Veitch

The House of Compulsion is the unofficial name of an experimental reformatory. Fern Terris, a twenty-four-year-old temptress, finds herself facing ten years in prison – unless she agrees to submit to Compulsion's disciplinary regime. Fern agrees to the apparently easy option, but soon discovers that the chastisements at Compulsion involve a wide variety of belts, canes and tawses, her pert bottom, and unexpected sexual pleasure.

£6.99   ISBN 0 352 33509 2

If you would like more information about Nexus titles, please visit our website at www.nexus-books.co.uk, or send a stamped addressed envelope to:

Nexus, Thames Wharf Studios,
Rainville Road, London W6 9HA

NEXUS BACKLIST

This information is correct at time of printing. For up-to-date information, please visit our website at www.nexus-books.co.uk

All books are priced at £6.99 unless another price is given.

- - - - - - ✂ -

Please send me the books I have ticked above.

Name   ....

Address   ....

               ....

               ....

               .... Post code....................

Send to: **Virgin Books Cash Sales, Thames Wharf Studios, Rainville Road, London W6 9HA**

US customers: for prices and details of how to order books for delivery by mail, call 1-800-343-4499.

Please enclose a cheque or postal order, made payable to **Nexus Books Ltd**, to the value of the books you have ordered plus postage and packing costs as follows:
   UK and BFPO – £1.00 for the first book, 50p for each subsequent book.
   Overseas (including Republic of Ireland) – £2.00 for the first book, £1.00 for each subsequent book.

If you would prefer to pay by VISA, ACCESS/MASTERCARD, AMEX, DINERS CLUB or SWITCH, please write your card number and expiry date here:

....

Please allow up to 28 days for delivery.

Signature ....

Our privacy policy

We will not disclose information you supply us to any other parties. We will not disclose any information which identifies you personally to any person without your express consent.

From time to time we may send out information about Nexus books and special offers. Please tick here if you do *not* wish to receive Nexus information.   ☐

- - - - - - ✂ -